SHAKA ARE DEAD

John Samson

TSL Publications

Published in Great Britain in 2016
By TSL Publications, Rickmansworth

First published in Great Britain in 2015
by TSL Publications (Lulu) 978-1-326-20513-3
& ebook ISBN / 978-1-326-20714-4 (e-book)

ISBN / 978-1-911070-14-6

Listen to the dialect of *Shaka are Dead* at
http://tslbooks.uk/authors/author-john
samson/#Shaka

BOOK I

ONE

If a ou were to of jump over a railings outside a classrooms on a third floor, onto a tarmac quadrangle below, you don't not always kill yourself. Old Zakes found that out a hard way. We all skrikked somethink chronic, aspecially a girls cause of girls is worserer as boys at getting frights. Theresa Dern were a worstest, screaming away like what she done, wouldn't not bleddy stop. But then I aspose she were sitting a closest to a drop zone which were what we did of called that spot from then on. Got blood all over her zarms. Why all a screaming though? It weren't like they was peanut butter zarms, they was egg. Zakes' blood could of only have made a taste betterer. Eggs make me puke big time, but maybe a blood were like tomato sauce what always do of make thinks betterer. If they had of beed peanut butter zarms I reckon I would of have probably finished Zakes off then and there for wasting, I don't not like it when a ou wastes peanut butter.

So anyways, like I said, there were old Zakes lying on a ground groaning, all a girls was screaming and ja, even some of a boys was screaming too also. David du Plessis, he were a biggest woosie of all time, screaming like a bleddy girl he were.

Miss Smit were a teacher on duty and you couldn't not of chosed a worser teacher acause she were a big woosie too, even by girl standards. She were like really pale normally, but she did of went even more whiter. I mean she were broek wetting skrikked seeing old Zakes like that.

She did of kept going, 'Oh my god, oh my god, oh my god,' which were quite funny as she are like a religious edumacation teacher and all. Old de Wit, a headmaster, sented her home with trauma so as we did of had a free period that arvie. Not many ous merembered to thank Zakes for that when he did got back, he done us a big favour by jumping. Not that I is saying ous must go and jump off a third floor corridor there by Dawnhurst Primary School. Zakes were lucky, he did of survived, but I reckon most ous what jump off there won't not live. It were like a million

5

to one chance that a ou could of jump and live, so that a next nine-hundred and ninety-nine thousand, nine-hundred and ninety-nine ous what acide to jump would become deaded, one shot. But old Zakes, he were lucky, he were a one in a million ou.

Not that he would of say he were lucky, I mean if a ou do of wants to commit sewerage pipe, then he do of wants to be deaded don't he?

It were Larry van Staaden what adventually sorted old Zakes out. He were a P.E. teacher. We do of call him Larry the Lisp. Not to his face like, I mean like that would be dof, but that were our nickname for him, Larry the Lisp or more like Larry the Lithp. To his face we did of called him sir or Mr van Staaden, but sometimes some ous, including yours troolie, would of say 'thir' or 'Mithter van Thaaden', but he did pretended that he never heard. He were a woosie too also, but I'll charf yous about all that later.

What I wants to know is howcomewhy are it always a P.E. teachers what have to take charge when there are a mess, like what old Zakes did of made, to sort out? I merember when old Mandy Wasserman puked up her breakfast in assembly one morning, there were old Larry the Lithp sorting her out with tissues and all. Then, there he were again stopping all a ous from checking out a sick. Serves Mandy right though cause of from what I sawed I reckon that she did of had eggs for breakfast. Eggs is enough to make anyone puke. But I already did of told yous that.

So Larry the Lithp thorted out Thaketh. He were in there organising and lisping, 'Thtay away, thtay away. Tharah, go call Mithter de Wit, Thuthan, run and tell Mithith Monroe to call the ambulance. Thtay back everyone.'

Thtay back? What? Is committing sewerage pipe like contagious? Can you catch it from an ou what tries? In that case maybe old Theresa Dern were right not to eat her zarms with Zakes' blood on them, she may of have runned off to try and top herself then. I wouldn't not of have beed sad if she had of cause she were a silly cow.

But Zakes, he weren't not a bad ou. He were kind of quiet and did of sat by hisself at breaks and all that, but he didn't not never have a problem if you did wanted to copy his homework or if you needed like a rand more to get a toasted zarm from a tuck shop, he did always have got one or two spare, he were that kind of a ou.

Old de Wit gave us a big spiel in assembly a next day, charfing us how Zakes did of had a terrible accident and that we must be more carefuller and all and not climb on a walls. It weren't not none accident I can charf yous, Zakes bleddy jumped. I sawed him done it. He did of climbed onto a wall and he jumped like a bleddy springbok he did. I scheme maybe

6

what old de Wit were trying to tell us were that we shouldn't not try and commit sewerage pipe in his school otherwise he would of donner us dead. I reckon Theresa Dern did of maked him charf all this. No, maybe not Theresa Dern, her old man. He were always in de Wit's office whingeing about somethink. It must of have beed him what were in there going, 'I did paid for those egg sangwidges out of a millions of rands what I earn.' He would of charf sangwidges and not zarms. 'I don't not want them messed up by some poor person's blood. If I had of wanted my daughter to have ketchup,' ja, he would also have charfed ketchup acause he are too larny like to tune tomato sauce, 'I would of have had my maid put some on them for her.' Ja, I reckon it were Dern's old man what did of make de Wit charf all that stuff.

Miss Smit were there at assembly too also. She still checked skrikked sitting up there on a stage, as white like as Casper a friendly ghost.

It were Jaapie le Grange what dared me when we got to Miss Smit's class for maths. He were my friend then.

'Jump, jump,' he charfs. So of course I did of had to. Not acause it were Jaapie telling me to do so, but acause it were important to skrik Miss Smit some more. I did climbed on a wall and jumped. Jaapie told me afterwards that she did wet her broeks. Dunno why, I mean Miss Smit's class were on a ground floor and it were only about a meter to fall.

But, Larry the Lithp were walking by just then and there was no broek wetting with him. He were like standing over me looking cross and all so as I had to of do somethink fast like.

'I think it'th thprained, thir.'

I did of start rolling on a floor holding my foot.

Howcomewhy are it that teachers can always tell when you is lying. I were in de Wit's office in no time and had a whole assembly spiel all over again. It weren't not even my fault, it were old Jaapie what made me to done it. How come didn't he not get a lecture from de Wit too also?

Still, I did of miss half of Miss Smit's maths class so as I did started to plan my next jump. Also, I had to check if what Jaapie had of told me were true so as I dropped my pen on a floor and tried to check out if Miss Smit had of really wet her broeks. But she were wearing a long skirts so as I didn't not see nothink.

David du Plessis, a big girl woosie what cried when Zakes did try to be superman, he bleddy goes and charfs Smit what I is doing so as she like screams my name. I skrik and hit my head underneath a desk. It were bleddy sore, but I did of get to check out Theresa Dern's panties so it were worth it. I acided that I would still donner du Plessis at break anyways.

But when break did came that little woosie must of knowed what I did wanted to do so as he did of just hung out round Larry the Lithp a whole time so as we couldn't not touch him none.

Jaapie and me adventually stopped waiting for Larry to leave and wented off to cause kak someplace else. I checked out Theresa Dern playing hopscotch so did of goed that way with Jaapie followink me. When we got near I starts talking loud like to Jaapie.

'He did of poohed his pants when Zakes went splat.'

'Who?' Jaapie asks. Hell, he are no Einstein.

'Woosie du Plessis,' I says and gives him a look as if to of say, 'you dof or what?'

'Oh ja,' he charfs, 'I remember now. Jis, did he stink afterwards.'

Now Theresa Dern are asposed to be a clever one in class so as you would of thinked she would of seed that Jaapie and me were joking, but she did of falled for it big time.

'He never poohed his pants, no-one poohed their pants,' she charfs and all a other girls are now watching.

'Course he did of. He did had a great big fat stinky nutty steamer in his undies,' I check her out all serious like, but Jaapie do of laugh. What a moron.

'Did not.'

'Did too.'

'Did not.'

That are when I realises. 'You is just saying that 'cause of you *love* him.'

'Do not.'

'Do too. Theresa loves Pooh Pants, Theresa loves Pooh Pants.' This are much betterer than actually donnering a ou.

'Do not.'

'Oh ja, then howcomewhy is you wearing those pretty pink panties. Did you put them on special like for him?'

Jaapie are killing hisself laughing and Theresa Dern looks down like as if we can all check her panties, then she do goes all red and charfs, 'Ugh! You boys are disgusting,' and she do walks off.

It do of takes Jaapie about ten hours to stop laughing. I adventually have to of punch his arm to make him stop.

We do go sit in a shade under one of a trees what grows there by a side of a playground and Jaapie becomes all serious like.

'Why d'you think he did it?' he do asks.

'Why did du Plessis pooh his pants?'

'No man, why did old Zakes jump like that?'

'I dunno, maybe he did just of wanted to make du Plessis pooh his pants,' I laugh, but Jaapie do stay serious. It are like as he really do wants to know. So I start to thinkink.

'I dunno,' I charfs again, 'why would a ou want to commit sewerage pipe like that?'

'My one uncle topped himself,' Jaapie charfs. He do like got this look on his face.

'Serious?'

'Ja, serious. He killed my aunt and my cousins too, first obviously before he like done himself in.'

'Serious?' I like can't not believe it. Why would a ou do that?

'Ja, true's Bob's got a knob. Come, let's go play soccer.' You can check that he don't not want to talk about it, but now I wants to know.

'So whycome did he done it?'

'Dunno. You coming or what?' He are like starting to walk away.

'You dunno. You didn't not ask no one?' I stay sitting so as he stops.

'Ja, I asked but you know what growed ups are like, they tell you boggerall.'

'So your oom committed sewerage pipe over boggerall.'

'No man, don't be dof. My parents didn't tell me nothink.'

'So whycome do you scheme he done it then?'

'Money.'

'Money?'

'Ja.'

'Why do you reckon money?'

'Cause that's what the newspaper said.'

'Your oom were in a newspaper?' Now I is like really interested.

'No, but I read of another ou what shot his kids and wife then committed sewerage pipe and they said it was because of money.'

'So you reckon your oom done it cause of money?'

'I dunno. You coming or what?'

'Maybe he did of wanted to get into a newspaper like,' I charf and do of start standink up.

Jaapie just checks me out like as I is dof. You can check that he don't not like thinkink about it so I just charf, 'Ja, I's coming. How long till break are over?'

He do of check his watch. 'Ten minutes.'

As we walk over to play I is thinkink like, so I asks Jaapie, 'You reckon old Zakes jumped because of money?'

'Dunno. Don't think so, you have to have a wife and kids to shoot them first if it's about money,' he charfs and do of run off ahead of me.

TWO

So now when my ma do of get home I asks her straight out cause I had of beed thinkink lots. 'Do pa have enough money?' I asks.

'Enough money? For what?' She are sitting reading a *Huisgenoot* magazine.

'I dunno. Stuff. Thinks like. I just wants to know if he are got enough.'

'Why?' She do check me out skeef now.

'Just asking,' I charfs. I don't not want her to get skrikked so as she do think pa might of come at us with his gun.

'I suppose so. We always have food in the house don't we not?'

'Ja,' I says and wonder if Jaapie's oom did of always had food.

'And we've always got clothes to wear?'

'I aspose.' Now I reckon we should of be okay cause Jaapie would of have told me if his oom did walked round naked. I do got R200 what I have of beed saving but I scheme I can keep that. Still, I don't not wants to spend it just yet in case pa do run out of money. I don't not want him coming after me with a gun.

I go into a kitchen and my ouma are there. She do of lives with us. I meremeber pa moaning to ma when she did came.

'And just how long is your mother planning to stay?' He charfs this even though I are sitting in a lounge there with them. Sometimes it are like as if I just aren't not there.

Anyway ouma did came to stay. She doesn't not do much as she do got very cross veins. She just sits round in a kitchen most of a time.

She are having a egg zarm which do of nearly makes me sick. How can she eat that? I goes and gets a peanut butter out and makes myself a proper zarm.

'You should of have a peanut butter zarm,' I charfs her, 'it will of make your veins betterer.' I says this but don't not offer to make her none. She just do of laughs at me.

'Do pa have enough money?' I asks sudden like. It are not like I don't not trust ma or nothink, it are just, I dunno, I guess I just want to make sure.

Ouma are not like ma, she don't not charf yous what she do of think yous want to heard, she charfs me straight out, 'No, your pa has never had enough money.'

Well I bleddy near choke on my zarm. This skriks me somethink chronic. If pa has of never not had enough money, howcomewhy has he not committed sewerage pipe and deaded us all with him? I check ouma out in case she are joking with me, but she do just chew on her egg zarm and charfs, 'He has never had enough to keep your ma in the manner in which she was accustomed.'

Now I is troolie skrikked so as I do take my zarm and goed to my room. I are poeping myself cause I now knows it are only a matter of time afore pa comes at us with his gun. I can't not hardly taste my peanut butter zarm none so as adventually I puts it in my undies drawer to keep it safe for later. Ma do some-times comes in my room and cleans so I can't not take none chances, she would of throwed a zarm away if she do of find it.

Then I sits there to think. It are not long afore I have this brilliant diarrhoea. I check to see ouma are still in a kitchen. She are drinking her tea now. Ma are in a lounge talking on a phone. I goes quietly down a passage and into ma and pa's room where I goes to pa's sock drawer. I get a key from there and then go to a gun safe. I had of seed pa sometimes getting his gun out so as I knows where it are.

A gun are heavier than what I aspected, but I do take it quick like then lock up and go back to my room and close a door. I start checking it out. It are a pistol, that much I knows, and it are black. I point it at a door like what a cops do on TV and nearly do of pull a trigger, but a door starts opening all of a sudden like so as I quickly shove it under my pillow.

'What you doing?'

'Nothink, bugger off.' Howcomewhy do Sally, my sister, always come in when I is busy? 'Bugger off!' I shouts and throwed her with a shoe. I do of misses and she do laughs but then buggers off cause she can check I will of donner her if she don't not. But now I are worried. I can't not keep a gun in my room. What if Sally do of come back and finds it. You can't not leave guns lying around with kids in a house. I heard ma tell pa that one day. So now I reckon I can't not leave a gun lying around, not with Sally in a house. I hided a gun in my undies drawer and were then lus for my peanut butter zarm, so I did chowed it quickly then goed and told ma that I were going over to Jaapie's. She like nods at me and carries on talking on a phone. I could of have shooted her and she would of still carry on talking like, '...and then he said, blah, blah, blah, so I said whatever, whatever, whatever...'

11

But I don't not shooted her cause she are my ma like. Instead I go over to Jaapie's carrying a gun in a Hypermarket bag. Jaapie's ma do answer a door and charfs me that he can't not come and play cause of he are doing his homework and didn't I not have none homework to do.

Silly cow. I is so pissed off now so as I take a gun out a packet and shooted her. Pow!

Ha! In my dreams like. I can't not shooted her, she are Jaapie's ma and all. I just charfs her that we didn't not have none homework today and that Jaapie must of have just said that so as she didn't not think he were a woosie doing extra studying.

She like laughs at me and I reckon that she don't not believe me none. I should of shooted her when I did of have a chance. Anyway it are too late now so as I just bugger off. I do of hope she gets very cross veins like ouma.

So now I dunno what to do with a gun. I were hoping old Jaapie would of keeped it at his house. His dad do got plenty of money so he will be safe. I aspose I could of go to Theresa Dern's. Her old man are so loaded you could of put him in a room full of guns and he wouldn't not never shoot no one. But she are such a woosie, she would most likely tell old de Wit or someone, asides I don't want to owe her nothink. Silly cow.

I aside to go down to a shops. Ma doesn't not like me going there alone, but what else is I asposed to do? I do of only got R10 still from my pocket money and I want some chips and a coke and some sweets, but that are like going to cost me R50 or maybe more. I check out old George whose cafe it are. He are like busy and all talking to some old toppie so as I chuck some stuff in a Hypermarket bag, then get a roll of humbugs and goes and pays. If George do of asks me what are in a bag I would of showed him and that would of have beed a last think what he did seed. But he are so busy talking to this old guy that he does of even give me R1 too much change. I bugger off out of there quick like.

I then sit on a wall and chow my feast what I had of put into a bag. While I is eating I check this black dude what are looking skeef at me. It are not like he are a tramp or nothink, he are not all dirty like, but when he checks me checking him out, he do grin and comes over.

'How you doing, boss?' he asks. I always wants to laugh when a black ou calls me boss. Why don't not white ous never do that?

Still I says, 'Okay,' but now I do hold a bag more tighter. I don't want this ou scaling my sweets. You got to be careful with blacks, my pa says, they'll steal any bleddy think. I just check him out proper like.

'Enjoying your sweets, boss?'

I nods and put a other Toff-o-lux in my mouth, but I is not offering him nothink. He can buy his own bleddy sweets, or steal them more like.

A ou laughs loud like and goes, 'Sharp my bro.' Then he checks me out again and charfs, 'you want to make some money so you can buy your sweets next time and not steal them?'

I do of poep my broeks. Are this ou going to tell George I zicked some sweets?

He laughs big time now cause of he can seed I is poeping my broeks. But then he do stop sudden like and checks out my Hypermarket bag again.

'I'll give you R200 for the gun,' he charfs me.

'R200?' I says, then think maybe I should of have told him I didn't not got none gun. How did he knowed anyways? I check down at a bag and see that you can check there are a gun through a plastic. Geez, I can be dof sometimes.

'Ja, R200.' He smiles at me now.

I sits and thinks for a bit. It are like pa's gun and he would bliksem me somethink chronic if he knewed I did of sold it.

A black ou takes out two R100 notes and shows me. 'R200, straight up.'

But, I think to myself, if I do of take a gun back, pa could then shoot us all and commit sewerage pipe.

'I don't know,' I charf a ou and he do puts a R200 away while I watches him. It would be lekker if I could of have a R200 and keep a gun cause then pa won't not be mad with me none and I could of give him a R200 and he wouldn't not commit sewerage pipe cause then he would of have enough money.

'Okay, I'll give you R300 then.' A ou takes out his money again.

'R300? I dunno. It are my pa's gun and he won't not want me to sold it.'

I is now really scared of what pa will do to me but I don't not want this ou to check that so as I stick a other Toff-o-lux in my mouth and chew.

A ou laughs again, 'Eish! Man you drive a hard bargain. R500 and that's my final offer.'

R500! Jislaik! That are big bucks. Pa would always then have enough money.

'Okay,' I charf and takes a gun out of a bag. A black ou quickly looks round, takes it and do of gives me a money. He puts a gun in his pocket and grins big time.

'Thanks, boss. See you around,' he charfs afore he buggers off.

I check a money out again. R500. I is a bleddy genius. Just call me Einstein. He were only going to gived me R200 and I did of maked him to pay R500. I put it away in my pocket to give to pa later, but then suddenly think, what if pa do of go and buy a other gun with a money and then we is poor again and he do got a gun?

I sit for a bit thinking, then goes back into George's shop and buy some more Toff-o-lux, some liquorice, a bag of chips and a other coke with a bucks what I did just gotted.

THREE

Miss Smit are like nervous and all when we goes there a next day. Jaapie do charf me to jump off a wall again but I can't be arsed.

'You jump if you do of think it are such a good diarrhoea,' I tune him, but he are a woosie.

Miss Smit do start with a maths and I sits there checking out a numbers on a bored. I never do of understand what's potting with all this maths stuff so as I checks round a class.

Theresa Dern are showing off and answering all of a questions. So are Pooh Pants du Plessis. They *love* each other. Then I do of have a brainwave. I do write on a piece of paper DdP ♥ TD and pass it to Jaapie. He do laugh which are like megadof cause of Smit will confiscate a note if she do check it out. I like nod my head to charf Jaapie to pass a note on to Theresa Dern. He do laughs again, but quiet like this time. I watch as a note are passed across to Theresa Dern and are almost wetting myself.

When she do gets a note and reads it, she goes all red like and checks at Pooh Pants who are checking her out anyways, cause he do of love her. *He* then do go all red and looks a other way.

I think of writing a other note making out like it are from Theresa saying, 'I want to kiss you', but Miss Smit are checking out a class now. She can like tell that somethink are going on, so as I charf, 'Miss, are Zakes alright?'

I dunno why I do asks this, it just do like come out. But it do stop old Smit from checking out a class too much. She smiles at me like as I had of done somethink good, which are not good. It are never good when a teacher do like what you have of done.

'Zakes is fine.' But I can check in her face that she are lying.

14

'So are he coming back soon?' Suddenly I like really wants to know, I wants to asks Zakes howcomewhy he did of done it.

'Zakes will be off for a little while.'

'Is he in hospital,' it are Miriam what asks this.

'Yes,' Miss Smit says and you can check that she are just about crying now.

'Is he going to die?'

'No, Patty, he's not going to die, but now we must get on with the lesson.'

I want to like ask a other question so as we don't not got to go on with a maths, but I can't not think of nothink, so old Smit do carries on.

But now I'm really thinking like. When are Zakes coming back? Are he going to die? I do of really wants to know howcomewhy he did done it. Don't ask me why I do of want to know, I just do.

I check out Miriam. Maybe she do loves Zakes. Maybe that are why she did asked about if he are in hopstibal. Sissy. Only sissies fall in love. I write a note what charfs Miriam ♥ Zakes, but then I screw it up. I don't not want to upset Zakes.

'You got a rand?' I asks Jaapie at break.

'Nope.'

He are chowing a zarms what his ma did made. I think they is marmalade ones. I do of quite like marmalade. I got a zarms my ma made, but I is not lus for them. Anchovy. Normally I don't not mind anchovy paste, but today I is just not lus so as I chucked them in a bin. But now I is like really hungry and I don't not got enough money to buy a toasted zarm at a tuck shop. I mean I do of got enough, I do of got R500, but most of that are in my undies drawer. I did got some with me, but it are not enough so as I can only buy a bag of chips and a chocolate log, it are all what I can afford.

Now if Zakes had of beed here, he would of had a R1 what I were looking for. I don't not share Jaapie none chips as he didn't not share me none of his zarms.

'Come,' I charf him afore he are finished his zarms, 'let's go check out a drop zone.'

'Why?' he do asks. You can check that he are more interested in his marmalade zarms.

'I dunno, somethink to do.'

'Why don't we go donner Pooh Pants?'

I check round a playground. Old Pooh Pants are playing cricket with some other okes. Larry the Lithp are not around, but then I check that Theresa Dern are there watching them. She loves him.

15

'Okay,' I charf. It would of be fun to donner him in front of his girlfriend, and we can check out a drop zone laterer.

Old Jaapie are still chowing his zarms as we do of walk over, but he do chuck a crusts away as we get nearer Pooh Pants. What a bloody waste. I do of hate ous what waste.

'Where you going?' Theresa Dern, a silly cow, has of checked us coming and she do stands in a way. She like knowed we is gonna donner her boyfriend. I do of want to donner her now to get her out a way, but you can't not hit girls. That's what pa do say to me. Don't never hit girls. So I don't not donner Theresa. I will of just have to wait till she do grows up to be a lady, like what pa done with ma.

'Just come to watch,' I charf Pooh Pant's girlfriend. Jaapie, a doffie, laughs funny like. Why don't he not just say to Theresa that we have of comed to donner her boyfriend so as she can go call Larry the Lithp and get us in trouble.

Theresa Dern just do of stands there in front of us and doesn't not move none, she can check what we is up to cause of Jaapie a Doffie did of laughed like he did done.

'Just watching,' I charfs again and check past her to where Pooh Pants are batting. And then it do of happens. Petrus Buthalezi bowls a ball and old Pooh Pants do give it a great big whack which were quite good for a woosie like him. But a ball flies through a air and donners Theresa Dern on a back of a head. It are not like a proper cricket ball, only a tennis ball, but acause of Theresa weren't not aspecting it, she do gets a huge skrik and do fall over flat on her face. That are when old Pooh Pants acides to shout, 'Look out!' A little late if you asks my opinion.

I is laughing so hard now so as I do of almost pee in my broeks. Theresa Dern are like crying and rolling around holding her head. She are not even worried nione that her skirt has of comed up and we can all check her blue panties. Old Pooh Pants' face are like full of skrik, he has of just donnered his girlfriend with a ball. I check his face out and start laughing more.

Then blerry old Larry the Lithp rocks up on a scene and checks this out. He like charfs me, 'Did you hit Theretha?'

I'm like, 'No, sir, I didn't not hit no one.'

'What happened here,' Larry asks everybody. And do yous knowed what did of happen then? Bleddy Pooh Pants points at me and goes, 'He hit her, sir. I saw him.'

Next think all a ous is pointing at me and going, 'he hit her, sir.' I turn to Jaapie so as he can charf Larry a truth, but he like just looks at me and doesn't not charf nothink. I did of thought he were my friend and all, but even he don't not charf a truth none.

Larry the Lithp checks all this out, then takes me off to de Wit's office. De Wit do of calls my ma and pa and that night when pa do gets home he bliksems me one shot in a face with his fist.

'That's for hitting a girl,' he charfs. Ma doesn't not charf nothink and ouma just sits in a kitchen with her very cross veins, drinking tea.

That night I do of hear ma and pa shouting at each other and a next morning ma do come into my room to wake me. She are wearing dark glasses so as I can't not check her eyes none. She like tries to hug me but I don't not want to be hugged, I is so blerry cross with every one so as I do just push her away and go lock myself in a bathroom. I check a mirror and I do got this great big black eye, like what old Neil Evans did of have when his face did of meet a other ou's knee at rugby. I can't not hardly open it none.

Ma comes to a door and charfs me to hurry up cause of it are time to go to school. I says nothink. Then I hears pa shout that I can bleddy well walk to school cause of he can't not be late for work. He then do also shouts that if he do of hear that I didn't not go to school he would take his belt to me.

I wait till I hear them bugger off then go to a kitchen. Ouma are there making tea. She checks me out but doesn't not charf nothink. Sometimes it are like as she are not all there. I check that ma has of made me zarms as usual. They is peanut butter ones. Ma do never makes me peanut butter zarms.

I go to a cupboard and get out a peanut butter and bread and start making my own zarms. That are when ouma checks me out and charfs me, 'Your mother made you sandwiches,' and she points at them.

'They is peanut butter zarms,' I charf her and start spreading my own zarms, 'I can't not eat peanut butter cause of I is allergic. I is making a egg zarm for me.'

She like looks at me and you can check that she are trying to work this out, but she can of be dof sometimes. Maybe she do got very cross veins in her brain. Anyways she do like adventually smiles and buggers off with her tea.

At school we do got P.E. with Larry the Lithp first period. I arrive just in time and old Jaapie checks me out as we is changing into our kit.

'What happened to you eye?' he asks, but I give him a blank and do of carry on changing. So he do asks again. You can check that he are sorry he never did of said nothink when old Pooh Pants charfed that I did of hit Theresa Dern, but I is still cross with him so as I blank him more.

Then Larry the Lithp do arrive and he checks out my eye so he do asks me what did of happened.

I look away and charf, 'Nothink.'

He checks me out then charfs me to come into his office. He gives a ous a soccer ball and tells them to go play, then he do sits down and do of asks again, 'What happened to you eye? You can tell me, you won't get into any trouble.'

I look up at him now and charf without even not blinking, 'Theresa Dern's pa hit me. She told him that I did of hitted her, which I never did of, but when he sawed me there by a shops yesterday he did of just punched me, sir.' I reckon I can of charf this acause Larry the Lithp don't not never believe nothink what I says.

But now this time he checks me out all serious like. I want to charf him that I is only joking but it are like as I can't not say nothink, so I just sits there while he asks me if I is sure. I do of nod but look away.

He then charfs me to stay in his office and he goes off. Next think de Wit comes in and I poep my broeks. I reckon I is in kak big time for lying.

De Wit do sits in Larry the Lithpth chair and checks me out, but all concerned like. You can tell he are checking my eye out special like so as I do look away. I don't not like him checking me out that way.

'Can I go play soccer please, sir?' I don't not want to be in there with de Wit none more.

'In a minute,' he charfs, but his voice are not normal like, it are as if he are not cross with me or nothink.

'Can you tell me what happened to your eye?'

Now I is poepping myself again. This are like serious. If I do of charf him that it were Theresa Dern's pa then I is in kak with Theresa and all her chinas, I can of see that now. I is probably already in kak for telling Larry the Lithp that.

'Nothink, I did of fell,' I charf de Wit and keep checking out a door hoping that Larry the Lithp will of come in and tune me to go play soccer.

'That's not what you told Mr van Staaden.'

'No, sir,' I charf.

'So will you tell me what really happened?' It are like as he do of wants me to charf that it really were Theresa Dern's pa what did of donnered me. I can check that there are like a whole big lorry load of cowkak coming down a road to be dumped on me, but then I merember that all this kak did of started acause of bleddy Theresa Dern wouldn't not let me donner her boyfriend none.

So I look at de Wit with my good eye and charf, 'I never did of hitted her none, sir. It were a tennis ball what Poo...David du Plessis hitted what hitted her. It were a accident like, but it weren't not me.'

I don't not call du Plessis Pooh Pants to de Wit cause of he wouldn't not of knowed who I were talking about.

'We went through all that yesterday,' de Wit charfs. 'Now I want to know what happened to your eye.'

I is now lank angry again with Theresa Dern and Pooh Pants cause of all this kak were their fault. I nearly do of say it were Pooh Pants' old man what done it, but just charf de Wit what I charfed Larry the Lithp, 'Theresa Dern's pa did of hitted me.'

De Wit checks all concerned again and I do of want to laugh acause of I reckon he do like Theresa Dern's pa and all. I think of how cross Theresa are going to be when she do of hear what I charfed de Wit about her old man and nearly almost laugh.

Meantime old de Wit are asking me if I is sure and all that and cause of what I had of already charfed him, I can't not say it weren't not what did of happen otherwise he would of think I were a liar which aren't not.

So now de Wit asks me if I had of charfed my ma and pa what did of happened. I skrik a little cause of I don't not want ma involved none.

'I did of told them that I gotted into a fight with some ous from Voortrekker Laerskool.'

'And they believed you?'

'Ja,' I nods. 'I have of had fights with those ous from that school afore so as they did of believe me.'

De Wit now checks me out straight in a eyes, 'And is that what really happened?'

'Oh no, sir,' I charf, but I can't not check him in a eyes as I do of says this.

'Then why didn't you tell them that Mr Dern hit you?'

I don't not like what are going on now and just wants to be out of there. I do of wish I hadn't not told Larry the Lithp nothink. I should of have just charfed that I felled.

'I dunno, I didn't not want to get Mr Dern in trouble.'

'I see,' de Wit charfs and I can check now that he do of knows I are lying. 'Well, I'm afraid that Mr Dern is certainly in trouble now. Because of your accusations I will have to call the police in on the matter.'

I skrik big time now. 'No, sir! Don't do that.'

'Why not? If Mr Dern hit you, I have to tell the police. I have no choice.'

I check out a filing cabinet in Larry the Lithp'th office. It are like all what he do got in a room, a filing cabinet, a desk and two chairs. It are not a lekker office and I just wants to get out.

'Well?' de Wit goes. You can check he do knows that I knows that he knows I is lying. Bastard! I hate de Wit. I hate Larry the Lithp. I hate Pooh Pants du Plessis and his stupid girlfriend Theresa Dern. I hate Jaapie cause of he didn't not say nothink and I hate Theresa Dern's pa cause of he hitted me. But I don't not say nothink, I just keep schtum.

'Okay,' de Wit charfs, 'let's go to my office. I will call the police from there.'

He checks me out again and I do of realise all of a sudden like that he do wants me to charf him no, it weren't not Theresa Dern's pa, so as I reckon to myself, 'Cool, he do of wants to play games, let's play.'

I check him in a eyes now and then I do of just start crying and charfing, 'I never hitted Theresa Dern, honest, sir, I never hitted her, that are what I told her pa, but he didn't not believe me none neither. I never hitted her, it were a tennis ball what David du Plessis hitted. Why don't nobody not believe me none?'

I can check that de Wit are skrikked big time and I do of want to laugh so hard, but I have of got to keep pretending to cry so as I put my head on Larry the Lithp'th desk and make crying noises while I keep charfing, 'I never hitted her, I never hitted her.'

'Come now, don't cry. I do believe you and I'm very sorry for what has happened.' You can hear in his voice that he don't not knowed what to do. I just lie there and sniff loud like and then real slow like stop pretending to cry. When I do of look up I can check that I have of fooled him proper like.

FOUR

If there are one think what I can tell yous, it are don't never get a cops involved in nothink. They is like de Wit, but like a hundred times worser. They don't not take kak from no one cause of it don't not take them long to check that I are lying about Theresa Dern's pa, but not afore I had of caused as much kak about it as what I could.

They did of have Mr Dern in a police station and you could check that he were skrikked big time. I weren't not asposed to check him, but a lady cop what were in charge of me had of gone to get some forms and I did of walked out of a room I were in so as I could check out what a cop shop did check like. That lady cop got into lank kak for leaving me alone like and I did of feeled a little bit sorry for her cause of she were nice to me and all, but then she did of talked to me about Mr Dern donnering me and adventually did of made me so confused so as I did of said that he didn't not touch me none.

I skrikked when I did of charfed that cause of I realised that this lady cop were clever at talking. I were much more carefuller when she did tried to ask me who really did of hitted me. I charfed her that I fell and that I did of said it were Mr Dern cause of what Theresa Dern had done at school lying about me hitting her.

A lady cop did of kept asking me if I really did of fell, but I were carefuller so as not to tell her nothink more than I did fell.

Pa took his belt to me after a cops had of left, but it weren't not as hard as what I aspected. He charfed me that it were cause of I had caused kak that he did hitted me. I didn't not mind so much as I had of caused lekker kak with that liar Theresa Dern and her boyfriend Pooh Pants.

A next day at school everyone did of blanked me. Even old Jaapie didn't not want to knowed me. So as I schemed, no fine, if he do wants to be like that then I will just find me some new friends. So I went and sat on my ace and chowed my zarms. I still couldn't not check so lekker out of my eye what pa hitted, but at least it weren't not sore none more.

I didn't not feel like causing none kak in Smit's class so as I did just sat there being bored. Larry the Lithp made me tidy a cricket kits at P.E. cause of I did forgotted my cozzie. He then did of let everyone have a free swim. This pissed me off big time, so as I stuck one of a stumps through some pads, then put a ones with a hole in at a bottom of a kit bag so as no one couldn't see.

After school I weren't lus to go home none so as I did of hung around till everyone were gone. When I couldn't not check no one around I went up to a third floor where Zakes had of jumped from and did of looked over to see how far it were that he had of jumped. It were like a long way and I reckoned it must of have taked lank guts for Zakes to of jumped cause I would of beed too poep scared.

I still did of wanted to know howcomewhy he done it, even more now that I could check how scary it were. I reckon old David du Plessis would of really have poohed his pants if he did of have to jump from there. Zakes never poohed his pants. Zakes were too tough to pooh his pants.

21

I checked over a wall again and spied where Zakes had of felled. There were a dark mark on a ground from where his blood were. I would of aspected it to be red, but it weren't, it were dark black.

Then I checked old Larry the Lithp come into a quadrangle so as I did duck down and wait for a bit till I do of thinked he were gone, then I did looked over a side again and he are bleddy well looking straight up at me. We both do of skrik, but I reckon him more an me.

'What you doing up there?' he charfs and you can tell that he are like worried and all. 'Come down here at onthe.' He are like trying to be like a teacher telling a ou off, but his voice are funny like and then I realises that he are like skrikking that I may of jump.

So I do of climb on a wall and jump. He are a P.E. teacher, he will of catch me.

No, I don't not jump. I is not that dof. Larry the Lithp wouldn't not of caughted me cause of he would be skrikking too much, but it would of have beed funny to see his face if I did of jumped. I probably would of squashed him flat if I had of fallen on him, cause he aren't not so big.

Anyways, I go down a stairs and he are still standing there by a drop zone. He are checking out a blood spot like, but do of look up quickly when I arrives.

'What were you doing up there?' he asks.

'Nothink,' I charf. I want him to bugger off, he won't not understand none. I just wants to donner him so as he goes away.

'Nothing?' Are he deaf or what, I just did of charfed him that. Nothink. I weren't not doing nothink, but I is not lus for his stupid questions so as I just do of stands there checking out a drop zone and a blood spot and stays schtum.

'You can't have been doing nothing. What were you up to?' he do asks again. He are angry, you can check and I do of reckon it are acause of what I did of said about Theresa Dern's pa. Stuff him.

'I were checking out a drop thone, thir.'

I do of says 'thir' to piss him off, but I dunno why I charfed a rest, it do of just come out like.

'The what?'

Boy, are this ou deaf?

'The drop zone, sir.'

'The drop zone?'

Jislaik! Growed ups are megadof, you do of have to got to asplain everythink to them.

'Ja, a drop zone, where Zakes dropped from a sky, sir.' I check him out now with my good eye to make sure he do of understand. But he doesn't

22

not understand nothink, you can check. He do look up at a third floor then down at a blood spot then at me.

'Why?' A other dof question, aren't teachers not asposed to be clever?

'I dunno, sir.' I check down at a blood spot again. It are like all sticky and dark.

Then old Larry the Lithp becomes all concerned and all. 'Thaketh is going to be okay. He wath very lucky to ethcape that fall. It wath a terrible thing that happened. That'th why you need to be very careful up there, acthidenth happen eathily. You have to be careful.'

'It weren't not a accident,' I charf still checking out a blood spot. 'Zakes jumped, sir. I did of sawed him done it.'

Old Larry the Lithp checks me out for a bit then says, 'Yeth, he did jump.'

It are a bit like he doesn't not want to charf that, but I is chuffed he did of cause teachers always do of treat you like you is dof and know nothink.

'Whycome did he jump, sir?' I asks. Maybe if Larry the Lithp aren't not going to lie for once, he can maybe tell me why.

'I don't know,' he charfs and sighs and I can check that he are not lying none, he doesn't not know why neither. We do of stand for a bit and I did get ready to go when suddenly he charfs, 'Maybe there wath trouble at home.' It are like as he are talking to hisself. 'Maybe he wath being bullied. He theemed thuch a nithe quiet kid. A bit of a loner though. Perhapth it wath becauthe he had no friendth. If only we had theen the thignth.'

Now that are weird like, it are like as he are upset that he hadn't of stopped old Zaked, so as I charf him, 'It weren't not your fault, sir.' I dunno why I charf that, but it weren't not Larry's fault.

He checks me out now as if he had of just seed me and then he do of smiles like this funny smile, it are not a happy smile. He do of bends down so as he are looking me in a eyes and do of put his hand on my soldier and charfs, 'Thankth,' afore he do of stands up again. 'Now I think you mutht go home young man,' he charfs and starts to walking off.

I check after him, then suddenly charf, 'Sir, I will of be Zakes' best friend when he do comes back. I will of make sure he don't not jump none more,' and I do of mean it.

He like looks back at me and smiles, this time it are a happy one. 'Good. You do that,' he charfs and then buggers off.

I do of stand there for a while and then check round. No one are there so as I lie down near a blood like what Zakes looked like when he had of jumped. My one ear are on a ground and it are like rough and all, but I lie there anyway and pretend that I are Zakes after he had of jumped. I lie really still like he did done for a bit, then he did of began to cry and all. Not girl crying, but hurt crying. Anyways I don't not cry none cause of with my ear to a ground I can hear a world talking to me. It are charfing me that I must of be Zakes' friend. It are not like a loud voice what charfs me this, it are more like as a whisper. Also it don't not come through my ear, but it are in my head like, 'Be Zakes' friend.'

It are a lekker voice, not like a teacher or ma or pa charfing you what to do, it are like asking me nice like. So I charf a world, 'Ja, I will of be Zakes' friend,' and I can of feel that a world are happy.

Then de Wit do come along. At first he skriks cause of he must of reckoned that I did jumped like what Zakes done and that I are dead, but when I do stand up to charf him that I is okay he do of get all cross. He don't not like me none, you can check that, but I don't care nothink. I wait till he are finished being cross with me then I just bugger off home.

When I gets home, ma are on a phone, I think she are talking to Aunty Sheryl. She checks me out when I walk in, but then do turn away. It are like as she never even noticed I were late getting home. I reckon she were crying also as well cause of her voice do sound funny. She doesn't not have her sunglasses on like what she did this morning so as I can check that she do got a black eye like me. Pa must of have donnered her as well too also.

Ouma are in a kitchen drinking her tea like as normal. She doesn't not even check me when I walk in so I do of grab a juice cause of it are too late for a zarm and bugger off to my room. I think about what Larry the Lithp charfed about howcomewhy Zakes had of done what he done. 'Perhapth it wath becauthe he had no friendth.'

FIVE

Pooh Pants aren't not at school a next day and Theresa Dern are crying and all. At first I reckon it are acause she loves him and she are sad acause of he aren't not there. But then I hear Petrus Buthalezi charfing someone else that Pooh Pants aren't not at school cause of his pa got shooted.

'Are he dead?' I asks Petrus.

I aspect him to blank me, but he charfs, 'Ja,' and then it are like as he merembers he do of have to blank me and so he do. All a ous is still not talking to me or nothink, even not Jaapie, but I listens to them talk and hear that some ous broked into Pooh Pants' house last night to rob them. Mr du Plessis went to check out what were happening and got shooted.

Of course Miss Smit are like crying during Religious Instruction and all, aspecially when Theresa Dern charfs, 'Can we say a prayer for Mr du Plessis.' Then all a girls and some of a boys start crying. Woosies.

While everyone are crying and praying I try to think what it would of be like if some ous came and shooted pa. I aspose ma would be crying and all. Ouma would probably sit in a kitchen and drink tea and eat egg zarms.

At break I goes and sits under a tree where Zakes used to of sit and chow my zarms. I wonder when Zakes were of coming back cause of it has of beed like ages since he did jumped. I reckon that maybe he are deaded and no one will charf us a truth. But then I merember that a world charfed me to be his friend. If he were deaded then a world would of knowed. It wouldn't not charf me to be his friend if he were deaded cause of a world are not dof.

I start to pretend like I is Zakes checking out a playground and all. A ous what normally play cricket is just hanging around, maybe cause of Pooh Pants aren't not there to bat none. I could go bat, but now I is Zakes and Zakes never did of played cricket.

I is busy checking out a ous when Miriam comes up to me and charfs, 'You can't sit here. This is Zakes' place.'

I want to charf her that I is Zakes but like some other ous have of comed and they also charf me that this are Zakes' place and that I must move. None of them were Zakes' friend so I charf them all to bugger off and leave me alone.

But like more and more ous are coming and checking me out and then some ous try and push me away from Zakes' place. I is like ready to donner them when old Larry the Lithp appears and I reckon I is going to get into trouble even though I didn't never done nothink.

But Larry are cool, he just charfs everyone to leave me alone. Everyone buggers off, but you can check that some ous is giving me a hairy eyeball. It are like weird that Larry the Lithp were on my side, he has of never beed on my side afore.

I check round now and see that someone did knocked my zarms onto a floor when I weren't looking. They did got dust on them and taste crunchy so as I throw them over a fence onto a street. Then I check this dog what were there what comes up and sniffs at them. It chows them afore it walks away.

We used to of had a dog once, not like a one what sniffed my zarms, our one weren't not as big. One day it did do somethink what I can't not merember, so as pa skopped it one shot with his foot. Ma charfed me later that it were sleeping there by a vet. It must of liked it there by a vet cause of it did of never comed back none.

I call to a dog, but it blanks me so as I throw it with a stone and it does bugger off. I check round a playground again, a ous is playing cricket now.

After school I check a black ou what boughted pa's gun. He are like hanging around outside a shops, but when I start walking home, he do of catches up with me.

'Hey, boss,' he charfs and smiles big time. I like say howzit but carry on walking.

'You spent all that money yet?' he asks me. I just do of shake my head cause of I still got about R350 left.

'You need some more?' I stop and do looks at him skeef and he laughs like. 'Now you want to talk to me hey, boss?' I just keep checking him out.

'You got bullets for that gun?' he asks.

I know pa did got a box of bullets in a gun safe so as I nods.

'How many you got?'

'A box, I think there is twenty in a box.'

A ou nods all serious like, then he charfs, 'I'll give you twenty bucks for that.'

I think for a bit them scheme that since pa don't not got none gun no more, he don't not need a bullets.

'Fifty bucks,' I charf a ou. I dunno why I charf fifty acause I don't not reckon pa paid more an R30.

'Eish, boss. I've only got thirty,' he takes a money out and shows me.

'Okay, thirty.' I scheme maybe I can use a thirty bucks to pay for ouma to have her very cross veins fixed.

A ou grins and charfs me to meet him there by a shops when I did got a bullets.

It are easy to get a bullets cause of ma are talking on a phone again and ouma are in a kitchen chowing her egg zarms and drinking tea. Sally are playing by a friend's house so as I go into pa's room and zick a bullets.

A black ou are there by a shops waiting. He are smoking and all and it do of smell like when you cut a grass. I did of showed him a bullets and he like grins at me then do laughs a bit afore he takes out a R30. I give him a bullets and aspect him to bugger off, but he don't not. He do of just sits there smoking and all, so as I sit with him. He blows out a smoke from his cigarette, checks me out again and laughs. He do of got very cross veins in his eyes.

'You still here, boss?' he asks.

I nods.

'You should go play with your friends,' and he points with his cigarette down a road to where Jaapie do live.

'I didn't got none friends,' I charf.

'No friends,' he laughs for like ten minutes, then charfs it again, 'No friends hey?'

'I did got one friend,' I charf and I is cross with a ou for saying I didn't got none friends. 'I got a friend Zakes, but he are in a hopstibal cause of he jumped off a third floor at school.'

Now a ou stops laughing and checks me out all serious like. 'Zakes is your friend?'

I nod. Is this ou dof, I did of just charf him that.

'Zakes Thabane? Your friend?'

Now I'm like weren't that what I just charfed you? But I just nods my head and charf, 'Are Zakes your friend too also?'

Now he laughs big time and then sucks on his cigarette afore he do blow a smoke out real slow like, checking me out all a time. Then he charfs, 'No, Zakes is my brother.'

'Zakes are your brother?' I'm like, really?

He do of nods his head and smokes again.

'Are he okay?' I charf and he like shrugs his soldiers.

'He's in the hospital.'

I know that, but are he okay is what I wants to know, but I don't not asks. I just check a ou out. But now it are like as he don't not want to talk to me about Zakes none more so as he do smoke again then offers me a cigarette. I take it and smoke big time.

No, don't be dof, I don't not. Pa'd kill me if he did heard that I had of smoked. I just shake my head so as he shrugs again and throws a stompie on a floor and stamps on it. Then he do just bugger off without not saying nothink. I go into George's and buy some chips and sweets with a money what I got for a bullets.

Later that arvie I asks ma if she can take me to a hopstibal to see Zakes, but she are like 'Who are Zakes?' so I charf her that he are a ou at school what are in a hopstibal, so she then charfs, 'They don't let children into the hospital.'

So I charfs, 'If they don't not let children into a hopstibal then howcomewhy are Zakes there?'

27

She just laughs and charfs that only sick children is allowed into a hopstibal. I do of want to charf that Zakes are not sick, he were just donnered by a ground there in a quadrangle there by school, but I can check that ma do of not want to talk none more.

That night I do of hear ma and pa fighting about a telephone, but he doesn't not hit her none then. It are only laterer when they do of go to bed that I hear ma crying funny like she sometimes does of do and pa are grunting from slapping her.

A next morning I aspect ma to be all quiet and everythink, but she are like as if nothink did of happened. I charf her that I want egg zarms for school and she doesn't not even check me out skeef or nothink. She do of just makes some egg zarms and don't not say nothink.

At break I wait till Larry the Lithp are nearby, then start chowing a egg zarms. I aspect them to make me sick so as I can go to a hopstibal and see Zakes, but a zarms don't not even make me feel funny. So I wait till Larry the Lithp buggers off, then throw what are left of a zarms into a road. A dog what were there yesterday comes again, but this time it doesn't not chow a zarms.

I is like really cross with a zarms cause of they didn't not make me sick or nothink and I is also hungry cause of I only ate one zarm. I wished I had of asked ma to make peanut butter zarms for me. She would of done acause this morning it were like as she weren't not there. I didn't got none money to get somethink from a tuck shop cause of I aspected to be sick and in a hopstibal and I didn't not want a ous at a hopstibal scaling my money like.

I think of asking Jaapie if I can of borrow some money, but he are like best friend with some other ous now so as I don't not ask no one for nothink. I just sits there by Zakes tree and watch a ous playing.

When I gets home I make three peanut butter zarms cause of I is like lank hungry and all, but after I have of chowed two I is not so hungry none more so as I put a other one in my undies drawer, then acide to go to a shops to check if Zakes' brother are there.

He aren't not there none so as I go into a shop. I did forgot to bring my money so I can't not buy nothink and old George are watching me proper like. Now I can't not scale nothink neither, so as I go to walk out. But old George calls me back and charfs me to empty my pockets. It are like as he do think I are a thief. So I empties my pockets to show him I aren't not one. He like looks at me all skeef and you can check that he are unhappy that I didn't not got none sweets in my pockets. I is pissed off big time that he do of thinked I are a thief, so as when he charfs I can go and a phone rings I grab a Tex Bar and some Rolo as I walk out a shop cause of George are answering a phone. That'll learn him not to think I is a thief.

SIX

I do nearly forget about Zakes cause of he didn't not come back for lank ages. I didn't got none friends neither now so as I just sits at break under a tree and chuck my zams at a dog what do come every day now. A zarms what I chuck are like a ones what ma makes cause of they is usually anchovy or marmalade. I make my own zarms in a arvie after school and hide them in my undies drawer for school a next day. They is not so lekker as what I make when I get home, but at least they is peanut butter ones.

Ma did of fell a other night and were bleeding so as she did have to go to a hopstibal and all, but it were when I were asleep. I only checked a next morning when she did of have a plaster on there by her eye. At least pa were being nice to her.

I didn't not check Zakes' brother round a shops much. I saw him like once, but it were like as he didn't not seed me. He looked, but it were like a very cross veins in his eyes was too much so as he couldn't not see none. He were still smoking his mowed grass cigarettes.

Some ous broke into Hester Lange's place and shooted her pa, but he didn't not die. He are not a woosie like David du Plessis' pa what just did of died. Still, I don't not call old du Plessis 'Pooh Pants' none more cause of his pa were deaded.

Larry the Lithp would like come and check on me every break, but now he don't not worry me none more, which are fine by me cause of a dog don't not come near till he buggers off. I like a dog, but when it do try to follow me home after school, I have to tell it to bugger off and throw it with a stone, otherwise pa'd kick it if it did of comed home.

One day after school, a dog comes to me and charfs me to run away with it. 'Let's go to Jo'burg,' it charfs. So I follow a dog to Jo'burg.

No, I don't not cause of dogs can't not talk none, but sometimes I do of wants to run away. It are not lekker having none friends.

When I think this, I merember what Larry the Lithp did said about Zakes. 'Perhapth it wath becauthe he had no friendth.' That are when I merember Zakes so as I go check out a drop zone again. You can still

29

check a little bit of a blood spot, but it are not like when he jumped cause of you can't not see it so lek-ker none more. After school I do of wait till everyone buggers off then go up to a third floor and check over a wall again. It are still blerry high up. I could never jump like old Zakes did of done.

Then I goes downstairs and lay by a drop zone to see if a world would of talk to me again, but it didn't not say nothink so as I think that maybe it didn't not actually speak to me last time and it were just my brain talking to me.

A next day I work out why a world didn't not say nothink and it are acause of Zakes are back at school. A world knew he were coming back. All a ous did of crowded round him like he are a big hero or somethink. He do got clutches to help him walk and all and Miss Smit are nearly crying and it do take ages to start a lesson, which are good.

By a time break comes, a ous have of forgotted about Zakes and, cause of I had to stay in class and clean a board, he are like sitting there under a tree afore I get there. His clutches are on a grass next to him.

I go talk to him, but suddenly I is like shy and all cause of I don't not knowed what to say or nothink. I can't not just go charf him that a world told me to be his friend, so as I stand nearby and say nothink. It are him what speaks first cause of he can check that I is hanging around.

'Hey,' he charfs, 'how come you not playing with Jaapie?' He like nods his head in a direction what Jaapie are.

I check Jaapie out. He are talking to Theresa Dern. I mean like really talking to her, like he loves her. I didn't not noticed this afore, so as I check out Pooh Pants. I call him that again cause of he told on me when I did hide Miss Smit's handbag that one time. Old Pooh Pants are like not interested in Jaapie and Theresa cause of he are playing cricket and all.

'Ag! We aren't not friends none more,' I charf Zakes and he like nods. Then I check a dog coming and I don't not even think afore I chuck him with my zarms. Ma did forgot that I don't not like egg zarms none and had of made me some. She were like all happy this morning but I didn't not know howcomewhy. So I is hoping that a dog will chow a egg zarms this time.

I is just checking out a dog what are sniffing a zarms when Zakes charfs, 'Hey, you been looking after Shaka for me?'

'Shaka?'

And Zakes are like, 'Ja, Shaka, the dog.'

I check him out, then check a dog out, then check him out again. 'This are your dog?' I asks.

30

He are all shy like now, but he charfs, 'Sort of. I feed him at break times. I was worried when I was in hospital because I wasn't here to feed him.'

Shaka. That are a lekker name for a dog. I check him out now, but he are not interested in a zarms.

'What you got on those sarmies?' Zakes asks.

'Egg,' I charf, but I are still looking at Shaka.

'He hates egg sarmies,' Zakes tells me this like I is dof.

'Me too,' I charf, pretending like I didn't not notice that Zakes do of think I is stupid. 'My ma forgot I don't not like them. I don't know why she did of made them.' I says this, then chuck my peanut butter zarms what I had of made for me, over a fence for Shaka. He like catches then in his mouth afore it do of hit a ground.

Zakes now checks me out like as he can't not believe what I had of just did. 'Peanut butter,' is all what he charfs.

'How did you know?' I asks cause of there are no ways he could of have knowed.

'Shaka only does that for peanut butter ones.'

I check him out some more, then I is like, 'I have of never chucked him none peanut butter ones afore. I like them too much so as I always chow them myself.'

'So what you going to eat now?' he asks me.

'I dunno,' I charf and then realises how dof I were to have throwed a peanut butter zarms, aspecially cause of I didn't got none money with me. I have of spent all a money what Zakes' brother gaved me and I didn't not have none pocket money cause of pa charfed I weren't not allowed none seen as how I broked a bottle of his whiskey when he did of pushed me.

Zakes checks me out for a bit, then at old Shaka who are sniffing around by a gutter. Then he do takes out some money all of a sudden like and charfs, 'Here, go get us some toasted sarmies. One each, and we can share a packet of chips. I don't mind what flavour, just not cheese and onion.'

I like check out a money and then take it. It are not often that a ou does of offer to buy you a toasted. Jaapie never did of and he always had lots of money.

Shaka are gone by a time I get back so as I sits next to Zakes and he moves his clutches for me. I want to ask him whycome he did of jumped like what he did, but I is all shy again so as I just charf him what has of beed happening while he were away. He has a lank laugh about me telling people that Theresa Dern's old man did hitted me and a kak what it did of caused. He charfs me that he doesn't not like Theresa none cause of she did called him a kaffir. I don't not tell Zakes that that are what my pa do call black ous.

By a time a bell goes to end break, we is talking lekker. I help Zakes with his clutches and we do of walk slowly back to class. As we is walking I asks him if he do want to come play after school.

'Can't,' he charfs me, 'I've got to go see my Psycho The Rapist.'

'Psycho who?' I charf.

'Psycho The Rapist. She's the lady that they told me to go and see because I jumped.'

'Really?' I charf cause of I don't know what else to say.

'Ja, she's not so bad. She's got big boobies.' He grins as he do says this and then stops to show me with his hands how big her boobies is.

I grin and charf, 'Big boobies,' but I is not so sure howcomewhy that are a good think. I make my hands like Zakes' and charf it again, 'Big boobies,' as if this would of somehow asplain but it don't not so as I just laugh and he laughs too also as well.

I check out Miss Smit when we do of get to class. She don't not have big boobies none. She are like got none boobies.

SEVEN

Zakes' brother are there by a shops a next day. I had of scaled R20 from ouma's handbag so as I could buy some sweets. I did bought some Cherrols and had of zicked a Kit Kat when George weren't not looking. I were just sucking on a Cherrol when I sees him. He are by a wall and like checking round lots and he do calls me over.

His eyes is only a little bit red and he do of grin at me then charfs, 'Hey boss.'

I laugh cause of he did called me boss again, but he don't not laugh none. He checks all round like he are looking for someone, then asks me if I did got more bullets. I think for a bit, then charf that I don't not think so.

'Eish! Boss!' He do shake his head. 'A hundred bucks if you can find me some.'

A hundred bucks! Are this guy for real! Now I is interested.

'I can go look,' I charf him and run off home.

There are no one at home when I get there, not even ouma are there. Then I merember that it are like a Wednesday and ouma sometimes goes on a Wednesday to see oupa in a hopstibal. He do got Old Timers disease that are why he are there. Pa always charfs that oupa got Old Timers so as he could forget he were married to ouma.

I do go to my room and make some noise there for a bit so as to make sure that ma are really not home, then I do go quietly into ma and pa's room. A bullets what I got last time were in a gun safe but now there were none more left and pa hasn't not of bought none more, so I check out his cupboard but can't not see none.

I then look in his drawers. He do got some lekker stuff in there, a lectric razor, a small whiskey bottle, a other bottle what smells like he do when he goes to work and his army medal.

I check all this out then put it all back careful like. Then I do go to his undie drawer and I lift up a undies. There are a box of bullets at a bottom of a drawer. I are just grabbing them when I hear a front door and ma's voice. She are like talking to some ou and they is walking down a passage.

I had of charfed her that I were playing there by Jaapie's cause of I didn't not want her to knowed that I didn't got none friends, but this did of mean that she wouldn't not of aspected that I were home.

I climb into a cupboard quick like, just in time. A cupboard door don't not shut proper like so as I can check out a little bit. Ma do of come into a room with Larry the Lithp. What are he doing here I do of wonder, then skrik cause of maybe he are going to tell her that I had of beed chucking my zarms over a fence for Shaka.

But they don't not hardly say nothink. Instead Larry do starts kissing ma big time. I like nearly drop a bullets cause of I is so surprised. Do Larry the Lithp love ma? I sit really still like, checking this scene out and holding onto a bullets really tight like. I had of never really checked out ous kissing what like ma and Larry were doing and I'm like really interested in seeing it.

Next think though is old Larry are taking ma's clothes off. Now I is like what to do? I have of never checked ma with no clothes on and pa charfs that it are like a sin to check a girl with no clothes on, but I can't not stop looking. I wonder if Larry the Lithp knowth that it are a thin to thee a girl with no clothth on. He doesn't not seem to be worried none and are even letting ma take his clothes off.

I jump out of a cupboard and charf them to stop cause of it are a sin.

Are you mad? Of course I don't not. I would of get into huge kak from pa, cause of ma would tell. Asides, this are too interesting to stop.

With none clothes on, ma do of check like a girls what I sawed in a magazine what I found once in pa's drawer. All I can check of Larry are his bum. I think of calling him Larry the Bum cause of this and I nearly laugh, but do of stop myself. Anyways, I don't not see Larry's bum for long cause ma lies down and he do lie on top of her. Next think are that he are bouncing up and down on ma. This checks really weird. And then ma do of start moaning like what she do when I can hear pa slapping her. All of a suddenly I realises that this must be what pa are doing with ma all a time cause of I can hear that slap sound as Larry the Lithp bounces on ma, a only difference are that Larry the Lithp are going, 'Yeth, Yeth, Yeth,' as he bounces. Pa never done that afore.

Ma and Larry go on bouncing forever so as I get bored and sits back in a cupboard. I do of start to wonder if old Pooh Pants had of ever got Theresa Dern to take her clothes off and then bounced on her cause of he loved her, but then I merember that Theresa don't not like Pooh Pants none more, she loves Jaapie. I think that maybe if I asks Jaapie nicely, he would let me bounce on Theresa with no clothes on to of see howcomewhy is are that ma and Larry do of like this so much. But I don't not reckon that Theresa would of let me any how cause of she don't not like me none and anyways, Jaapie are not my friend none more. I acide to asks Zakes about it cause of Zakes knows lots of stuff.

I are just thinking all of this when all of a sudden like I hear ma shout, 'I'm coming,' and I skrik big time cause of maybe she are like now playing hide and seek and are coming to find me. I quickly check out through a crack in a door, but ma are not coming none. She are still lying under Larry the Lithp and he are like shaking on top of her going, 'Yeeeeeth!'

This are all just too weird for me and I want to run off and sell a bullets to Zakes' brother and pretend like none of this never happened. But I can't not do nothink, so as I sits still in a cupboard and wait. After lots of time they shut up and all I can hear are them breathink hard. I wonder if Larry will ever bugger off so as I can get out of a cupboard. But at last I do of hears them move and check that they is starting to put their clothes on.

'How's my son doing?' Ma asks when she are almost got all of her clothes on.

'Much better,' Larry charfs, 'He theemth to have made friendth with that boy Thaketh, the one that tried to commit thuithide.'

'Is that a good thing?' ma asks and I is like, stuff you ma, asking Larry if it are a good think. Of course being friends with Zakes are good, I didn't not got none other friends.

'I think their friendthip will be good for both of them,' Larry charfs, 'Thaketh is theeing a thighcomanologithst. I think that were a word what he did of used, a psychomanologist, but he are wrong cause of I knowed that it are a psycho the rapist what Zakes are seeing. He also charfed me that he do have to see a fizzy ou the rapist also as well. I want to charf old Larry that he are wrong, but geez man, that would be megadof. So I do of charf nothink and ma charfs nothink but she do just smile at Larry the Lithp, then gives him a big girlie kiss.

'You'd better get going, people will be home soon,' she charfs and I do of almost wet my broeks laughing.

EIGHT

I couldn't not find Zakes' brother afterwards, so did of hided a bullets in my undies drawer and it were lucky that ma didn't seed them when she put some clean ones in there later.

A next day at school I charfed old Zakes what I had of seed, but I never charf him that it were Larry the Lithp what were with ma. He like checks me out with these big eyes what looks like them eyeball sweets. I did want to grab his eye and put it in my mouth but I don't not cause of they is real eyes and not sweet ones.

'You saw your ma doing it? And it wasn't with your pa?'

I like check him out. So that were what 'doing it' were, bouncing on top of someone with no clothes on. I can under-stand why old Zakes are like, 'You saw your ma doing it?' but don't not really knowed howcome-why he were like, 'and it wasn't with your pa?' Anyways, I don't not let him knowed that I didn't not knowed what 'doing it' were, so I just nods like and charf, 'Ja.' I did of wanted to ask him if it were wrong that ma were 'doing it' with someone what weren't not pa, but I didn't not cause of it would make like I didn't not knowed these thinks.

'Did you see her boobies? What were they like?'

He are getting all excited and all and I don't not really like it cause of she are my ma and if she shouldn't not be bouncing with Larry, then I reckon that Zakes shouldn't not be seeing her boobies, even if they are in his brain like, so I just charf, 'No, I didn't not see nothink cause of I were in a cupboard. I only sawed a ou's bum. Where are Shaka?' I don't not want to talk about it none more.

'He'll be along. I think that sometimes he hangs round the shops first as there are ous there that give him some hamburgers and stuff.'

That's when I merember and charf, 'I sometimes see a ou round a shops what says he are your brother.'

Zakes checks me out big time now. 'You stay away from him, he's trouble.'

He are like quite angry when he charfs this and I's like, what are a problem?

'You stay away from him, you hear me?' he like charfs again and I can check that he are really serious and all.

'Okay, okay,' I charf, 'keep your undies on.'

He checks me out good and proper for a while and I want to ask if this ou are like really his brother, but can check that he doesn't not want to talk about it none so as I look round and see that Shaka are coming up a road.

'Here comes Shaka,' I charf and we is cool again.

I throw Shaka with my zarms and we watch as he chows them. While this are happening I check round and see old Larry the Lithp are watching us. He's like got this smile on his face, but as soon as he sees I is checking him out, he do of walk away and goes and talks to Miss Smit.

I still haven't not of asked old Zakes whycome he did jumped, but I reckon it aren't not so important as what it used to was. In fact, I only merember that he did of jumped when I do of walk past a drop zone that arvie. Zakes had gone to see his fizzy ou and I were hanging round school for a bit cause of I felt like it. I checked hard on a ground but could hardly not see nothink of a blood spot. It were like as Zakes' jumping never did of happened.

There were nothink going on at school so as I acide to bugger off home. I were just coming near a shops when suddenly some ou grabs me from ahind and I nearly do of falled over.

'Where my bullets, boss,' Zakes' brother are like standing there and it checks like he are about to donner me. His eyes is full of very cross veins and he are like checking round lots. He are not friendly like afore, you can check that he really do of wants a bullets and that he would donner me hard if I didn't not get them.

I like skrik and nearly wet my broeks, but then I is not a woosie, so I don't not. I just charf him, 'R150 cause of it are a last box.' I don't not knowed howcomewhy I charf him this cause of he are like biggerer as me and could of cause some serious damage if he did give me a klap like pa do. I wait, poeping myself as he checks me out.

Then all of a sudden like he laughs and charfs, 'Okay, boss, R150, but don't mess with me today. I've got to have them by four o'clock, okay?'

I nods big time even though I can't not tell a time proper like. I just reckon if I do of run home and get them and then run back, I should be there afore four o'clock.

When I gets home I check that ma are on a phone and ouma are in a kitchen as usual. So I grabs a bullets and run back to a shop. Zakes' brother are not there so as I hang around for a bit and is just about to bugger off when he do of come. He don't not say much to me, just charfs, 'Thanks,' when I give him a bullets. He gives me a R150 and buggers off quick like.

'That are a last box,' I shouts after him, but it are like as he don't not hear me none. I hang around for a bit longerer then go buy some Toff-o-lux and chow a whole roll afore I go home.

When I get home ma are sitting round reading a magazine in a lounge. When she checks me she like calls for me to come sit there by her. I skrik, but only a little. Ma has of never asked me to sit with her, but I can check that she aren't not cross with me none, so as I go and sit on a chair near her.

'How things going?' she asks.

What sort of a question are that? How thinks going?

'Fine,' I charf and check out my takkies. Ma always makes us wear takkies when we go out. I much affer to go out barefoot, but pa did of caughted me one time I didn't not wear takkies and he bliksemed me really hard, so as I don't not do it none more.

'How's school?'

Now this are really weird. Ma don't never ask about school.

'Fine,' I charf again. My laces is undid on my one takkie and I do of want to tie it, but don't not, cause of ma are looking at me.

'What did you do at school today?' she charfs.

Can't she not check that I don't not want to answer none questions?

'Nothink, bugger off and leave me alone,' I shouts at her and runs out of a room.

Don't be dof, I would never of talk like that to ma, cause of she would of tell pa and he would bliksem me.

Still, I were a bit a moer in that I do of have to answer all ma's questions so as I acide to stir a kak.

'We had P.E.,' I charf. 'Mr van Staaden,' I do of call him Mr van Staaden cause of ma wouldn't not of knowed him if I had of said Larry the Lithp, 'did make me do push ups till I were sick.' I check her out now as I charf this.

She are like all, 'He didn't did he?'

'Strue's God,' I charfs.

'And what did you do to make him punish you like that,' you can check that she are not sure.

'Nothink,' I charf and give her a look what says that I really don't not knowed whycome old Larry the Lithp would of do this.

'You must have done something,' she says.

Why don't growed ups never believe me?

'I didn't not do nothink,' I charf, 'we just gotted to P.E. and he like told me to start doing push ups and then let a other ous go play cricket. I had to do push ups a whole period. He even came there to check that I were doing them.'

'I don't believe it,' she charfs and now I get pissed. She just don't not want to believe me cause of she loves Larry the Lithp.

'He did too,' I nearly do of shouts but stop just in time and say it instead. I check out my takkies again. I do of need new ones, but pa says I can't not have none.

'How's Jaapie?' Ma do of asks sudden like, 'He don't come play none more.'

'No,' I charf, 'Jaapie's ma don't not let him out to play none more. I do of have to go play there.' I is not going to charf her that we is no longer friends cause of then I can't not say I's going to see Jaapie when I wants to go out.

Ma just nods now like she do believe me. Howcomewhy don't she not believe me when I charfed her about old Larry the Lithp making me do push ups?

'Do you have any black friends?' she do of asks next.

Now I can check what she are doing. She are like trying to check if Larry the Lithp were telling her a truth. Part of me do of wants to lie and part of me don't. A part of me what don't, are a one what speaks.

'Ja, there are this ou called Zakes what I do of hang out with sometimes.'

Ma nods and you can check that she do of wants to ask if he are a ou what tried to commit sewerage pipe. If she had of asked then a part of me what do of wants to lie would have charfed her, 'No,' cause of I were worried that she would of say that I can't not play with Zakes cause of it would make me want to commit sewerage pipe too also.

But she don't not asks that. She just charfs, 'You know you can ask him round to play if you like, but just not when your pa are around. You know how he feels about blacks.'

I didn't not really knowed how pa do of feels about blacks other than that he do of calls them kaffirs and that are bad according to de Wit.

Still I nods and then says, 'Thanks ma, but Zakes has to go see this Fizzy Ou most afternoons.' As soon as I say this, I want to donner myself for being so dof.

'A physio? Why?' Ma asks. Now you see howcomewhy I reckon I were dof?

'I dunno. What are a fizzy ou anyways? Zakes just do say he must of go see this ou, but he didn't not say whycome.'

Ma smiles like and then charfs me what this fizzy ou does. I is like a bit disappointed cause of I thought that maybe it were like this ou what did gave Zakes sherbet and that maybe he would of give me some one day. But I didn't not want to let ma check that I had of beed dof, so I is like, 'Oh, so it must of beed cause of a car accident what he had that he do of needs to go see this fizzy ou.'

Ma do of smile again and nods like as she believes me, but I can check in her eyes that she do of knows different. Of course she do of knowed different, Larry would have told her all about Zakes.

'Can I get some new takkies, please ma?' I asks this cause of I don't not want to talk to her about Zakes none more and cause of I also do want new takkies too.

Ma checks out my takkies and charfs, 'I'll speak to your pa,' but you can check that she won't not cause of she are scared pa will donner her.

'Can I go play now?' I asks and she do of nods.

I don't not like that ma were 'doing it' with Larry the Lithp cause of now she would of knowed all what were potting there by school and I reckoned it were only going to get worser.

NINE

I didn't not really knowed Sunette Snel too good, but I did of feeled sorry for her when I hear that her ma were shooted dead by some ous what came to her house and stole a car. Sunette never really blanked me like all a other ous did of, but that were more cause of we weren't not in a same class so as I didn't not knowed her too good. But when I did of heard that her ma were killed, I were sorry for her, but didn't not say nothink.

All a ous are like worried at school now cause of this were a second person what were killed. I like skrik a bit and start to think that maybe I shouldn't not of sold pa's gun to Zakes' brother cause of if those ous do of come to our house, pa didn't not got none gun to shoot them with. I begin to reckon that maybe I should buy a gun back like, but I didn't not got none money cause of I did of spended it all on sweets.

At least, I reckon, Zakes would of be safe if those ous did come to his house cause of his brother do got a gun. I have of never charfed Zakes that I did sold his brother pa's gun cause of he like told me he doesn't not like guns nothink.

So at break I don't not talk to Zakes about Sunette Snel's ma. We do of sit and throw Shaka with a zarms what I make special like for him and then Zakes do of starts talking about Mrs Wentzel's boobies. Mrs Wentzel are a geography teacher and she do of got big boobies. I still don't not knowed howcome-why Zakes do thinks boobies is so important, but I talk to him about it cause of he do likes it.

I still haven't not asked him whycome he did of jumped, but I is not that interested none more. I charf him instead that he can of come round and play anytime, so long as my pa aren't not there.

'Why don't you want me to see your pa?' he asks.

'Cause of he'll donner you,' I charf.

Don't be dof, I don't not charf him that. I don't not even charf him that pa do of not like blacks none, cause of that would also be dof as well. I just charf him that my pa are so ugly that he do of scares people.

'He do of even scare me,' I charf, 'so as my ma do of only let me see him a little bit.'

He like checks me out like I is lying to him, so I charf, 'Cross my heart and hope to die.' I can check that he still doesn't not believe me none, but he doesn't not charf nothink none more, he just do of nod like.

Shaka are giving us a hairy eyeball to check if we is going to give him more zarms. I do of got one piece left, so as I chuck it over to him.

'What are your pa like?' I asks Zakes. I is still watching Shaka chow a zarm.

'My pa's dead,' he charfs.

I skrik a bit at this. Not like a big skrik, but it are like not what I were aspecting to hear.

'Did he get shooted?' I asks this cause of I think maybe that are why he don't not like guns none.

But he do of just shake his head and charf, 'No, he died of Aids. Him and my ma.'

'Your ma are dead too also?' Now I do of feel dof cause of that were what he did of just said, but Zakes don't not check me out like I are dof, he do of just nods his head.

40

I don't not know what to charf then. What do you charf a ou what tells you his ma and pa is dead. So I don't not charf nothink.

At assembly, de Wit charfs us that we must be careful cause of a ous what is shooting people.

Zakes are still going to see a fizzy ou and a psycho the rapist so as he can't not come play none, but I still charf him where I do live so as if he ever do wants to come play he will of know. He never do of asks me to come play there by him.

It are only laterer that I merember that he did of said that his pa had of died of aids. I merember it cause of I did cut myself and ma wanted to put a band aid on, so I charfed her, 'No, cause of I did heard that people died of Aids.'

I don't not charf her it were Zakes' ma and pa what died. Ma checks me out and laughs like as if I is being dof, but then she just charfs, 'Okay, we won't use a band aid.' She did of goes away and then comes back. 'This are a plaster, not a band aid,' she do charfs me and do of puts it on my cut.

I check out a plaster. It do of check like a band aid, but I is chuffed that I made ma not give me Aids. I is not so dof you know.

A next time ouma goes to visit oupa and his Old Timers, I tell ma that I is going to play at Zakes'. She like smiles and charfs me that are fine. I go out, but I don't not go to Zakes', I go out a front door then round a side of a house and in through a kitchen door at a back. I can hear ma on a phone in a lounge so as I go quietly to her room and climb in a cupboard. It are not long afore her and Larry the Lithp is 'doing it'.

I check out ma's boobies proper like this time cause of Zakes did wanted to know what they looked like. I is not really interested in watching them 'doing it', I just really do of want to see if they charf anythink about me afterwards.

But they don't not say nothink about me. They talk a bit about pa and how he do of donners ma. Larry charfs ma that she mutht leave him, but ma charfs that she can't not. They do of argue a bit but it's not like shouting argue. Then ma charfs Larry he must go, cause of I will be home soon.

I wonder if ma has of told Larry that pa do of also donner me and did gived Sally a hard klap once that made her fall over.

I's glad that I did of moved quickly from a cupboard while ma were saying goodbye to Larry cause of she went back to her room and I could of heard her crying there. I don't not like to hear ma crying, so as I went to a shops and zicked some Rolos while George weren't not watching. I also wanted to zick some chips too as well, but didn't not get none chance.

41

I were cross with Larry the Lithp for telling ma to leave pa, what would happen to me and Sally then? I didn't not want to stay with pa if ma weren't not there.

I is busy thinking this when I check out Zakes' brother. I go over to asks him if I can borrow a gun. He charfs me ja and do of give it to me. I then goes to school and check Larry the Lithp are in his office. I go in and point a gun at him and he's like wetting his broeks and all and charfing, 'I'm tho thorry for telling your ma to leave your pa,' and all that. But I just charf him to shut up and then I do of shooted him.

Of course it don't not happen in real life, only in my brain like. I did really seed Zakes' brother though, but he don't not seed me. He looks skrikked and all and are running, but he are running funny cause of he are holding his one soldier with a other hand. I chow my Rolos there near a shops then start to walk home. It are then that I check a blood on a road where Zakes' brother had of beed running.

TEN

I are still wondering about a blood when I do of get home. There are a ambalance outside of our house with all a red lights going and all, and a ou running to a ambalance. It do of drives off with a sirens going, as soon as what I gets there.

I goes inside and check pa sitting in a lounge and he are like talking and all. He doesn't not even check me when I walks in. His eyes is all red and he do keep charfing, 'I'm sorry Maggie, I'm so sorry.'

I check round a room cause of Maggie are my ma's proper name, but I can't not see no one there none, so as I charf, 'Pa?'

He do look up and checks me out for a bit like he can't not tell who I is. I want to charf him that it are me, but then he do of charf my name so as I knows he do of knows it are me.

'Where are ma?' I asks.

He do of look like he are about to cry and I skrik cause of I do suddenly think that maybe somethink not lekker has of happened.

'Has ma beed shooted?' I asks and do of feel like I is about to cry myself.

Pa do of looks at me like I are mad.

'Shot?' he charfs.

I charf him, 'Ja, David du Plessis' pa were shooted and Hester Lange's pa were shooted too also, but he didn't not die and Sunette Snel's ma were shooted dead also, so were ma also?'

Pa do smell of whiskey. He checks me out for a little bit, then charfs, 'No, your ma has not been shot, she's been mugged.'

I don't not know what he means when he says *she's been mugged* but reckon that maybe pa did of hitted her hard with a coffee mug or somethink this time. At least he were sorry, so I charf, 'Okay,' and leave him in a lounge and go through to a kitchen. Ouma are there, but I never sawed her like this afore. She are also talking to herself.

'That's it. This time he really did it to her. Nearly killed her. I can't believe he did it. No, I can believe it. Animal! She was on the floor, on the floor and unconscious and he still kicked her, my poor baby. Why? She was unconscious, she never did him no harm.'

Who were on a floor? Who were unconscious? Who did of kicked who? I are so confused and I check ouma out, but she don't not check me none.

'We'll be lucky if she survives this time,' ouma do of charf her cup of tea and I skrik big time. She were talking about ma and pa. Had pa really skopped ma when she were on a floor? I thinks back to a dog what we had what pa skopped. That dog did of never comed back and now I are scared that ma had of gone to sleep there by a hopstibal and that we wouldn't not never see her again.

I check ouma out a bit more and she are like seriously talking to her tea, but you can check that she are upset about ma. I leave her to her tea and go to Sally's room. She are like sitting on her bed playing with her dolls and all, so as I asks her what are happened.

'Pa comed home and started donnering ma,' she charfs and don't not even look up none from her dolls.

'Ja, and?' I charf. Pa do often donnered ma but somethink weren't not lekker this time.

Sally like stops playing with her dolls and do of looks at me.

'What are a slut?' she do of asks.

'I dunno,' I charf, 'whycome do you want to know?'

'Cause of that are what pa called ma afore he hit her, a slut.'

'A slut are like a snail what didn't got none shell,' I charf, but I don't not know howcome pa would of call ma that.

Just then we hear ouma shouting and screaming and she do of run through to a lounge. She are like trying to bliksem pa, but he are too strong for her, so as he fights back and donners her one shot. Ouma falls over backwards and klaps her head on a coffee table big time. She then like just lies on a floor doing nothink.

I check up at pa and he are like checking ouma out. He are super skrikked and all, but thinks are not lekker here. I scheme that maybe ouma are dead so as I grab Sally by her hand and pulls her out of a lounge and we go awards her room.

Sally are now screaming and all I can check are that pa are coming for me to bliksem me also. I is nearly almost poohing my pants cause of a look pa what gives me. I reckon he are going to donner me into next week, and then Sally too also.

I run into a passage and get a huge skrik cause of Zakes' brother what are standing there. He sort of checks me out, but he are not so lekker none neither and I don't not reckon that he do of knows who I is. I check round and see pa in a passage ahind me.

He then checks out Zakes' brother and stops. Now it are pa's turn to skrik which he does big time and then I see whycome he are skrikking so much, it are cause of Zakes' brother did got a gun and are pointing it at me.

'Hey, boss,' he charfs and then do laugh, but it are not really a laugh proper, more like a cough and I can check that some blood are coming out of his mouth. 'You got any more bullets for me?'

Now I pooh my pants big time. Not as in real pooh, but I is really skrikked somethink chronic cause of now pa will of knowed I did of sold Zakes' brothers a bullets and a gun.

Now pa gets a moer in and like shouts, 'Get out of my house!'

Sally are crying and pa do of comes down a passage awards me. I check him out, then Zakes' brother then Sally. I do of want to run but my legs don't not got a cat's clue what to do, so as I just stands there.

Pa keeps coming and shouting at Zakes' brother then suddenly there are a moerse loud bang, I mean this bang are even louderer as a crackers what me and Jaapie scaled from his pa once and then went and set them off there in a veldt.

I check round and see that pa has of falled down and it checks like Sally are screaming and all, but I can't not hear nothink cause of a bang. Then, slowly I can start to hear Sally, but I can check that thinks are not lekker with pa cause of there are blood all over his shirt.

'Pa?' I charf, but he doesn't not move or nothink.

Then I hear Zakes' brother. He like coughs and goes, 'Heh, sorry boss, I shot your pa.'

He says this then do of just sits down really slowly like. There are more blood coming out of his mouth and his eyes check all funny like as they is not seeing nothink. This are a big time kak scene and I don't not knowed what all to do. All I knowed is this are not good none and we do of need to be out of here. So I grab Sally's hand and run outside with her, telling her to shut up and stop screaming.

ELEVEN

The veldt are not lekker in a dark and Sally are scared and crying. I are poep scared too also, but I keep charfing Sally to stop crying, but nice like. I is not shouting none cause I do of need to think what to do and Sally crying are making me not think proper.

I make like to donner her shut her up, but she do just cries even more, so as I stop and charf her nice like again to stop crying. She still don't not stop so I give her a hug even though she are a girl. This makes her go quieterer and I charf, 'Don't cry Sally, it are going to be okay. Don't cry, please.' There are snot coming out of her nose and all so as I use my t-shirt to clean it and she do adventually stop crying.

I find a place in a veldt where Jaapie and me let off crackers. It are quite a lekker place and there is some nice rocks there to sit on. I do of make Sally sit and she are like just sitting down when I hear a noise.

'Shh!' I charf and check round into a dark. I can hear that someone are coming and I skrik myself silly. Maybe it are Zakes' brother with pa's gun what are coming to shoot us. Maybe pa has of come to donner me for selling his gun.

'Shh!' I charf again even though Sally are not making none noise. Then I do check a movement in a dark and I wet my broeks.

It are like only afterwards what I laugh about it cause of it were quite funny that I did of wet my broeks. It weren't not pa or Zakes' brother, but it were Shaka. I dunno where from he had followed us, but it were lekker to see him. Sally skriks though cause of she don't not knowed Shaka.

'It are okay, Sally,' I charf her, 'It are okay, this are Shaka, he are a good dog.'

I pat Shaka to show Sally that he are a good dog and all, but Sally are like scared so I pat Shaka some more and take Sally's hand to try to make her pat him also too as well. She like cries, but only a little bit so as I pull her hand some more till she can pat Shaka and then she are cool. Shaka are cool too cause of he lets Sally pat him and he don't not do nothink.

It are good that Shaka are here now cause of Sally are cool with him and she do play nicely and is quiet so as I can of try to think. I wish Zakes were here also cause of Zakes are clever. Zakes would of knowed what to do.

I check out Sally with Shaka. She are now like stroking him lekker, then suddenly, Shaka do of checks round and his ears go up straight and me and Sally skrik lekker cause of someone else are coming.

Then I hear some ou calling, 'Shaka! Shaka!' and I charf Sally that it are okay cause of that are Zakes and Zakes are my friend. Shaka runs off and we wait. It aren't not long afore Zakes comes. He can walk now without his clutches but he do still walks a bit funny. He checks me out, then Sally. It are dark, but a moon are making it light so as I can check his eyes are like eyeball sweets.

'This are Sally, she are my sister,' I charf Zakes afore he charfs anythink and he do nods. His eyes is not so much like eyeball sweets now, cause of he knows who Sally are.

Zakes leans his head to tell me to come over to one side so as we can talk so as I charf Sally to stay with Shaka.

'The police came,' Zakes says when we is far enough away from Sally, 'they shot my brother. I don't know where he is, but I know he's wounded.'

I check him out and like merember Zakes' brother falling over at our house. I reckon that he were deaded, as were also pa and ouma and ma. I want to tell Zakes all this, but all I can charf are, 'Howcomewhy did a police shoot him?'

Zakes do of looks at me and charfs, 'Cause he's a bloody tsotsi, a gangster. He was the one that shot David du Plessis' pa and all the others. He was a small time crook till he managed to get hold of a gun, then it got out of hand. He was into drugs and all that. That's why the police came for him, because he shot those people.'

I check out Zakes big time now cause of what he are charfing me. It are cause of Zakes' brother had a gun that Pooh Pants' pa are deaded and Sunette's ma are deaded and Hester's Pa were shooted. And also my pa were shooted cause of Zakes' brother did of have a gun. I is like, it must of have beed some other gun what he did used cause of he would never of used pa's gun to shooted people with.

'I think your brother are dead,' I charf Zakes.

'Dead?' Zakes charfs giving me a hairy eyeball. It are not cause of he are dof that he do of asks this, Zakes are not dof, it are cause of he are surprised that he do charfs, 'Dead?'

I then charf him all what happened when I got home and he like does a eyeball sweets again. Then Sally do says, 'I want to go home.'

I charf her to play with Shaka cause of we can't not go home right now cause of what did of happened. She do of start crying and I have to go hug her to make her stop and I check out Zakes to make sure he are not like checking me out skeef cause of I is hugging a girl. But he are cool, he can check why I is doing it.

I charf Sally to play with Shaka and that me and Zakes is going to sort out thinks. I can check that she do of wants to cry more, but she don't say nothink. Shaka goes and sniffs her hand and she are cool again.

I go back to Zakes and asks, 'What can we do? Sally do of wants to go home.'

He charfs straight out, 'You can't go home. If you do, the cops will take you and Sally away because your parents are dead. They will make you go stay with horrible people.'

I check him out and I'm skrikking a little cause of I don't not want to go stay with none horrible people.

Zakes goes on, 'That's what the police did with me and my brother when my ma and pa died of Aids. They made us go stay with these horrible people. We ran away then. I wanted to go to my grandparents in Mpumalanga, but my brother said that that's where those horrible people would look for us, so we came here. My brother pretended he was my father because he looks old. He looked after me at first, but then he got mixed up with this bad crowd. That's when he started with the drugs.

'I tried to run away, but they caught me and made me go back home with them. I hated it there. They were always drunk or stoned. I had to cook and clean for them all, I was like their slave. That's why I jumped off the third floor at school. I couldn't take it anymore.'

He checks round now and I is like just checking him out cause of now I knowed howcomewhy he did of jumped. But somehow it aren't not so important none anymore. What are important is that we sort out what to do.

'Can we go back to your place?' I charf, but Zakes do of look at me like I are dof.

'The police are all over the show at my place, that's why I'm here. I ran when they raided and shot my brother. I found Shaka and have been following him around ever since, till he found you. We can't go there.'

47

He do of think for a bit then charfs, 'And we can't go to your place cause the cops are most probably there also.'

'So what can we do?' I asks. I feel a bit dof that I can't not acide what to do, but I can't not none.

'I'm going to try and find my grandparents,' Zakes adventually charfs, 'You can come with if you like.'

I is like, 'ja, I want to go with,' and are just about to say so when I do of hear, 'I need to go wee.'

'Go there behind that bush,' I charf Sally. 'Shaka will go with you, so as you will be okay.'

She checks me out for a bit then goes off.

'Can Sally come with us?' I asks Zakes.

He do of shakes his head and charfs, 'No, she's small and also a girl. It will be hard for her. Is there someone nice you can leave her with, someone who will look after her?'

Now it are my turn to think for a bit. Then Larry the Lithp come into my brain all of a sudden like. I think that maybe if he do of loves ma then he will look after Sally okay.

'Ja,' I charf and nods.

TWELVE

Pa are still lying on a floor in a passage and Zakes' brother are lying on my bed, but he are dead now, I reckon. Ouma are on a floor in a lounge. Zakes reckons that a cops is too busy chasing a ous what hung out with his brother, so that is howcomewhy they is not there by our house.

We did of have to wait to go in cause of our neighbour, Mr Louw, were outside checking around, but he adventually wented inside again. I climbed in through a bedroom window cause of I knowed how to open it. A first think what I do is get all my money. Zakes charfed me to see if my pa or his brother did of had any money as well. I roll pa over, aspecting him to wake up at any time and donner me, but he don't not. I get his wallet and take a money out.

Zakes' brother are more difficulter cause of all a blood, but I like check his pockets. He do got lots of bucks what I take. He do also got some pills and a plastic bag what do got stuff what checks like grass in it. I chuck these away, then go to a kitchen and load whatever food I can find into my satchel after throwing all my school books out. I check a small bottle of pa's whiskey what I also put into a satchel as well. I then go find ouma's handbag cause of I knowed she always do got some bucks in there. I had of zicked from her lank times afore, but there is not too much in her purrs this time when I really needs it.

I are just about to go back to Zakes and Sally when I do of merember and go into Sally's room. Her doll are on her bed like, where she did of lefted it when pa donnered ouma. I are just about to grab it when I hear a knock at a door.

'Police! Open up!' some ou charfs outside and I poep and wet my broeks all at once. Not real poep and wet, like what Pooh Pants did, but just as in proper skrik. I grab Sally's doll and run quick like to my room while a police bang some more. I grab a shirt and stuff it into my satchel, then chuck it all out of a window. A police is banging lank hard on a door now, so I jumps out a window, grabs my bag and runs like mad to where Zakes and Sally is. A police are like so busy breaking a door that no one checks me out.

'Come, let's go,' I charf Zakes and Sally as soon as what I get to them. 'A cops is at a house.'

We do of run down a street and Sally keeps going, 'I'm scared, I'm scared.'

'Come on,' I charf and keep running.

She like stops in a middle of a street and I like get a moer in with her and wants to shout, but Zakes, who can't not run lank fast cause of his legs are still funny from when he did of jumped, he do of stops and says to Sally all nice like, 'Sally, we're taking you somewhere safe and then we will go and sort things out. Is that okay?'

I reckon it are cause of it were Zakes what charfed this and not me that she do of believes him and Shaka like sniffs her so as she are cool and we run a bit more till we are there by Larry the Lithp's house.

Cause of Zakes can't not run that fast we acide that he and Shaka will go to a veldt and I will sort out Sally with Larry the Lithp. We give Zakes a few minutes so as he can get away, then I charf Sally to go up to a house and ring a bell.

At first she doesn't not want to cause of she are scared and all so as I charf her that if she don't not go ring a bell then a police will come and take her to live there by some horrible people.

'I just want to go home to ma,' she charfs and is sort of crying. It are then that I do of merember her doll and take it out my satchel. She do of smile and takes it from me.

'Larry the Lithp will take you to ma later when all this stuff are sorted,' I charfs. I do of feel bad cause of I is lying, but I can't not tell Sally that ma are deaded cause of then she would of never go to Larry.

She like looks at me and I charf, 'Strue's Bob.' You can check that she are still not sure but I do of push her a little so as she goes down a path to Larry the Lithp's house.

She makes like a few steps then stops and looks back at me. I charf her to go on by like pointing and all. After checking me out for a bit, she adventually goes down a path again. I check her go all a way and then check that she are too short to reach a doorbell. She looks round at me and I'm like what to do now?

Sally do of start to walk back to me so as I run up to her and take her to a door again. There I charf her that I's going to ring a bell, then run away so as Larry don't not stop me cause of if he do, he will send us to stay there by a horrible people, but if he don't not stop me, then he will send her to ma.

She like checks me out again like she don't not believe me none, but she don't not charf nothink.

'Okay?' I charf, 'I is going now. I will see you when me and Zakes have of sorted thinks out.' I feel a bit sad cause of I don't not knowed if I would never see Sally again ever. I give her a hug cause of girls like hugs, then jump up and ring a bell and run like mad.

When I gets outside Larry's garden I duck down ahind a bush and check out a house. Larry do of comes to a door and you can check that he are lank surprised to see Sally. She like starts crying and all which are good and not good cause of I don't not like to see Sally cry but at least she can't not tell Larry where I are if she are crying. I check that Larry takes her inside, then bugger off fast like to a veldt.

THIRTEEN

Shaka are a library door dog. I knows this cause of one day I checked Shaka when we was driving with ma and I asked her what kind of a dog are that one and did pointed at Shaka.

Shaka, a library door, gave like a small bark when I did of got near our place in a veldt. It were a bark what did of told Zakes it were me and there were no trouble.

It were darkerer now as what it were earlier cause of there is clouds in a sky what is not letting a moon shine so bright. I can just check out Zakes and Shaka when I get there.

'Okay?' Zakes charfs and I nods. 'We must get moving. We want to put as much distance between us and the police tonight as we can.'

I nods again then charfs, 'Do you know where your grandparents' house are?'

Zakes are trying to stand up, but it are hard for him cause of his legs is funny.

'Ja, Mpumalanga,' he charfs and gets his legs right so as he can stand proper.

'Where are that?' I asks.

'This way,' he charfs and do of start walking. It are like easy to keep up with him cause of he can't not walk so fast, but I are getting hungry cause of I didn't not have none supper. I wants to charf him to stop so as we can chow somethink, but I can check that he wants to walk, so as I just follows.

It are not easy walking in a dark cause of you can't not see where you is stepping so as we do of walk slow like across a veldt till we gets to a road. There is not so many cars around cause of it are late and all. Zakes charfs that we must walk along a road so as we can see a sign what tells us where Mpumalanga are. I is scared that if we walk by a road then maybe a cops might see us so as I charf Zakes this.

'Good thinking, Einstein,' he charfs and I are chuffed that I did of think of somethink clever. We checks up and down a road. There are a shop like George's what do of have a Coca-Cola sign that are a little bit up a road.

'I think that there is a stream just past that shop,' Zakes charfs. 'We can go and sleep under the bridge there. I think that we are far enough to be safe for the moment.'

We check up and down a road again so as to make sure there is no cars coming, then we starts walking. We is almost by a shop when I check back and see blue lights flashing.

'Zakes!' I charf, but he had of already seen a lights.

'Quick!' he do of pulls me off a road and we duck down by a bushes nearby. A cop car comes screaming along and turns in there by a shop. We can check lekker what are happening cause of a lights in a shop. Two cops jump out a car, they do of have their guns out and all.

I were skrikking somethink chronic when I did check a blue lights, but now I are more relaxed cause of a cops isn't not after us none. I wants to go closerer to a shop so as I can check what are happening, but Zakes charfs, 'Are you mad?' when I says I wants to go.

And Zakes are right, cause of a cops run into a shop and we hear like a whole lot of shots and all going off, so maybe I are not such a Einstein after all.

We wait for lank ages for a cops to come out again but nothink do of happens so as we wait some more, but still nothink do of happens so as adventually I charfs Zakes, 'Come, let's go check what are potting there.'

He are like, 'No,' but you can check that he really do of wants to go, so as I just like get up and walk real slow like awards a shop, checking a place out all a time and checking to see that there is bushes and all by a road so as if a cops do of come out we can jump ahind them quick like.

I can hear Zakes walking ahind me when I get near a shop and I like check round to him and then point to a dustbins what he can hide ahind while I go check what are happened. He must go ahind a dustbins cause of with his legs, he can't not run if there are trouble.

When Zakes are hidded I go really slow like to a door of a shop and check inside. There are a ou what are lying up to a counter. A sweets what should of beed there is all over a floor and I is like checking out all these sweets and thinkink how much we can of zick.

A ou what are lying up to a counter has blood all over his shirt and I do of think he must be deaded, cause of if he were alive, he would of already have taked a sweets hisself.

Then I check one of a cops lying by a fridge and there are a milk carton what are fallen over and it are dripping over his head and all, so as I scheme that he are deaded too also as well, cause of no ou would lie and let milk drip on his head, unless he were deaded.

I can't not check no one else, but I reckon that a other cop must of also be deaded or he would be helping out Mr Milkhead. I call Zakes to come and he checks all this out afore we go inside a door. He like gives this whistle and shakes his head.

'That guy was one of those who hung out with my brother,' he charfs really quiet like and points at a sweet ou.

Shaka goes into a shop afore we can of stop him and he do of sniffs a ou what are by a counter, then goes to Mr Milkhead and do start licking up a milk. Zakes charfs him to come away, but he don't not even look up none, so as we go into a shop.

I walk to a ou by a counter cause of I want to zick some sweets. There are lank of them all over, Cherrols, Meth-o-lyptus, Humbugs, Wilson's XXX mints, Toff-o-lux, Tex bars, Crunchies, Kit Kats, Flakies, Mint

Imperials, Chappies, PS Bars, Astros, Liquorice and even some eyeball sweets.

I are just of about to pick up a roll of Toff-o-lux when I do of hear some ou breathink really funny like. I skrik big time and drop a toffees and they do of roll over to a Sweet Ou. I check round and there are a other cop lying against a Simba Chips rack. He are all covered in chips and his eyes is like as a eyeball sweets. He checks me out and I check him out and he charfs, 'Help,' but I can't hardly not hear him none cause of he don't not speak too good.

I skrik some more and charf Zakes to of come over. We then check out Mr Chips together till Shaka comes and do of seed all a chips and goes to eat them.

'Shaka! Come away!' I charf, but he don't not listen to me. Mr Chips have of closed his eyes and he breathes funny like some more while I charf Shaka again to come away. Shaka checks us out, then do of carry on eating.

Mr Chips opens his eyes and charfs really slow like and breathink funny all a time, 'Go call for help.'

I check out Zakes and he checks me out and I is like, 'What should we do?'

Zakes thinks for a small bit, then charfs, 'Shaka! Come away!'

Shaka checks him out, then do of come over to us this time. Whycome don't Shaka not listen to me none?

'We must get away from here quickly. Go check if there is any money in the till, push all the buttons till it opens.'

'What about this ou?' I charf and points at Mr Chips.

Zakes checks him out then charfs, 'He's too far gone, we can't help him now. Go! See what money you can find. Move! There will be more cops here soon and we need to be gone.'

I like stand there for a bit, cause of I don't not knowed what to do, then I check out Mr Chips again and you can check that he are almost deaded.

'Go!' Zakes charfs again and he are like looking around a shop for I don't not knowed what. I runs ahind a counter and there are a other ou there what are also deaded, I think, cause of he are not moving none and also he are bleeding from his head. I reckon that maybe this ou are a one what owns a shop cause of he are ahind a counter and also cause of he do look a bit like George.

'Zakes,' I charf. I can't not see him none cause of I is too small to check over a counter. 'Zakes, there are a other deaded ou here.'

'Get the money,' Zakes just charfs.

53

I push all a buttons on a till and a drawer do of adventually opens. There are not lank money there, but I grab it all anyways.

When I gets back round a counter Mr Chips are still lying there doing nothink so as I reckon Zakes were right and that he are completely deaded now also as well.

I can't not check Zakes so as I go and grab as much sweets as what I can and stuff them in my satchel which are now full and quite heavy. Then I check Zakes at a door and he are like, 'Come on.'

I can check that he do have a plan cause of a way he charfs, 'Come on', so as I follows him out of a shop.

'I've got their car keys,' he charfs me when I get to a door and he like shows me.

I check them out, but can't not understand none what old Zakes wants to do with a keys. But then when we goes outside he climbs into a cop car ahind a steering wheel and charfs me to get in next to him.

I is like, 'Can you drive Zakes?'

And he are like, 'Of course man, it's easy. I've seen my brother do it.'

So I is like, 'Okay,' but that are only what I says cause of I don't not reckon he can of drive none, but I still do of get in next to him. He can hardly not check over a steering wheel none, but he do still reckon he can drive so as he do of start a car and steps on a pedal and a next think is that we is rerersing like big time.

Afore I can even shout nothink, old Zakes had of drived a cop car over a side of a road and into a little stream. I is laughing much better now cause of Zakes are also no Einstein.

Old Zakes checks me out and I don't not reckon that he are going to laugh none at first, but then he do of also as well and we is cool. Then suddenly a cop car starts talking to us and asking if everythink are okay and we skrik, so much that old Zakes even do a eyeball sweets think.

'We'd better get out of here,' he charfs. 'They'll send some more cops soon because those guys are not responding.'

'Good thinkink, Einstein,' I charf, but I don't not knowed where to go now and my satchel are lank heavy so as I can't not run fast. But that are okay cause of Zakes' legs, he can't not also run fast neither, so as I just follows him to a bridge what goes over a stream and we run underneath it. It are really dark there and Shaka are started barking at somethink so as Zakes do switch on a torch. I don't not knowed where he had of got a torch from, but I wished that he didn't not of had switched it on cause of he shines it on this black ou what are sitting there and he do got blood all over him. Jislaaik, did I skrik big time.

54

FOURTEEN

You know when you skrik like that, it are like as if your brain are not thinkink none cause of you poep first and asks questions later. There were nothink really to poep your broeks at with this black ou, but cause of we weren't not aspecting it, we did of poeped first.

It were only after we had of poeped and we did of have got Shaka to shut up, cause he were barking somethink chronic, that old Zakes do charf, 'Duma?'

This ou, Duma, checks us out, but he can't not seed us proper like cause of a light from a torch.

'Is that you Zakes?' he asks and I reckon he must of knowed Zakes' voice cause of there weren't none ways what he could of have seed us.

'Ja, Duma, it's me,' Zakes charfs, but you can hear that old Zakes are like not so happy to see Duma.

'Is Sharp okay?' Duma asks.

'Sharp is dead, I just saw him in the shop.'

I want to charf that Sharp were not so sharp cause of he did got killed, but I don't not say nothink.

'Zakes, you got to help me man, I've been hit, bad,' Duma charfs and he do of cough.

But old Zakes do just laughs and charf, 'Ja, like you helped me when my brother was beating me up. No Duma, you can take your chances with the cops.' Then he like turns to me and charfs, 'You coming?'

I check this scene out and it don't not take none Einstein to work out what are a best think to do.

This Duma ou are shouting ahind us and are saying bad words and all, but Zakes just keeps on walking like as he can't not hear nothink, so as I do of pretend not to hear nothink too also and walk ahind him. I is tired now, but Zakes charfs that we need to get far away from here cause of a other cops would be coming soon to check out what are happening to Mr Milkhead and Mr Chips so as we walk.

And we walk and we walk and we walk. We is like quite far away when we check a blue lights going awards a shop, so as we get off of a road. I dunno how long we did of walked for, but it were starting to get light when Zakes asides to stop. I can check that he are lank sore cause of he are not walking so lekker. Shaka are also panting lots and my soldiers were hurting cause of carrying my bag what were heavy with all a sweets and stuff.

'We'll rest here for a while. Hopefully we're far enough away,' Zakes charfs.

A sun are just starting to come up and I could of check that we weren't not so far from a road, but cause of we was nearby some big rocks, no one could check us out if we did went round a other side of them. There weren't none houses or nothink what I could check, which were a good think.

'This will do nicely,' Zakes charfed when he checked that there were also a small tree on a other side of a rocks. 'We'll need the shade when it gets hot. What food you got?'

He sat down and you could check by his face that his legs were lank sore, but he didn't not charf nothink.

I opened my bag to show him all a lekker stuff what I did of have. Chips, sweets, cokes. It were a proper feast, I tell you. But old Zakes just checks this out, then checks me out.

'No bread? No milk? What's with all this stuff?'

I'm like, what do you mean? This is like the bestest stuff ever, I had of never had so much sweets at once afore. But Zakes, all he do of wants is bread and milk. So I charf him, 'What are a matter with this? This are all lekker stuff.'

Zakes checks like as he are going get a moer in with me, but then he chills and smiles. That's what I likes about Zakes, he are never angry long.

'This is lekker stuff,' he charfs me, 'but it's not going to fill us up and give us strength for the long journey. We need bread cause it's really filling. And what's Shaka going to eat? This stuff is no good for him. Next time, I do the shopping, okay?'

He charfs this in such a lekker way that I can understand what he are saying, but don't not feel stupid none.

'Chuck us a bag of those Fruit Chutney chips, we'll buy bread at the next shop we see.'

I chuck him a chips and start chowing some myself. Poor old Shaka, shame man, he do eat some of a chips, but doesn't not like a sweets what I offer him. Also he don't not drink coke none, but there are a small stream nearby what he do of drink from.

After we is finished eating, Zakes did of lied down and charfs that he are going to sleep. I are also lank tired too, so lie down, but my brain are like all over a show. I is wondering if pa were really shooted dead, or if he were only just shooted wounded. He did check proper dead, but I

56

have checked those fillums where a ou checks dead and then gives you a skrik when he do all of a sudden like shoot a other ou or, if he are a baddie, he do of tries to shoot a goodie but are shooted dead proper like.

Maybe pa weren't not proper dead and would come and find me in Mpumalanga and donner me somethink chronic for not calling a ambalance, and then he would of donner me more for leaving Sally there by Larry the Lithp.

I then worry more. What if Sally are not safe with Larry the Lithp. Maybe he are got one of those Peter file thingies. I want to ask Zakes if he do think Larry the Lithp are dangerous, but Zakes are already kipping.

A sun are coming up and Shaka are back from a stream. He do go and lie next to Zakes.

I miss my ma all of a sudden like. It would of be nice to have her here to make me a peanut butter zarm and tuck me into bed, but I reckon ma are proper dead. I don't not know how I knowed this, I just knows it. Pa donnered her so hard, like he donnered ouma.

I think more an more of ma and then I start to cry a little. I check out Zakes cause of I don't not want him to see me being a baby, but he are still lights out and all. Shaka though, checks me out like what only dogs can do, you know when a dog checks at you and it are like he are charfing, 'What are a matter?'

I don't not mind Shaka checking me crying cause of he are a dog and all, so I cry for a bit, but quiet like. Old Shaka are great though, he checks me out for a little bit, then gets up and comes and sits by me and I feel much betterer.

I stroke him for a bit, then do fall asleep. Normally I don't not dream much, but now I did. In my dream I can check Sally and she are playing with her dolls and she are happy. I like this dream. But then I do of dream more and it are like as thinks didn't not happen there by a house as what I did of told yous. This are not a lekker dream cause of I don't not like how thinks did of happen in a dream.

FIFTEEN

It are cool when old Zakes do wake me up. He are already standing and all.

'Come on, time to move.'

I check round and see that it are late arvie. I do of want to sleep some more cause of a dream what weren't not lekker what did of maked me wake up lots so as now I were tired, and also cause of my legs is sore, but old Zakes are standing there and I scheme if he can of do it with his sore legs, then I can too also. So I get up and chuck my satchel on my back. It are lighterer now as afore cause of we have of drinked most of a coke.

'Which way?' I asks Zakes and he checks out a road.

'This way,' he charfs, but I can check that he are guessing. He don't not have a cat's clue where Mpumalanga are none, I can of seed that now, but I don't not charf nothink cause of I is happy to be away from pa and Larry the Lithp and Theresa Dern and Pooh Pants du Plessis and de Wit and Smit and all. It are only ma what I miss. Oh ja, and Sally too also, but only a little bit.

We starts to walk, checking out a road all a time for cars. There are not lots what come on a road, so as we can walk without having to hide all a time. But we did get a skrik one time. We checked a car coming so as we hidded ahind a big tree. This bakkie comes near and then it did slowed down and stop. I check out Zakes and he are like Shhh!!! and all and points for us to move ahind a other tree what are furtherer from a road. He do move quick even though his legs are sore and even Shaka are moving with us.

We is just ahind a other tree when this old toppie what must of beed about a hundred comes round a first tree and he are unzipping his pants and all. At first I skrik cause of I reckon that he do of got a Peter file in his pants, but he do just turn to a tree and next think is he are taking a huge piss.

I do of want to laugh, but reckon that I don't not got to be a Einstein to know that I mustn't not. I check Zakes out and he are also trying not to laugh, but cause of I check him out and he checks me out we both laugh, but only a little bit and not loud like.

Fortunately, this old toppie are a bit deaf cause of he don't not hear us none and cause of he are talking to hisself too also.

'It's good to be free to pee on a tree,' he charfs and Zakes and me are like killing ourselves laughing, but also trying not to laugh as well at a same time.

Then old Shaka, I don't know why, maybe he must of reckoned that this old toppie were a problem for us, but he runs out and bites a ou on a bum.

This makes me and Zakes stop laughing cause of we do now skrik that a old toppie will of come and find us. But he don't not, cause of he gets such a skrik that he do try to run off, but do of lets go of his pants what fall down and then so do he too also.

Zakes and me don't not knowed if to laugh or not. A old toppie jumps up and are in his bakkie and away really quick, it are like as I did of never seed a ou that old move so quick. And it were good that he moved so quick cause of Shaka would of have bitted him on a bum again.

Now Zakes and me can laugh and we do so big time. We can hardly not walk cause of we is laughing so much.

It are Zakes what stops first and becomes all serious like cause of he are checking Shaka out.

'What is it boy?' he charfs and I stop laughing too also so as to see why Zakes do of charf this.

Shaka are busy sniffing around where a old man were peeing and he are making like whining noises and all.

'What is it boy?' Zakes do of asks again and we go check out what Shaka are sniffing.

I sees it first and skrik a little.

'A old toppie's teeth felled out,' I charf Zakes and point at a false teeth what are sitting in a small puddle of pee. I start do of chuckle, but then check that Zakes are all serious like, so as I stops and charf him, 'what?'

'We must move. Now.' He are not happy none.

'Why?' I is okay with moving, but I like don't not see a problem.

'False teeth cost money. That old guy is not going to leave them here. He'll be back soon.'

'What? Even if they is in a pool of piss?' I pull a face.

'Ja, even then,' Old Zakes has of hardly charfed this when we hear a car coming.

'Quick!' Zakes like points to where we was hiding afore and we run back there just in time for a old toppie to pull up.

He don't not get out of a bakkie, but rolls down a window.

'Hello?' he charfs.

I check out Zakes and he are like, Shh!! and all.

'Hello,' a old toppie charfs again, 'I'm not going to hurt you, I jush want my teef back, pleesh. Wash that your dog?'

'He sawed us,' I whisper to Zakes and he nods, but we don't not do nothink.

'Hello?' A old toppie don't not sound like a bad ou. 'Pleesh man, I jush want my teef.'

'We do of got to help him,' I whisper to Zakes who like checks me out and shows me a whites of his eyes afore he nods.

I walks out from ahind a tree while Zakes do of hold Shaka back cause of he are growling and all.

'It are okay Shaka, it are okay. He do of only wants his teef.' I can't not help myself from saying 'teef' and then do of start to laugh a bit so as old Zakes donners me with his elbow, but not too hard like, so as I just pat Shaka to tell him it are okay.

A old toppie checks us out, aspecially Shaka, but he don't not get out of a bakkie.

'It's okay,' Zakes charfs him, 'Shaka won't bite you, he was just surprised last time. I promise he won't bite. Gary will hold on to him, you can come get your teeth.'

I like check round to see where this Gary ou are, then I realises what old Zakes are doing. He don't not want to tell this old toppie our real names so as he are calling me Gary.

A old toppie checks this out but he still don't not want to get out of a bakkie.

'I'd brefer it if you got my teef for me, pleesh.'

I laugh cause of I can't not help it and old Zakes donners me again with his elbow, but harder like.

'I'm sorry sir, but your teeth fell...well they fell where you had just relieved yourself.'

'Ag no man!' He like can't not hardly believe it none.

'We could fish them out for you in return for a lift.' I check old Zakes out now, what are he doing?

'That'sh very kind. Where are headed?' A old toppie checks like he did of just won a lotto.

'Mpumalanga,' Zakes charfs.

I aspect a old toppie to ask lank questions, but he do of just nods and charfs, 'That'sh a long way. I'm not going all the way there, but I can take you shome of the way. You'll have to travel in the back though.'

'That's fine, thank you,' Zakes says. 'Hold on to Shaka, Gary, I'll get the teeth.'

I check round again for this Gary ou, then bliksem myself in my brain for being dof. Old Zakes disappears, then comes back with a 'teef' on a stick. A old topppie takes a 'teef' and shoves them in his mouth.

That would of have beed lank funny, but he don't not, it would of beed megadof if he had of. He do of just lets Zakes drop them into a packet what he found and we jump up onto a back of a bakkie.

It are a bit cold so as we do sits with our backs to a cab. Shaka, like all dogs, stuck his head round a side so as to eat a wind.

'It's too soon for us to have been reported missing, so this guy won't think too much about reporting us. Also, he's so old he won't remember even if we do get into the papers. Besides, it's better than walking.' Old Zakes were a Einstein.

We did drived for about five hundred hours and it were getting dark when a old toppie adventually acides to stop. I reckon we must of be almost in Mpumalanga cause we had of beed driving for so long. Zakes did sleep lank lots, but he are awake when we pull into a garage.

A old toppie gets out and charfs a garage ou to fill up while he do goes to a toilet. When he comes back he are got his 'teef' in, which he has of hopefully washed. At first he checks us out like as he don't not knowed who we is, then you can check that he merembers us.

'Where was it you gents were headed again?' he asks us and do of smiles to show off his 'teef'.

'Mpumalanga,' Zakes charfs all polite like.

A old toppie checks down at a ground, scratches his head, then do of looks up at us. 'Ah, Mpumalanga. You need to head down this road, but you'll need to get a lift, it's a long way.'

Zakes and me check out each other then check down a road where a old toppie is pointing. It were in a direction what we had of just comed. He bleddy took us a wrong way. I like do my nut and charf Shaka to bite a old toppie in a balls.

SIXTEEN

Being bitten in a balls are not lekker, I can of told you that. It don't not take none Einstein to work that out, but I can of told you this acause it did of happened to me once. That dog we did of have, a one what pa kicked so as it had to go to sleep, it did bited me in my test tickles once. It were only a small dog then so as its 'teef' weren't not so sharp, but it did still of hurt me lank sore.

It are cause of what I merembered how sore it were that I don't not charf Shaka to bite a old toppie in a balls. Also, it were cause of a way a old toppie charfed us that we did of need to go in a way what we had just come from, to get to Mpumalanga that you could check that he didn't not mean to take us a wrong way. It were like as he didn't not knowed what he were doing. I reckon he do got Old Timers sickness like what my oupa do.

Zakes also checks this but I don't not reckon that he do of knowed what Old Timers are, cause of he don't got no oupa what I knows of, he do of only got grandparents. He just checks a old toppie out and charfs, 'Thank you for the lift, sir, we'll be fine from here.'

A old toppie smiles again to show off his 'teef'.

'You boys take care now,' he charfs then gets into his bakkie and buggers off.

It are got dark now and there are not nobody there by a garage accept for a lady what are in a shop and a ou what serves a petrol. Old Zakes checks round then charfs, 'Let's get some bread and milk then move off, I don't like it here.'

We like go into a shop and a lady there checks us out big time. I don't not like it neither and Zakes are also unhappy too.

'No dogs in the shop.' This lady's voice are strict and we check that Shaka have of followed us inside. 'And only one of you allowed in here at a time. I don't want you stealing from me.'

I don't not like this lady nothink, but don't not want to cause kak and neither do Zakes also, so as he do of take Shaka while I get a bread and milk. When I are paying for it, and a lady are busy counting a money what I gived her, I grabs six rolls of Humbugs and stuff them in my underpants.

Old Zakes are grinning big time when I get outside and I reckon it are cause of he checked me zicking a humbugs. That'll learn that stupid cow to think we would of steal from her.

We starts to walk down a road to where a old toppie had of pointed us to where Mpumalanga are and Old Zakes starts laughing and I laugh too. I is happy that Zakes are laughing at me zicking a sweets, so I take them out from my underpants and give him a roll. He stops laughing and looks at me cross like.

'More sweets, I thought I said we must get bread and milk, that will fill us up, not waste our money on sweets.'

Now I are confused like, but I still charf, 'I didn't not buyed these, a lady gived them to me.'

'She gave them to you? Why?' Now it are his turn to be confused.

'Cause of she said that when I did pay for a bread, she sawed that we weren't not crooks and she were sorry she were horrible to us.'

Zakes checks at me, then smiles a little bit. 'Hmm, so I shouldn't have done it then.' He says this, but it are like as he are not talking to me.

'Done what?' I asks.

He checks up and grins big time. 'No, while you were in the shop I went into the ladies and lifted all the toilet seats up.'

I is like, 'Why?'

'It's the one thing in life that really pisses women off the most, if you leave the toilet seat up. Didn't your mother ever moan at your father for doing it?'

I wants to charf Zakes that my ma would never of have moaned at pa for nothink, cause of he would of donnered her if she had of. But I don't not want Zakes to think my ma were a woosie, so as I just charf, 'Ja, I think so.'

'Well then, when that woman back there goes into the toilet, she's going to be well pissed about the seats being up,' and he then laughs so as he has to sit down.

I still don't not knowed what a big deal are and why women don't not like to have a toilet seat up, but I laugh too also and Shaka goes and licks Zakes' face.

It are nice being there by a side of a road laughing and Shaka being friendly and all and I want thinks to stay like this forever, so when I see Zakes are stopping laughing I charf, 'We should put a seats up at every place we go to.'

Old Zakes don't not laugh more, but do of just grin and charfs, 'We'll see, but we need to find somewhere to sleep tonight.'

I are not so tired cause of we did sleep lank during a day, but Zakes are a boss so as we find a place not too far from a petrol station. It are a old house what are all broked down, so as there are no roof or nothink, but a walls stop people from seeing us. There are lots of rubbish in there and it do also smells like some ous have pissed here big time. I want to charf Zakes that this are not such a lekker place and I don't not want to stay here, but he are already sitting down and Shaka have of already lifted his leg on a wall in a other room so as I just charfs myself that this are where we is going to stay. Even though I don't not reckon I are tired, I is faster sleep soon after I lie down.

I don't not knowed how late it were, but it were dark when Zakes are waking me up and charfing me to be quiet cause of someone are coming. Shaka are growling already and I can hear this ou what are walking nearby, cause of he are like talking to hisself and all, but it are not like proper talking cause of he are not using real words.

'He's drunk,' Zakes whispers to me and he puts his hand on Shaka to stop him from growling like. Shaka goes quiet, but you can check in a dark that he are still wanting to bark.

A ou is now like coming into a broken down house and are almost falling over. He do of say a bad word what if pa were here he would of donnered a ou like what he donnered me once when I did said a bad word. Only pa are not here, so as a ou isn't not donnered, but Shaka don't not like a bad word nothink and he do of growl. Zakes pats him like as to make him keep quiet, but a ou did heard.

'Is that a puppy or a big bad wolf?' he do of asks and then laughs like.

'I is a big bad wolf,' I charf, but make my voice really deep like. I don't not knowed whycome I did of said this, but it were really funny cause a ou do nearly falls over, you can hear cause of a noise of a stones in a other room.

Shaka acides that it are time to go check out this ou, so as he goes through a door, still growling.

'I is coming to eat you up,' I charf. Old Zakes are like killing hisself laughing and we go to this small hole in a wall so as to check out what are going to happen. Cause of a moon, we can sort of check a ou what are trying to stand up. He then checks Shaka and do of laughs.

'You're not a wolf, you're a puppy. A cute little doggie. Here, boy.'

You can check that Shaka are confused cause of a ou are talking nice like and he are holding his hand out and all.

'Here boy,' a ou charfs again. 'Hey, big puppy, what's your name?'

Old Shaka are sniffing a ou's hand now and he must of reckoned that this ou were okay cause of he don't not growl none more and do of let a ou pat him.

'My name are Shaka,' I says in my Shaka voice.

'Hmm, a dog with a grammar problem,' a ou charfs while still patting Shaka.

I check out Zakes cause of I've skrikked. How could this ou have of knowed what did happen to my Gran'ma. But Zakes do of just shake his head like I is dof and goes back to checking a ou out.

'My name,' a ou charfs, 'is Theodore Roosevelt Biggles-worth Crumpington Mandela van der Merwe.' Then he do of nearly fall over laughing while Shaka checks him out. 'But,' he says while still laughing lekker big time, 'but, you can call me Ted.'

Now he do of have to sit down cause of he are laughing so much.

Poor old Shaka don't not know what to do so as he just barks. He are got a lekker bark and Ted pats him and do stops to laugh, slow like.

'And what's a nice dog like you doing in a place like this?' A ou looks at Shaka now. 'Not that I'm complaining mind you. We don't get much by way of company up here, so you're most welcome. Just wondering what you are doing here.'

'I is on a journey,' I do of use my Shaka voice again.

'A journey? I see. And where are you headed?'

I is about to charf Mpumalanga when Zakes donners me, but not so hard like, with his elbow and shakes his head.

'I is going to…um...a moon.' I dunno why I charfs that but I want to laugh big time after I do says it, but I don't not.

Ted laughs lank loud though. 'The moon. That's a good one.' Then he stops laughing and charfs, 'And are you taking your friends with you?' He now looks right at us and it checks like he are going to donner us big time.

SEVENTEEN

Ja, I did of nearly poohed my pants there. Not like as in real pooh, like old pooh Pants du Plessis did, but it were a nearly almost. It must of have beed a way a light were shining from a moon onto Ted's face what did made us think he were going to donner us. Of course laterer I charfed Zakes that I weren't not scared none and he charfed me that he too also weren't not, but strue's Bob we was both skrikked lekker big time there.

Old Ted were killing hisself laughing when he checked out how much he did of skrikked us, but it were a nice laughing what made us stop skrikking and we also did of started laughing.

'Come, my young friends, won't you join me and Shaka. I'll get Mildred to put the kettle on and we can relax in the front room.'

I check out Zakes and I is like 'Who are this Mildred ou?' and he do shrug his soldiers. But we go sit there with Ted in his front room cause of we would of feeled stupid not to. He do smell like of pa's booze and all, but also like of wee.

'Come in, come in.' Ted points for us to sit there on some rocks nearby to where he are sitting. When we is sitted, he leans over to us and do of whisper, 'I'm afraid I can't let you sit on the new settee,' he like points to some other stones, 'but Mildred is very particular about who can sit there. A fine woman Mildred, but she can be a bit fussy at times.' The he do of look at us as if he had of told us the biggest secret in a whole world.

Old Shaka checks Ted pointing at a rocks so as he goes and sits there. I aspect Ted to shout at Shaka, but he don't not say nothink, he just sits and smiles at us so as I reckon that when this Mildred woman do of adventually pitch up, she will shout at Shaka and all to get him off a set tea, but only if she are as mad as what Ted are.

'I am Samuel, and this is my friend Gary,' Zakes charfs Ted.

'Pleased to meet you Samuel, Gary,' he like shakes our hands as he charfs a names what are not really ours. 'Ah, Mildred, these gentlemen are headed to the moon, they'll need some tea to sustain them for the trip, and do you think you could see fit to spare some of those lovely scones you made?'

Now Zakes and me do of know for sure that this Ted ou are mad, cause of he are talking to Mildred what aren't not there. And we is not going to get none tea and scones neither, but that are okay cause of I don't want to be sustained nothink, that did of sounded painful.

Meantimes, Ted are still talking and charfing what a fine woman Mildred are and all and that her scones were a bestest in a world. He are talking so much that neither me or Zakes can get a word in sideways. But cause of he talks so much about these scones, when Mildred do of comes back, in Ted's brain anyways, I is really wanting some real ones.

Ted do of serves us a tea and scones and we take it from him. I takes a bite of my scone and it tastes really yukky so as I throw Shaka with it when Ted are not looking. Shaka are not stupid though cause of he do sniff it but don't not eat it none.

Don't be dof, there is no real scones, so they don't not got none taste or nothink and even if I had of pretended to throw Shaka with them, he are too clever to sniff at nothink. We just sits there and pretends to eat a scones and drink a tea cause of we is scared that Ted would get psychomad if we did of told him that there weren't not none tea and none scones neither.

Ted then starts to asks us how we is going to get to a moon and I is just about to charf him that we weren't not actually really going to a moon, when old Zakes chirps up and charfs, 'We are planning to carry a ladder to the top of Mount Everest, then use the ladder to get the last bit of the way.'

I nearly pee myself laughing, but old Ted nods all serious like, it are as if he reckons you can climb to a moon on a ladder.

'There's just one problem,' Zakes charfs, 'the ladder we need to use is a very special one and the man who has it is in Mpumalanga. We need to get there first, but we are a bit lost at the moment. Do you happen to know how to get to Mpumalanga, sir?'

My friend Zakes are a real Einstein, no, actually he are like a Einstein squared.

'Mpumalanga?' Old Ted do of thinks for a bit. 'Mildred comes from Mpumalanga, we could ask her. Mildred, my love,' he calls out.

Okay, so Einstein must of had bad days too also.

Anyways, Mildred comes back, like in Ted's brain only merember, and he asks her where Mpumalanga are and she charfs us and Ted charfs, 'Well, there you go. Wonderful woman, Mildred. Thank you my dear.'

A problem, Ted, are that Mildred are a most wonderful woman what never existed. She are like a bestest invisible woman in a world, you mad old toppie.

I aspect Zakes to give up then, but he are not phased. He like nods and charfs, 'Thank you, Mildred. So we go to the Petrol Station and turn left?'

I is like all worried now that maybe it are me what are mad, cause of I is a only one what can't not check this Mildred woman none.

'No, right at the petrol station,' Ted charfs.

'Oh, sorry. Right at the petrol station then...?' Old Zakes checks at Ted like as he can't not merember what next.

'Right at the petrol station, then left at the first stop street. Two blocks down is the mini bus station. Lots of them go to Mpumalanga.' Old Ted checks out Zakes like, you understand now?

This are like a time when old Einstein jumped out of a barf shouting 'You reeker'.

EIGHTEEN

Ted are faster sleep a next morning when Zakes charfs that we should go. I are glad to go cause of I did dream of that night again, but a dream were differenter as to what I did of already told you what happened. We is just about to leave when I merember pa's half jack what I put in my bag and reckon we need to of give Ted somethink for helping us, so as I charf Zakes that I will catch up to him and go back. Ted are snoring somethink chronic what makes me laugh. I leave a whiskey bottle and run to catch up with Zakes and Shaka.

I don't not reckon pa would of beed cross cause I gave his booze to Ted, cause of pa are deaded and you can't not drink nothink when you is deaded.

After Ted had of went to sleep, which are not long after he charfed us how to get to Mpumalanga, Zakes charfed me that he reckoned Mildred were Ted's real wife, but that now she were deaded and that Ted just pretended like she weren't not, so as that were why he spoked to her and that he had of done this for so long that he now really did of thinked that she were there and alive.

As I do of turn to catch up with Zakes I did think, what if I started to pretend that ma were still alive and did of talked with her and all, would I get like Ted and start to think that she were still really alive? But I don't not want to be like Ted, cause of I don't not want to have to get drunk.

I didn't not say nothink to Zakes when I caughted up with him and Shaka, I did of just gave him some Toff-o-lux from my bag and we eated them as we wented down awards a garage. It were all quiet like round a garage so as I ranned into a ladies toilets to put a seats up like what Zakes told me to do, then we did walked up to a taxi rank.

'I is glad we is getting a taxi,' I charfed Zakes as we did of walked, 'my legs is lank sore.'

He do of stops and checks me out skeef. Then he smiles, but not too happy like. 'We're not geting a taxi, we'll have to walk.'

I'm like, 'Why?'

Old Zakes shakes his head and charfs, 'You ever seen a white person in a taxi?'

I thinks for a bit, then charfs, 'No, I never have of.'

'So?' he asks and I is like, what are a problem?

'What colour are you?' he asks.

'I is white,' I charfs and then I check what he are charfing me. 'So I can't not go in a taxi then?'

'Nope.'

'But that aren't not fair. I can't not go in a taxi just cause of I is white?'

'Blacks only.' Zakes charfs.

'But you is black.'

'Ja, I am. But do you want me to go off in the taxi and leave you to walk to Mpumalanga?'

'You wouldn't?' I are skrikking now. I don't not want to be left alone with Ted and you can check that Zakes are thinking about it.

'What about Shaka, he are not black, he are yellow,' I charf cause I have of just looked at Shaka.

'That's a point, they won't allow Shaka in the taxi either.'

'Cause of he are not black?'

'No, because he's a dog.'

Now I is like, what are these taxis all about hey? No whites? No dogs? But I don't not charf nothink cause of I don't not want Zakes to think I is dof cause of I don't not understand none.

'We'll have to walk. Maybe we can get a lift here and there. Come on, let's go see what direction the Mpumalanga taxis go. At least then we won't get lost. We can do that in all the towns, just follow the taxis.'

You is probably reckoning that Zakes are a Einstein to go check a taxis out, but I are also a Einstein cause of if I didn't not of asked about Shaka going in a taxi, old Zakes would of have gone off in a taxi and left me to go live with Ted and Mildred what isn't.

A day are only beginning so as there is like lots of people what is going to work and all. Most of a ous what is in cars is whites while all a ous what is walking or in taxis is blacks. There is some blacks in cars but they is not that much.

We walk down a road to where a taxi rank are. There is lots of ous there what are talking and shouting and all. Old Shaka don't not like it nothink. When we get closerer, Zakes charfs me to wait with Shaka while he do of go and checks out which are a taxis what is going to Mpumalanga.

I is not happy with this cause of I reckon that maybe old Zakes are going to just get a taxi and skedaddle and leave me and Shaka alone. Zakes must of checked a worry in my face cause of he like grins and charfs, 'Hey, relax, I won't leave you here. Besides, you've got all the money. I don't have any to pay for a taxi fare,' and he pulls out his pockets to make elephant ears and shows me that he are got nothink.

So I is like cool now and I watch Zakes go off to check out a taxis. I do of have to hold Shaka back cause of he wants to go with Zakes, but he don't not fight me too much cause of I reckon he don't not like all a people nothink.

It do of take Zakes like a hundred years afore he comes back and in a mean time, I is getting a lot of skeef looks from a ous what is coming to a taxi rank. There are a lady nearby what are braaiing mielies on a fire in a big oil drum. Pa once braai'd mielies but I afer them when they is boiled and soft and you eat them off a cob with lots of margareem.

A lady are checking me out lank and adventually she do of charf, 'Are you okay? Are you lost?'

I skrik a little and wish that Zakes were here, but I don't not want this lady to check that I have of srikked so as I just charf, 'No, I is waiting for my friend. He are just gone to check on some taxi info.'

This lady nods, but still keeps checking me out and I begin to thinks that maybe a cops are looking for us cause of what did of happen with pa and all and that maybe our pictures is in a newspapers and that maybe this lady are seen our pictures and she are going to call a cops and all and then we will of never get to Mpumalanga.

And still old Zakes are not come back. I check up a road where he did gone but all I can spy is lank people so I look back at a Mielie Lady.

'You hungry?' she asks me and it are like as her asking me has of made me lank hungry, but I don't not want to buy none mielies cause of maybe it are not a kind of food what Zakes wants to spend a money on. But I nods anyhow.

'Here,' she charfs and picks a mielie off a fire.

'I don't not got none money,' I do of lie to her.

'That's okay. This is for free.'

I check her out skeef cause of nobody has never gaved me nothink for free accept maybe for Ted what gave me invisible tea and scones.

'Go on,' a Mielie Lady charfs, 'it's free. All I want is for you to stand here by me and eat it.'

'Why?' I is confused.

A Mielie Lady gives a lank big laugh, then charfs, 'Because, if people see a white boy enjoying my mielies, they will come and buy them.'

This don't not make none sense to me, but I had not checked nobody buying none mielies from her all a time what I were there so as I reckon maybe she are desperate. Anyways, I take a mielie and start chowing it. It are much lekkerer as pa's mielies on a braai and I finish it up chop chop.

Suddenly, I check up and there are a queue of ous wanting mielies, so much many that a Mielie Lady are hardly not got enough. There is only two left when a queue stops and I am checking out a last two thinkink maybe I should of buy one from her.

She like finishes counting her money then checks me checking out a last mielies.

'Want another?' she asks and do of picks it up. I is about to take it when I spy old Zakes coming back. I check at a mielie, then at Zakes, then at a mielie.

'My friend are coming,' I charf and a Mielie Lady checks round at Zakes and it are like as she skriks big time, but only like a short skrik. Then she makes like to hug Zakes, then don't. Then she like starts to give him a mielie, then don't. It are like as she don't not got a cat's clue what to do.

Old Zakes and me don't not howcomewhy a Mielie Lady are acting so strange and Shaka are checking out Zakes, then a Mielie Lady, then Zakes.

But now you can check that a Mielie Lady are normal again and she starts charfing Zakes somethink, but I can't not understand nothink cause of she are charfing him in black language. So I just check them out and when Zakes and a Mielie Lady laugh, I do of laugh too also, not cause of I did understood, but cause of I just did. Then I stop quick like when I check that a Mielie Lady's laugh aren't not a happy one.

They charf each other more in black and I hear Zakes charf, 'Mpumalanga,' and they talk more and then Zakes are nodding and smiling and all.

Adventually he checks me out and charfs in English, 'Apparently I look a lot like this woman's son. He died a year ago, but when she saw me she thought she was seeing a ghost.' He like smiles a little now and so do a Mielie Lady.

'Anyway, she says that her husband is a truck driver and that he's heading to Mpumalanga tomorrow. She thinks we may be able to get a lift with him.'

This are excellent news and I charf a big 'thank you' to a Mielie Lady. But then I like reckon if her husband are only going to Mpumalanga tomorrow, then we is going to have to go sleep there by Ted again tonight. Old Zakes are sharp though, he are already thinking this cause of he starts talking black again and afore I knowed it, he are organised for us to sleep there by a Mielie Lady's house. I is not so sure about this, but Zakes do of knowed what he are doing, I aspose.

NINETEEN

A rest of a day we did of help a Mielie Lady. We like kept a fire in a oil drum going while she wented to find more mielies, then we did of help peel them. It were lank fun ripping a green leaves off and checking a yellow mielie underneath. Then we would chuck a mielies on a fire and have to watch them so as they didn't not burn none.

A Mielie Lady were like amazing, cause of she would turn a mielies with her fingers. When I did of try, I burnted myself big time.

Sometimes, a ou would pay for a mielie with like a R50 note and she wouldn't not have enough change and all, so as she would asked me and Zakes to run to a ou what were selling sweets or to a cafe to get change.

All a time she were letting us chow a mielies, aspecially Zakes. I reckon he must of eated about five hundred mielies. I knowed this cause of he were gived two every time I were gived one and I must of have eated about a hundred. I felt lekker fat.

A ous what came to buy a mielies were like all talking and smiling with a Mielie Lady. I didn't not understand nothink cause of they did spoke black, but you could check that they did of liked her and she did of liked them too also. It were all good fun and it were properly a lekkerest day what I had of had since afore Zakes jumped off a third floor.

Zakes also checked happy. It were like he were really a Mielie Lady's son and she were really his ma. It made me think of my ma and Sally and I did of want to see them again. Maybe one day, I reckoned, I would see Sally again, but ma...

Ag! I hated pa then. I were glad he were deaded cause of he did of killed ma. Ja, it were definitely pa what did of deaded ma. I think anyways.

Still, it were lekker hanging out with a Mielie Lady. Even Shaka were happy cause of ous would come from a café with stew and stuff and then would throw him with a bones. Sometimes a ou would even chuck him with some meat and Shaka would catch it in his mouth afore it did of touch a ground.

I gave a Mielie Lady a roll of Meth-o-lyptus and Zakes and me chowed lank of a other sweets. It were quite late when we did of adventually packed up all a stuff and started to walk to a Mielie Lady's house. She were all smiling and everythink and charfing that we was good luck for her cause of she did make a mostest money ever today.

A Mielie Lady's house were not so lekker. It were like not even bricks for walls but more like a metal stuff what were on a roof of our house.

'It's better than Ted's place,' Zakes charfed when I told him that it weren't not so lekker. I could check that he did of had a point. At least there were a roof. A lousy think were that a Mielie Lady said that Shaka weren't not allowed inside, but he did of check okay sitting outside a door.

There was only two rooms in a house, so I reckoned a Mielie Lady and her husband would of sleep in a other room what I thinked were a bedroom, and me and Zakes would of sleep in a room where there were a sofa and a chair, but a Mielie Lady charfed that, cause of her husband were going to be late, we could doss in a bed in a small room and she and her husband would doss on a sofa.

We didn't want none supper cause we had of chowed so many mielies, so a Mielie Lady made us some coffee. I had of never tasted coffee afore cause pa always charfed that I weren't not allowed none. It didn't not taste so lekker none but I dranked it all so as not to make a Mielie Lady feel bad. When we was finished, both Zakes and me felt tired, so a Mielie Lady showed us a bed in a next room and we were lights out really quick like.

We must of have slept lank lots cause it were hot when we did of waked up and a sun were shining in through a cracks in a walls. I needed to pee somethink chronic and Zakes were still faster sleep, so as I got up and tried to open a door, but it were locked. I did tried to push it harderer, but it wooden not open and it were making a noise so as I did of stopped trying a door and checked round a room to see if there were somethink what I could pee in.

I did of found a empty tin can under a bed what I started to pee in, but then Zakes did of waked up.

'What you doing!' he charfs me in like this angry voice.

I skrik cause of I didn't not seed him waked up and do of nearly miss a tin.

'I is taking a leak,' I charf and turn my back to Zakes, cause of I don't not want him checking me out while I do of pee.

'Why don't you go to the toilet like the rest of us?' I can of hear him sitting up in a bed ahind me.

'Cause of a door are locked,' I don't not like talking when I is peeing cause it do of make me loose consternation.

'Locked?'

'Ja,' I charf and do of finish off.

Zakes gets off a bed and tries a door, but it are locked like I did of told him. He like rattles it hard but nothink do happen.

'Hello?' he shouts, 'anyone there?' I start to skrik a little cause of no one answers and it are getting hotterer in a room.

Zakes and me bangs on a door lots and shouts and all, but nothink do of happens. We can hear Shaka barking outside, but he are a dog and he don't not got none key to open a door for us.

Adventually, Zakes stops and sits on a bed. He are sweating lank.

'It's no use,' he charfs, 'no one's there.'

I stop banging and sits down too also.

'Why did a Mielie Lady lock us in here and leave?' I asks.

'I dunno. Maybe we've been reported as runaways and she's gone to the police to get the reward.' Zakes do of look too serious to be joking.

TWENTY

It do got hotterer and hotterer in a room. Zakes also did of have a pee in a tin can what were now nearly almost full and every now and then we did of tried banging on a door or a walls for someone to let us out. It were weird that a house were just made of roof, but a Mielie Lady could lock it up so much so as we couldn't not get out.

We was lank thirsty and we could sometimes hear Shaka outside. There was people what did of walked past, but they never did stop none, even if we did bang on a walls and shout, 'Help!' Some of a people must of have heard us, but they would go on, aspecially if Shaka did of growled at them.

'If a Mielie Lady are really just gone to a cops to get a reward, howcomewhy are she not back already?' I asks Zakes when we have of beed waiting for lank long without not no one coming back none.

'I dunno,' he charfs and do of lay down on a bed. It were like really hot so as it were making us tired.

'I reckon she drugged us last night with the coffee.'

I did of want to ask him what 'drugged' were cause of I didn't not knowed what he were talking about none, but I were too sleepy too also. Asides I didn't not want him to think I were dof.

We must of have gone asleep for lank ages cause of when we did waked up again it were not so hot and it were getting a bit dark outside. My mouth were like so dry that I couldn't not of spitted even if I did of want to.

I merembered a time when pa did of locked me in my room cause of somethink what I done. Of course he had of donnered me first. I can't not merember now what it were what I done, but pa must of had thought it were bad cause of he did normally only donner me, he hardly never locked me in a room. I were hungry cause of I didn't not have none supper and I hadn't not got none peanut butter zarms in my undies drawers. I sometimes would of put zarms there just in case, aspecially if I had of done somethink bad.

Anyways, it were lank hot that day also and I were hungry and thirsty like we was now, so this must of beed howcomewhy I did merembered this. A difference were that when pa did of locked me in my room, I did

74

of jumped out a window and go to Jaapie's place. He were still my friend then and he gaved me some coke and a fish paste zarm cause of he didn't not had none peanut butter.

There weren't not none windows in a Mielie Lady's house so as Zakes looks at me skeef when I charf him my story. It weren't not like I were trying to tell him what we should do, I were just meremberng. Anyways, if he were such a Einstein hisself, he would of have comed up with a diarrhoea, but he didn't of had none.

Adventually, we did heard a Mielie Lady come home and we banged on a door cause of maybe she had of just forgot us. But she hadn't not of forgot us, she just meremberd us a bit skeef cause of she hears Zakes shouting to let us out and she charfs, 'Vincent, my son, quieten down.'

Zakes checks me out and I check him out. What were a Mielie Lady on about? Zakes do of bang again and charfs, 'Let us out.'

'Vincent! Be quiet now,' A Mielie Lady charfs, 'or there will be no supper for you.'

'I'm not Vincent,' Zakes charfs and you can check that he are worried now.

'Don't be so naughty, Vincent. One more word out of you and you'll definitely get no supper.'

Zakes makes like to bang on a door again then stops. He are thinkink.

'What are she...' I start to asks what a Mielie Lady's problem are, but he do like tells me to shh with his finger on his lips.

'I'm sorry I had to lock you up, my son,' a Mielie Lady are talking again, 'but you ran away and I won't let you do that again.'

I check out Zakes to see what he are going to do, but you can tell he are still thinkink.

'You'll stay in your room till I'm sure you won't run away again,' a Mielie Lady charfs.

'She's as mad as Ted,' Zakes charfs quiet like. 'She thinks I'm her dead son.' It are like as he are talking to hisself, so I don't not charf nothink. He starts to walk up and down a room and I have to move a tin of pee, cause of he did nearly almost kicked it over, but he are thinkink too lank to of check.

I try also to think, but I is not sure what Zakes are thinkink about, so I don't not knowed what I should of think, so as to help.

Then I hear like a man's voice in a other room and he's like talking to a Mielie Lady and all. I make to go bang on a door, but Zakes do hold my arm back and charfs me to shh! again. He then do of puts his head to a door to listen.

I listen also as well, but they are talking in black so as I can't not understand none.

'It's her husband,' Zakes whispers. He listens some more and then charfs, 'She's telling him that their son has come home...he's telling her that their son is dead...she's saying that he isn't and that he's in the bedroom.'

All of a suddenly like Zakes pulls me back and we sits on a bed as we hear a door being unlocked. A ou what opens a door checks skrikked for a bit when he do sees Zakes, but then he do of charfs somethink in black.

Old Zakes nods, then charfs in English, 'Yes, your wife said I looked like him.'

'I'm sorry she locked you up in here,' a ou charfs, also in English. I reckon he must of seed that I weren't not black so as that are whycome he do speaks English. He like shakes his head then.

'Come, you must be hungry,' he charfs and we follow him into a other room. A Mielie Lady are there and she are checking Zakes out, but she don't not say nothink.

A ou goes and cuts some thick slices of bread, then charfs, 'Jam or peanut butter?'

What a question! There can of only beed one answer.

'Jam, please,' Zakes charfs and I'm like Nooooo! Even though I don't not actually say nothink.

But a ou then asks, 'And you?'

'Peanut butter, please.' I aspose he didn't not knowed me nothink, that are whycome he did of have to ask.

He do of finishes making a zarms and also some tea, then charfs for us to follow him outside. There are quite lank people around now and we go sit on a little bench outside a house chowing our bread. I give Shaka some and so does Zakes too also. In a meantime, a ou are asking all these questions and Zakes are answering.

'I'm Samuel and this is Gary,' he charfs, 'We are heading to stay with my grandparents in Mpumalanga for the school holidays. We were trying to organise to get a taxi, but ended up helping your wife as all the taxis had left for the day. We were hoping to get one this morning, but, well, you know what happened.'

It weren't like one big sentence what Zakes charfed. A ou would of ask questions innertween, mostly in black so as I can't not say what his questions were, but cause of Zakes do answers in English, I think I knowed what he were asking.

A ou like listens to all what Zakes charfs him and adventually he charfs, 'My wife was right that I am a truck driver and that I am heading to

Mpumalanga province tomorrow, she did get the day wrong, but you are welcome to come with. I'm only going as far as Mbombela if that's okay?'

I check out Zakes cause of now I is like not so sure to believe a ou or not. It were beginning to seem like to me that all ous were a bit mad in this world and that only me and Zakes and Shaka were normal.

TWENTY-ONE

We slepted in a front room of a house this time so as we weren't not scared that a Mielie Lady would of locked us in none. Also I think that a ou and a Mielie Lady 'did it' in a other room cause of a noises what we did of heared. Me and Zakes were laughing lank and even Shaka, what were allowed to sleep in a room, did make a whine.

A next morning, a ou woked us up really early like, even afore it were light and, after we had of peed in a stinky toilet what were for all a houses around a place, we did of walked with a ou to where he picked up a truck.

He charfed us to wait round a corner from a truck place cause of he weren't not really allowed to give ous lifts nowhere. It were a little cold waiting and there were also nobody around. I did of thinked that he weren't not going to give us a lift cause of he took lank ages, but Zakes just reckoned that he were making his paper work.

Zakes were right and a ou, what had of tolded us that his name were Moses, came with a huge truck not so long after Zakes charfed this.

I did of want to laugh when a ou charfed that his name were Moses cause of old Jaapie would always of charf, 'don't ask me, ask Moses,' when he didn't not knowed a answer. I reckon that maybe this ou were a Moses what Jaapie were talking of cause of he did knowed lots.

As we drived, he would charf us about a places what we was going through. He kept talking of a struggles and a think what he did of called apart hate, as in like, 'during the struggles, there was an uprising in that township,' or, 'under apart hate, we couldn't go sit in that park.'

You could check that Zakes knewed what he were talking about, but I didn't not. I also didn't not want to check dof in front of Zakes, but I really did of wanted to knowed what this were all about, so as I reckoned Zakes wouldn't not say nothink in front of a ou if I asked, so I asked Moses.

It were hard to amagine that Zakes and me would of not beed even allowed to be friends if we had of beed born when Moses were. We wouldn't not of even beed allowed to go to a same school or nothink cause of a guvamint would of said we couldn't not.

How can a guvamint charf ous who can and can't not be friends? It were weird. I were glad that there were no more apart hate cause of then I wouldn't not have had no friends after when Jaapie didn't not say it weren't me what hit old Theresa Dern.

Moses also charfed us lank other thinks what even Zakes didn't not knowed, dof thinks like black ous weren't not aloud to go in a same door of a shop as of white ous, and black ous had to of live in one place and white ous in a other. I couldn't not understand howcomewhy white ous weren't not allowed to stay where black ous stayed or go into a same door of a shop. It must of beed horrible for a white ous.

I acided that a guvamint must of beed dof and I charfed Moses this.

He like laughed and charfed that a old guvamint were dof, but so were a new one too also.

'Why are a new one dof?' I asks.

'Don't get me started,' Moses charfed. So we didn't not, he just did of started all on his ace. He charfed us about edumacation and hopstibals and a houses problems and a conny me and lank other stuff.

A next time Jaapie charfs me to ask Moses, I'll charf him, 'ask him yourself,' cause of Moses answers big time with thinks that not even Einstein would of understanded.

So while Moses were talking and all, I do of just check out a window at where we is driving. It were nice cause of there was mountains and veldt and not so much houses. I schemed that maybe me and Zakes could of come live in a veldt, but then I merembered that there weren't none shops here so as where could I buy my chips and sweets and cokes and all. But then I schemed that we could of go into a town with my rucksack whenever we needed stuff.

I then did of started thinking about when ma were deaded by Zakes' brother and pa did of donner him, but then I did of shooted him, but he did of deaded pa afore I could of shooted him. But this are not right as it did of happened, so as I acide that I must of not be thinkink proper like so as I reckon it are betterer to go to sleep, cause of I don't not like what I are thinkink.

It were Zakes what waked me up to charf that we did needed to get out soon. I were like 'Why?' and was a bit a moer in cause of he waked me cause of I were having a lekker dream. But then he charfed that there were probably a cop stop up ahead and that Moses would be in a doggy doo if a cops founded us in a truck with him.

'There is a Shell Ultra City just past where the police usually are, I need to fill up there and will wait for you,' Moses charfs.

I could check that a cars were stopping just up ahead so that must of have beed where a cops was. We do of jumped out quick like and it were good that Zakes wented first, cause of I would of just have walked along by a road, and probably would of have beed caughted by a cops. But old Zakes and Shaka did headed off a road into a field. It were a farm field cause of all a plants were in a row. They was quite high, a plants, so as once we got ahind a first row, we could hardly not see a road none.

'Come on,' Zakes charfs and he are like almost running and all, 'we don't want to keep Moses waiting, he may go without us.'

I skrik a little and start to run too also as well, not just cause of I don't not want to be left ahind by Moses, but also cause of my bag with all a sweets and a money were still in Moses' truck.

It were not so easy to run cause of a sand were soft and a leaves from a plants kept of hitting us in a face, but it were lekker to be outside and doing stuff. Shaka were also happy cause of he were barking a bit and running in and out of a plants.

I did of goed into a next row so as I could overtake Zakes. I did almost charf, 'Race yous,' but then did of merember that his legs weren't not so lekker cause of he did of try and commit sewerage pipe, so I just ranned a little bit in front, enough so as I could win him, but not so much so as he didn't not felt bad cause of his legs.

We got to a end of all a plants and all and I checked back to see whereabouts Zakes were. This were a dof think to do, cause of I did trip and fall and slided in a sand right up to a shoes of a policeman what were standing there.

TWENTY-TWO

If I had of beed Pooh Pants du Plessis, I would of have done a world's biggest pooh then. But I aren't not a sissy like he are. I mean, I did skrik a bit, but not so much as a cop ou what did of skrikked big time and he like did of pulled his gun out and shooted at me, but acause he were so skrikked he did of missed.

79

No, that didn't not happen actual like that cause of Shaka did jumped and bitted his hand afore he could of shoot any.

No, that didn't not happen none neither. A cop did grab for his gun, but he checked I was just a children afore he could of done nothink. Also Shaka were too far ahind me to of did nothink neither, but he did of bark.

Zakes done a eyeball sweets look when he checked a cop, but we all stopped skrikking quite soon.

A cop did of say a bad word afore he charfed, 'What the hell are you boys up to?'

That were when I were such a Einstein that I could of won a Einstein of a year award. I checked a cop straight in a eyes and charfed, 'We did come from a farm over there,' I did of pointed back at a plants, 'and we was going to a Ultra City to get some sweets.'

This weren't not a lie cause of my sweets were in Moses' truck, what were hopefully waiting for us at a Ultra city. You check that I didn't not charf, 'buy some sweets,' cause that would of maybe have beed a lie.

A cop checks us out and old Zakes like nods to charf him that, ja, that are what we is doing.

'Why don't you use the road, why were you running through the field?' he asks and do points at a dirt road just furtherer up, 'it's a much shorter route.'

Now it were Zakes turn to play Einstein. 'We started out on the road, sir, but our dog ran into the field to chase a rabbit. We ended up way over there before we found him.'

A cop nods like as he do of believes us.

'Why is you here by a field and not there on a road with a other cops?' I asks. It are not like I were wanting to cause kak or nothink, I did of just want to know.

'That's none of your business,' he charfs and you can check he are cross and all, but he does like check at a ground near a plants. I check out where he are looking and there are a puddle of fresh pee there.

So I like laugh and charf, 'A man's gotta go when a man's gotta go,' which were somethink what pa would of sometimes always say.

A cop then also laughs which do makes us cool and we did of all walked up a road to where a other cops were. Old Zakes don't not want to hang around by a cops so as we leave a peeing cop there and go on to a Ultra City.

At first we can't not see Moses' truck cause of it were parked round a back with a other trucks and all, but then we do of seed him sitting in a Wimpy drinking a coffee and eating a toasted zarm. He do of buys us a milkshake and a toasted zarm each too also, which were really nice and then we did get back in a truck and drive some more. Zakes reckoned that he did of only buyed us a food cause of he did still felt guilty about a Mielie Lady locking us up in a house. He did only of tell me this laterer cause of he couldn't not talk about Moses in a truck cause of he were there.

I did of really like Moses, he were a only ou what had beed proper nice to us since we did of left Sally with Larry the Lithp. It were like as that were so long ago past that it were a other me and Zakes what did of done that.

We did of have to get out of a truck again to miss a other cop stop, but this time there weren't none problems, but also nthere weren't one Shell Ultra City so as we didn't get toasted zarms more.

I did of have some Toff-o-lux and gaved some to Zakes and Moses. There weren't not much of my sweets left from what we did of we gotted from a shop where a cops were of shotted by that ou Sharp. I reckoned we must zick some more at a next place.

It were getting awards dark when we check a sign post what charfed, 'Welcome to Mpumalanga'. That were really lekker to see cause of now we could be with Zakes' grandparents and all. But old Moses still droved more and more and I checked out Zakes cause of now I were worried that perhaps maybe Moses weren't such a cool dude after all and that he were taking us someplace else. But old Zakes just like laughs at me and charfs so as Moses can't not hear, 'Mpumalanga is a province. It's a big place. My grandparents live somewhere here. We'll go to Mbombela with Moses and then find them from there.

I do of feel a bit dof now, aspecially cause of I did now merember learning it at school that Mpumalanga were a province, so I just check out of a window so as even if Zakes were checking me out like I were dof, I couldn't not see him doing it none.

When we did of started to drive though a big town, Moses do asks us if we did got somewhere to stay for a night cause of it were dark and all. Zakes did shake his head.

'I've got a friend that I'm going to stay with. Do you want me to ask him if you can stay as well?'

We both nods and I reckon Shaka did of nod too also as well, but he couldn't not of have done cause of he are a dog and dogs don't not understand people none, so as maybe perhaps I did of just amagined it.

Anyways, Moses asplains to us that he are going to drop us off by a township where his friend are, then take a truck into town to drop it off and make his paper work, then he were going to catch a taxi back to find us and his friend.

81

It were a little cold when he did of dropped us off, but not so bad as to need a jersey. There were lank people walking everywhere, like it were at a place where a Mielie Lady did of sell her mielies. They all checked me out skew, but no-one said nothink. So I asks Zakes howcomewhy are everybody checking us out and he charfs me that it were cause of I are white.

'What are wrong with being white?' I wants to know.

'Nothing,' he like shrugs, 'it's just they don't get many white people round here. You're a novelty, that's why they're checking you out. Do you see any other white people around?'

I check around and he are right, I are a only one what are white, unless you count Shaka who are a almost white library door, but he are a dog not a person. Still I don't want to be none novel tea.

I also don't not like it that all a ous are checking me out skew just cause of I is white, and I don't not think Zakes are too happy none neither, but when I start to charf him that I is not happy, he like charfs, 'We should perhaps do something, we don't want to attract attention, we still don't know if the cops are looking for us or not.'

I nods, but what can we do? If we did of goed off somewhere, then Moses won't not never find us and then we won't not sleep there by his friend and I is not feeling very Einsteiny cause of I is tired. Zakes are also not a Einstein now neither cause of he just stands there checking round. There is ous what is selling stuff all along a street. Some ous is selling fruit – apples, bananas and naartjies and I feel lus for some so as I charf Zakes, 'Let's go get some naartjies.'

He's like cool with this plan cause if it are betterer as just standing around. I did still got lots of a money from what I tooked from pa and Zakes' brother and a ou there by a café where all those cops were shooted. A ou what are selling a naartjies are like nice cause of he smiles and all and doesn't not check me out skeef. When we is paying for a naartjies, I check a table next to a naartjie ou's. It are got like all this grass and trees and bones and bottles on it. A bottles are got like green cream soda juice and what do of check like pa's half jacks.

There are an ou what are sitting by a table but he don't not check so lekker. He are sitting holding his head in his hands like he are about to puke up his lunch. I give Zakes a elbow and then check out a ou.

'Witch doctor,' he do of whispers at me.

I'm like, really? I had of checked witch doctors on a TV sometimes, but they weared skins and made strange noises. This ou were in jeans and a purple t-shirt, and weren't not making none noises or nothing.

'What's wrong with him?' I asks.

'Dunno. Maybe he took some of his own medicine,' he charfs and then laughs, but not so loud like.

I check out a witch doctor, then Zakes, then a witch doctor again. I scheme that maybe Zakes are a little bit scared of him.

Shaka aren't not scared though, cause of he do go and sniffs at a ou, but it are like as he must of smelled bad, cause Shaka don't not hang around him too long none.

We wented back across a road to of wait for Moses and begined to chow a naartjies. A skins came off lank easy which were cool and they were a lekker orange colour with not too many lots of those white strings what do of hang to a segments. They were also lekker juicy as well. I were just about to chow my third one, when Shaka do of begin to growl so as we checked up. A witch doctor were almost across a road and he were looking straight at us and I don't not like a way he were checking us out none.

TWENTY-THREE

I are glad that Zakes are my friend and also too Shaka, even though he are a dog, cause of I wouldn't not of wanted to have to deal with a witch doctor without Zakes not being there.

A Witch Doctor Ou comes up to us and looks at me, then at Zakes, then at me, then at Shaka, then at me. I can check that Zakes are a bit skrikked too as he are looking round to see where we could of run to.

'You the boys that are travelling with Moses?' a witch doctor asks. He do got a really deep voice what didn't not match to his face none.

Old Zakes are still skrikked so as he don't not charf nothink. I don't not charf nothink neither also. A witch doctor checks us again, then charfs, 'You must be, not too many white kids hanging around with a black one and a dog.' He are not charfing us this cause of he are not looking at us, but looking round a street.

'It's okay,' he do says, but now he are checking at us. 'Moses just called, he's been delayed at the truck depot. He is staying with me tonight and asked if you guys can stay too. You are welcome, but the dog will have to sleep outside.' He then smiles big time and it are a nice smile.

'Is you a witch doctor?' I suddenly asks cause of I wants to know. Old Zakes like donners me with his elbow, but a Witch Doctor Ou just laughs big time.

'No, I'm not a witch doctor. Why would you...' he then checks round at a table where he were earlier. I can check that there are a other ou there what were looking after a stall.

He then laughs big time and charfs, 'No, I was just watching his stall for him for a few minutes.'

Suddenly it are like as Zakes aren't not skrikking none more. 'Did Moses say how late he's going to be,' he do of asks now.

'Not too long,' a ou what aren't not a witch doctor charfs. 'You can wait here for him if you like, but I've got to get home. It's up to you. You can come now and sit in comfort with some food, or wait here in the cold. Your choice.'

A ou weren't not a witch doctor, but he did of say a magic word – food!

As we did walked ahind him, I asks Zakes howcomewhy a ou had checked me out so skeef at first.

'Dunno, he was probably just checking that we were the ous that Moses was talking about.'

I asposed that were why, but I still didn't not of liked a way what a ou checked me.

It weren't not too far to a ou's place and as we did of walked there, he did charfed us that his name are Joshua. He did also live in a house like what a Mielie Lady's house were like, you know that congregated iron stuff, but only his house were biggerer as what a Mielie Lady's was. There were one room what did had a bucket of water in what he did of call a bathroom. Then there were a room what did of have a sofa and a chair and even a TV and a place where a food were cooked at a end of a room. I knowed this cause of Joshua's wife Lizzy were busy making food there when we camed in. There were also two other rooms what I reckoned were bedrooms but I didn't not get to check inside of them.

Joshua did of have two children kids what were sitting on a sofa when we did get there. One of them were a boy and a other were also a girl. Ben and Zondi was their names. Ben were a little bit tallerer as what Zakes were, but Zondi were much more smallerer.

'You boys can have a wash if you like, then we can eat,' Joshua charfs. Ben and Zondi did of just check me out big time. When we did of went into a bathroom to wash our hands and faces, they did stand by a door, just checking. Old Zakes charfed them somethink in black and Ben did charfed him somethink back and then Zakes charfed somethink more and they did of all laughed. I did of laughed a little bit too also as well, but I didn't not have a clue what they was charfing.

Zakes checks me laughing and charfs somethink more to Ben and they then do of laugh even more. I can check they is laughing at me, but acause I can't not understand them, I can't not say nothink so as I just do of wash my face.

A food were stew and rice and it were really lekker. I did say thank you to Lizzy when I were finished, like pa did taughted me, and she did check lank chuffed which were nice. I were begining to like her and also Joshua too as well, cause of they was nice to us.

Moses did comed just when me and Zakes and Ben were going outside to play soccer. Ben didn't not have a proper soccer ball, but had of taken lots of packets and tied them up with a string to make a ball. It weren't not as good as a proper ball, but we did of had lank fun. Even old Shaka did tried to play with us, but Ben and Zakes were much betterer an me.

When it did of started to get dark we wented inside so as to watch TV while Moses were finishing his food. He and Joshua talked lots and laughed lots and it were really lekker sitting there. It were like as a days when pa did come home and didn't not shout at us, but did play nicely with us.

It weren't not too late afore I were tired and I could check that Zakes were too also. Joshua and Lizzy did sleep in one room, Moses in a other one and me and Zakes and Ben and Zondi did of sleeped in a room with a TV.

I don't not knowed how long it were that we did of sleeped, but it were lank dark when Zakes did of waked me up.

'Get dressed, we've got to go,' he like whispers.

'Why?'

'Shh! Just get dressed and grab your stuff, I'll tell you outside.'

We do of get outside without not waking nobody. Shaka were there by a door, but he did of woked up when we came out and he did sniff us and wag his tail. It were not too dark outside cause of a moon and we did walk quick like back to a road where we did first meet Joshua, a whole time Zakes were charfing, 'Come on', and he were walking lank fast. I weren't not too happy none cause of I had of beed sleeping lekker and all and now Zakes were making me walk in a cold. But now I were more awaker and I did of charf myself that Zakes wouldn't not of made us leave Joshua's place none unless it were important. He are not dof like that.

TWENTY-FOUR

It weren't till we were lank far away from even a town afore Zakes did of slowed down and charf, 'Keep your eyes out for somewhere to hide.'

I had of tried to ask him howcomewhy we did have to leave, but he just kept charfing, 'I'll tell you later.'

I were reckoning that maybe he had of checked somethink in a house what made him think that actually Joshua were really a real witch doctor. I merembered a story once on a TV what said that a witch doctor had of cut up a children kid into pieces. I did of asked ma howcomewhy a witch doctor would of do that, but pa charfed that I must of goed to bed and that I shouldn't not of beed watching such stuff on TV. I did of asked ma again, but pa klapped me on a back of my head, not hard like, but it were a bit sore and I knewed that if I didn't not goed to bed then, that he would donner me a lot more sorer.

A next day when pa weren't there, I did of asked ma again and she did charfed me that a witch doctor did it to make muti with a boy, and that were why I mustn't not never talk to strange black ous cause of in case they was a witch doctor what did want to make medicine out of me.

So that were why I were reckoning that maybe Zakes had checked somethink what did of maked him think that Joshua were a witch doctor.

Anyways, it were starting to get light and we could of check that there were some mountains by a side of a road. Zakes charfed, 'Come, there should be a cave or some rocks we can hide behind up there,' and he did of start to walk off up a hill.

We did of find a lekker spot what were ahind a big rock so as none ous could check us from a road, but there were also a small hole atween a rocks from what we could check down onto a road. Also there were some mountains what were sticking out so that if it did of rained, we could sit under it and stay dry. It were like a small cave.

Just afore we stopped though, Zakes did of picked up some rocks and chucked them into a cave. 'To frighten away any snakes,' he charfed. It nearly did of frighten away me, but I couldn't not say nothink cause of I would of looked like a woosie.

We did of go into a cave and then sitted down. I were lank tired now, but afore Zakes could of charf nothink, I did asked him, 'Were Joshua a real witch doctor what were going to cut us up?'

He checks me out like I were dof. 'What? How did you come up with that?'

Now I do of feeled a bit dof, but I still charf Zakes about what were on a TV and he like nods all serious like.

'Yes, there are a few witch doctors like that, but not many. Most of them only use plants and maybe chickens or birds. But what made you think that Joshua was like that. He told us that he was only helping out his friend, you saw the other guy take over the stall.'

'I dunno,' I says, 'it were just you skrikked me by saying we had to go and all and you didn't not even tell me howcomewhy.'

Then Zakes do smiles and it are a nice smile. 'You're right, I should have said more, but I was skrikking myself and we had to leave, there was no time to explain. What happened was that I wasn't sleeping well and so got up to go wash my face. I got into the bathroom really quietly and before I could start splashing my face, I heard Joshua and Lizzy talking. Basically, Lizzy was worried that we were runaways and that they should check with the cops. At first Joshua wasn't interested, but Lizzy went on at him, so he eventually agreed to go see the cops in the morning.'

Now I could check howcomewhy we did of have to leave. 'It were good that you had of wanted to wash your face, you must do that every night,' I charfed and we did of both laughed.

'We should be okay here for a bit, so let's get some sleep.' He then do start to lie down. 'Later we can take stock of where we are.'

I started to lie down too also and closeded my eyes.

'Moses were a nice man,' I charfed even though I were really tired, 'it would of have beed lekker to stay with him.'

'Mmm,' Zakes were already almost asleep. 'He reminded me a lot of my own father.'

I did feeled really sorry for Zakes then cause of his pa were deaded and he did of sounded sad meremembering his pa. I wish Moses had beed my pa instead of my real one, but I don't charf this, I just thinks it. Then I do of start to thinks of that night again when ma were deaded. Somethink are not lekker with what I do of meremember cause of what I do of meremember now is that it weren't not Zakes' brother what deaded pa like what I did of told you earlier. I also don't not like what I do of meremember acause of it can't not be right none and it do of also make me want to cry, so as I do of make my brain think of sweets so as not to meremember nothink.

87

TWENTY-FIVE

Zakes were still sleeping when I did of waked up. A sun were shining but you could of check that it were already a arvie. When Shaka checked that I were awaked, he did come over and sit by me and I did of stroked him. I didn't not want to waked up Zakes so as I just sat quiet like and thinked, but also didn't not like what I were thinkink cause of it were more about pa. Maybe it were acause of we were charfing that Moses would of have made a lekker pa that I did thinked of my own real pa.

Anyways, I were merembering that last time what I sawed pa and how of Zakes' brother were outside a house when I checked a ambalance what tooked ma. He did of ask me if I did got more bullets afore I went inside, but I just did charf him no. I could check that he had of beed shooted, but didn't not say nothink. Maybe if I had of gived him more bullets, he would of have buggered off and not shooted pa.

It weren't not lekker thinking about this, so as I did of try and think of Sally and did wonder if Larry the Lithp would do it with her like what he did of done with ma. I did hoped not, cause of Larry were so much biggerer as Sally, so as he would of have squashed her.

This weren't not a lekker thought neither, so as I just thinked of all a stuff what I did of zicked from George's Cafe. That were much betterer to thinked of, but when Zakes did of waked up then, I felt lank hungry.

'Let's get some bread and milk, then when it gets dark we can move on. I don't think we should travel by day for a bit.' He were like a mind reader what knowed exactly what I were thinkink. Not about travelling by night, that were his own thoughts, but about getting food and all.

'I think there were a café back that way a little bit, let's go.'

'No, you wait here. If they have gone to the cops, then they'll be looking for a black kid travelling with a white one and a dog.'

'Or maybe they will of be looking for a white kid travelling with a black kid and a dog,' I charf.

'I think they are most probably looking for a dog travelling with a black kid and white kid,' Shaka do of charf.

'Shaka, you stay here with the white kid,' Zakes charfs him, even though Shaka hadn't not really said nothink.

When Zakes are gone, I don't got nothink what I can of do and I can't not think of nothink lekker to think of. It are like as either pa or ma or Sally or Larry the Lithp or Zakes' brother what comes into my brain, so as I acide to count my sweets. I did of got three Cherrols, two XXX Mints, four Humbugs, a box of Astros, a bag of cheese and onion chips and five rolls of Meth-o-lyptus. I didn't not got none Toff-o-lux left and I wish I had of asked Zakes to get some more.

He do of take lank ages afore he comes back and by then I have of chowed two rolls of Meth-o-lyptus and half a box of Astros even though they is not my favourtist sweets. He did of got bread but also some stew which were really lekker.

When we is finished eating, Zakes shows me a game what you plays with stones. It were a bit like noughts and crosses but like biggerer and more difficulter. Zakes always did of won cause of he knewed a rules betterer as me.

When it did of start getting darkerer, we did of stopped playing and ated a rest of a bread, then started to of walk again.

'Is this a way to where your grandparents live?' I asks Zakes after a bit.

'Ja, I think so,' he charfs, but you can check that he don't not really knowed still. Maybe we would adventually got to somewhere and he would like go, 'This is the right road,' or somethink, but I were quite happy just to keep going round with him.

We walked lank lots more that night and by a time it were nearly light, we could of check a small town not too far down a road. It were just after we checked a town that Shaka did of stop and did started to growl. Of course me and Zakes skrikked cause of Shaka didn't not often growl like what he did then.

Then we did of heard a other dog what did bark a angry bark. Me and Zakes checked at each other like, should we run? But afore we can of do nothink, we heard a ou what charfs, 'Spider! Come here Spider!' and a other dog did of stopped barking, but Shaka did still growl so as Zakes did pat him till he did stopped.

Then we could see a ou what did speak. He were holding on to a dog what were almost as big as what Shaka are, just a little bit down a road.

'You boys are out early,' a ou charfs when he checks us.

'Just walking the dog, like you,' Zakes charfs afore I can say nothink.

A ou starts walking awards us and he are looking a bit skeef at first, but then do smile nice like and charfs, 'Hmmm, jolly good.'

I can of check now that a ou are quite old. Not old old like a toppie what did of lost his false 'teef', but olderer like as pa.

'That's a lovely dog you've got there,' he are almost by us now and he like puts his hand out to pat Shaka, but Shaka does try to bite him and he do of pulls his hand back just in time. A ou do of almost say a bad word, but then he do smile again like as he were never not cross with Shaka, it were more like as he did of think it were funny.

A ou's dog what were called Spider did of barked at Shaka, but a ou had a lead on him so as he couldn't not bite and Zakes were holding Shaka too also.

'Perhaps we ought to let you gentlemen pass, our canine friends are not getting along.'

I didn't not like that a ou were calling Shaka a canine cause of he were a dog, but still, Zakes reckoned that it were betterer if he did of move Shaka so as a ou and his canine could of pass. I could check that Zakes weren't too happy none also, but I weren't not sure if it were acause a ou did of called Shaka a canine or if it were acause he had to move for a ou to pass.

'Let's get out of here, quick,' he charfs me once a ou were passed. 'I don't like that guy, there's something creepy about him.' He starts to walk quick like and I do of follow. We get to a end of a street and Zakes turns into a other one. As I turn, I check back and see that a ou are turned round and are following us. I skrik and charf Zakes what are happened.

'Come, move!' he charfs and starts running as best as what he can which are not that fast cause of his legs. We get to a next road and turn. It are only after we turn that we check that it are a dead end and all. There are like factories on both sides and a other one at a end of a road.

'Here,' Zakes charfs and he like goes in by a gate of one place. I can check that a ou with his canine are just by a factory road and are checking down awards us but I don't not knowed if he have of seed us.

'Hey! What are you doing here?' There are this really big black ou what are blocking our way and I skrik cause of I didn't not of seed him afore. Shaka do of starts to bark like, but Zakes pats him quick to stop him.

You can check that a big ou are a little scared of Shaka and he is like starting to get his gun out. He must of have beed a scurity god I reckon cause of otherwise he wouldn't not of have none gun.

'Don't worry, he won't bite,' Zakes charfs quick like. I is just about to charf that Shaka did of bited a ou what had false 'teef', but then reckon that maybe I shouldn't not.

'What do you want? You can't come in here,' a scurity ou charfs. I check up a road and see that a Canine Ou are not there none more.

'Sorry, boss,' I charf, 'There were a man what were following us, we think he might of had a Peter file.' That must of have beed a right think to said cause of a scurity god comes to a gate and checks up a street. You can check that he are worried.

'Where? There's no one there.'

'He are gone now, but he were there, honest. He did got a dog called Spider what are a canine,' I charf and Zakes like laughs a little when I charf this, but I is not sure howcomewhy he do.

A scurity ou checks us out for a bit, then charfs, 'Okay, you can wait here for a while, but not too long, my boss won't be happy if he catches me letting you hang around.'

I check up a road again and there are still no Canine Ou. Meantime, old Zakes starts charfing a security ou in black language and they talk for a bit so as I just stand there like a lemon.

Adventually Zakes charfs me that he had of asked a ou if he do of knowed Zakes' grandparents. A ou said that he didn't not, but knewed a other ou what knowed lots of people in Mpumalanga and that if we did come back at five o'clock that arvie, he would take us to this other ou.

'Have you seen the Canine Man?' Zakes then do asks me and like laughs a little when he charfs this.

'No,' I charf and laugh too also even if I don't not want to ask Zakes whycome it are funny, cause of he would reckon I is dof.

'Okay, let's go.'

We go back up to a main road and check up and down, but can't not see a ou none.

'Where is we going,' I asks as Zakes do of start to walking back to where we did comed from.

'Dunno, we can just walk around, maybe find a park and sit there and wait.'

I is okay with this cause of I is now feeling tired. We have of walked so much in a night and we didn't not sleep none. When we do get to a corner then suddenly a Canine Ou did of turn into a road.

'Ah, there you boys are, you disappeared in such a hurry, I was wondering if you would care to join me for breakfast, you look hungry.'

I check Zakes and he checks me and I can check that he are thinkink what I are thinkink – food!

But what if this ou are got a Peter file?

'I don't live too far away, I can rustle up some bacon and eggs if you like.'

I reckon Zakes are a Einstein so he would of knowed if it were okay. Anyways, I now want to knowed who this Russell ou are.

Zakes checks a ou up and down meanwhile. Shaka are stopped barking and are now sniffing Spider's bum. It are a good think Pooh Pants aren't a dog cause of no one would of wanted to sniff his bum. I laugh when I thinks this and Zakes checks me out like, 'what?'

'That's settled then,' a ou charfs, 'come on.'

He does of start walking away and I'm like, 'did Zakes said okay while I were thinking about Pooh Pants and I didn't not heard?' I reckon that this must of beed a case so as I start to follow a ou.

Zakes do of walk ahind me, but I is now not so sure if it are acause his leg are sore or if it are acause he didn't not say ja to a ou while I were thinking. Anyways it were too late, we did of goed with a ou.

His house are not so lank far away, we only had to of walk past this small veldt and along some roads. It are a really larny house with a big fence and lekker veranda and garden and all.

'You boys want to clean up while I make breakfast?' I check round to see if this Russell ou are anywhere, but there don't seem to be nonebody else by his house.

'Yes, please,' Zakes charfs.

'I'll get you some towels.'

He do of shows us a bathroom which are really lekker and clean and do give us some nice soft towels, then charfs, 'Don't take too long, breakfast will be ready soon.'

I let Zakes go first and check out a window of a bedroom what a ou said we could of get changed in. Shaka are playing with Spider in a garden. A room are lekker with a big bed and mirror and all. I like check a bed out and think it would be lekker to doss there for a bit cause of I is now feeling lank tired.

Zakes don't not take too long in a shower and I do of feel betterer when I have of showered too also. A breakfast what a ou made were really nice, two fried eggs each. Fried eggs are okay, it are when they mash them up on a zarm that I get sick. Lank bacon and fried tomato and toast and jam and orange juice as well. It were a huge feast and we did stuff our faces silly. A ou didn't not eat too much, just some toast and jam and he did of also drink a cup of tea. He did of checked us out all a time and did of asked us questions like where we was from and where we was going and all that. I did of let Zakes answer cause of he are much betterer at making stuff up as me.

I didn't not really listen cause of I were now lank tired and are almost sleeping. I wish they would of stop talking so as I can go lie down in a bedroom.

'You look tired, you want to go lie down for a bit?' A Canine Ou are now suddenly a Einstein, but afore I can of charf nothink, Zakes charfs, 'Yes, please, we've had a long journey.'

We don't not have none pyjamas with us so as we just sleep in our underpants. A bed are nice and soft and lekker so as I did of snuggle down. Just afore I did of goed to sleep though, I did of heard what were maybe perhaps a door being locked, but I were too tired to of care.

TWENTY-SIX

Afore I charf yous what did of happened there by a Canine Ou's house, let me charf about a dream what I did of have when I did of sleeped. It weren't not a lekker dream or nothink, but acause I did of merembered it after I did waked up, that are why I is going to tell yous.

I were in a house afore pa did of killed ma and ouma and afore Zakes' brother did of killed pa. Me and Sally was playing in my room and ma and pa and ouma and her very cross veins were in a lounge and they weren't not even fighting none cause of we couldn't not hear them.

I were charfing Sally that I had of checked Zakes' brother outside and that he were bleeding and all. I were charfing her this to scare of her, but she were just laughing. Then there were a moerse loud knock at a front door what did of maked us jump acause it were so loud and I did of charf Sally it were Zakes' brother what had of come to shooted her. Sally did of just laugh more, but we did heared someone go to a door and open it and suddenly there were a loud bang. Sally did of just keeped laughing, but I did wetted my broeks, only in a dream of course, I don't not wetted my broeks normal like.

'Stop laughing,' I charf Sally, but she did of just laughed more. I can heard people what are shouting now and I check out of my bedroom door. Ma are lying on a floor and Zakes' brother are pointing a gun at pa who had of comed out of a lounge to see what were happening. Afore I can do nothink, Zakes' brother did of shooted pa and were walking into a lounge. I could of check that he weren't lekker cause of he were holding onto a wall and all and walking funny.

I did of followed him into a lounge, but he had of already shooted ouma afore I did of getted there. He were sitting on a sofa when I checked round a door and when he checks me he like laughs and do go,

93

'Hey boss. Sorry, I didn't know you lived here.' Then he like coughs and this blood do of come out of his mouth and he do of wiped it away with his hands. That are when I run back to Sally and make her run out of a house with me.

It didn't not really of happened like that, but when I do wake up it were like that were what really did of happened and I is feeling lank cross with Zakes' brother for killing my ma. I don't not opened my eyes straight away like and even when I do of merember that it didn't not of happen like that, it still do of feel like it really did and I is not sure none more what potted there by a house that night cause of I can't not merember it too lekker now. Somethink are charfing me that my brain are not telling me everythink what did of happened then and that there are somethink not lekker what I isn't not meremembering. It do of make me feel not so lekker none, but I acide to wake up proper like to of make these thinks go away, but afore I do of open my eyes I can of feel ma's hand what are on my face. She are moving my hair out of my eyes.

Then I hear a Canine Ou's voice and so I don't not open my eyes none, but pretend to still of be asleeping.

'What do you think? It looks like it could be him,' a Canine Ou charfs.

'Yes, you could be right.' It are a lady what speaked, and she are sitting right there by me but it aren't not ma. 'He looks too young, though,' a lady are talking more and I is wondering if it are me what are too young or Zakes, and also too young for what?

'It must be them,' a Canine Ou charfs, 'the picture was blurred, but there is certainly a resemblance. If I'm wrong we can always apologise later.'

'Apologise now! We is not a ous what you is looking for,' I shouts and jumps out of a bed.

No I don't not. I don't not knowed what's potting with a Canine Ou and a lady, but I reckon I better of wait and see more afore I do nothink, so as I just lies there like I is asleeping. I can of feel that Zakes are lying in a bed next to me and I do of wonder if he are also awake or not.

'I think he's waking up,' a lady charfs and I skrik cause of growed ups can always tell if you is asleep proper or not. Ma were always catching me out when I were pretending to be asleep when I didn't not want to go to school none.

'Come, before they realise what's happening.'

I can feel a lady leaving from next to a bed and then she and a Canine Ou do go out. But when they do of close a door, they do locked it. I knowed that sound good from all a times what pa did of locked me into my room.

94

'Zakes, wake up.' I is up now and getting my clothes on. 'Zakes!' He are slow to of waked up, but suddenly his eyes do of open big time and he does do a eyeball sweets think with them.

I charf him that we is locked in and what a lady and a Canine Ou did of said and how they did of charf that I had a assemblance with a picture.

'What picture? What are you talking about?'

'I dunno. A Canine Ou must of seed a picture of me.'

'Damn! So they *are* looking for us.'

'Who?' I asks.

Zakes checks me out like I is dof. 'The cops.'

I skrik. 'We had of better get out of here, quick like. I don't not want to deal with none cops.'

'Check the windows.'

There is burglar bars all over them so as we can't not get out even though a windows do of open. I can check Shaka outside. He are still playing with Spider. I do of start to call him, but then reckon that a Canine Ou will come if I do of call, so as I don't not shout none.

Meanwhile old Zakes are checking through a keyhole.

'The key's still in there,' he like whispers, then starts to looking round a room. 'See if you can find some paper, quick!'

'Paper? What for?'

'You'll see,' he do smiles.

Now I did of already told you that Zakes are a Einstein, but what he done next even Einstein wouldn't not of thoughted of. Einstein are dof compared with Zakes. We did of found some paper at a bottom of a drawer what Zakes then did push under a door, but not all a way. Then he gotted a bic pen what were on a table and did taked out a bit what do of has a ink in what he do uses to push a key out through a keyhole. Then he do pull a paper back really slow like and there are a key lying on a paper.

We open a door proper quiet like and check up a passage. There are no one there, but we can of hear a Canine Ou talking and as we goes on tip toes to a front door, we can heard what he are saying.

'I'm pretty sure it's them, officer. The picture in the newspaper is a bit blurred, but I'm sure it's him.'

We check into a room where a Canine Ou's voice are. He are standing by a desk and are talking on a phone. He did got his back to us and Zakes do points so as we go quickly past a door. There is noises coming from a kitchen too also, so as I reckon it must of beed a lady, but we don't not have to go past a kitchen door so as I can't not check none to make sure.

We is just opening a front door when a Canine Ou shouts from ahind us, 'Hey! Come back!'

'Run!' Zakes do of shouts and I head out quick like, but old Zakes are not fast enough and a Canine Ou has him afore I can of do nothink.

'Go! Run!' Zakes shouts. He are trying to kick a Canine Ou and all, but he are being held too tight. I then check a lady what are coming down a passage. I don't not want to leave Zakes ahind, but he are shouting so much for me to run that I does.

'Spider, get him!' a Canine Ou do of shouts and I check round and do see Spider coming for me. I can tell you I nearly almost did of changed my name to Pooh Pants then, but just afore Spider do of get to me, Shaka does of jumped on his back and cause of Shaka are biggerer he do knock Spider over and then he are trying to bite Spider and Spider are trying to bite him and a lady are shouting and running after me and Zakes are shouting for me to run and all and I is skrikking somethink chronic now, but then I just did turned and run big time fast. I don't not stop running none till I can't not hear Spider and Shaka and Zakes and a Canine Ou and a lady none more.

I check round and don't not knowed where I is. There are a tree there and cause of there are nobody around I climb up into it quick like so as I can of think.

But when I is in a tree I can't not think nothink like cause of I is worrying about Zakes and Shaka and now, even if I did of want to go back and try to of save them, I didn't not knowed where I are so as to get back.

A street what a tree are in are quiet, all a people what are in a houses there, must of have beed at work. A houses is quite larny, like what a Canine Ou's house were and now I is not so tired from running so as I check up and down a street. There are no one there. I did still got my bag with me, but there are hardly not nothink left in it. I wished it were me what a Canine Ou had of caughted and not Zakes, then Zakes could of had thinked of how to free me cause of he are a Einstein.

I is busy thinkink this when I do check through a window of one house that there are a ou what do looks a bit like Zakes' brother. He are putting this stuff in a plastic bag and checking round all a time, but he don't not see me in a tree.

It don't not take a Einstein to knowed that he are buglaring a place, but it do of take a Einstein to come up with a good diarrhoea what I did of just had.

TWENTY-SEVEN

'All what I need to do now,' I charf to me, 'are to find out where a Canine Ou's house are, then I can of rescue Zakes.'

I is walking down a road, checking this way and that so as I can hide if I do of check anyone, cause of I is worried that maybe a Canine Ou are looking for me.

A burglar ou did bleed quite lank from a brick what I did of dropped on his head from a tree, but he didn't not check me take his gun or nothink cause of he were sleeping after it did of hitted him. I were lucky cause of he were still burgularing a house so as I could of climb down a tree and get a brick from some what was lying near a house's driveway and then get back up a tree in time for him to of walk under it.

I gets to a corner and check round. There are a car what are coming slowly up a road so as I jump quick like over a small wall there by a house what I is walking past and watch as a car do of go past. I skrik a little when I check that it are a lady from a Canine Ou's house, but she don't not check me none so as I is okay.

I waits till she are far gone, but afore I can of jump back over a wall, I hear an ou shout, 'Hey, what are you doing in my yard?'

'Playing hide and seek,' I charf and I is chuffed I did of said that cause of I didn't not even think it.

'Not here, you're not. Bugger off!' He are like shouting from a window.

'Bugger off yourself,' I charf and take out a gun and shooted him.

No, I don't not shooted him, but I still do charf him to bugger off hisself. A car with a Canine Ou's lady are gone so as I go back onto a road and walk in a way what a car did of comed from cause of I did reckon she must of have beed coming from a house and not going to it. I is worried that a cops might already have of taken Zakes away, but I do still have to go and check anyways.

I did of walked down lank streets but none did of looked like a Canine Ou's one. I were just scheming that maybe I wouldn't never find Zakes again when I did heared a dog barking. I checked round and it were Shaka. I were so glad to see him that I didn't not check that he did got blood on him till after I had of hugged him lank.

'Are that Spider's blood?' I did of asked Shaka.

97

'Ja, most of it are, but he did of bited my ear a little bit,' Shaka charfs. I check out his ear and can see that he had of beed bited there.

'I bet you donnered him good and proper,' I do of laugh and Shaka nods his head.

'We need to go and rescue Zakes, but I did of forgot where a Canine Ou's house are, can you merember where it are?'

Shaka like straight away do of starts running down a road, then do stops to check that I are followink him. I is so happy to see Shaka that I don't not care none more if anyone did of seed me.

We was only about two roads away from a Canine Ou's house and I knowed a place as soon as what I did of seed it. There weren't not none cop cars outside a house so as I didn't not knowed if they were still coming or if they had of already comed and taken Zakes, but I did of have to check anyways, so as I wented up a driveway. I were about halfway up when I do of check Spider lying on a lawn. There were lank blood all over a place and he weren't not moving none so as I schemed that maybe Shaka must of have killed him.

It were not so lekker checking Spider like this, but if he didn't not of had tired to catch me, then Shaka wouldn't not of donnered him dead, so it were his own fault. But now I is like poohing my pants a bit cause of I did got to sort out a Canine Ou and I is right there by a door. I gets out a gun what I did of taked from a burglar dude and take a big breath afore I ring a doorbell.

'You took your time...' A Canine Ou do of stop talking when he checks me and then he do of make like to grab me and then he like makes a lank big shut up and starts to walking backwards and trying to close a door when he checks a gun.

'Leave a door, or I'll shoot,' I charfs quick like afore he can do nothink. It do of feel a bit like when I did of shooted Zakes' brother there by a house, at least what I merember it did of feeled like.

A Canine Ou do of steps back more, but he do at least leave a door open. I can check that he are skrikking lekker big time.

'H-h-hold on, y-y-oung man, be reasonable.' He are like not totally hands up, but are half hands up like what a cops are sometimes on TV when a baddie are pointing a gun, most time just afore they shoot a ou so as I do of check him out good and proper like to make sure he don't not do nothink funny like.

'Where are Zakes,' I charf in a angry cross voice acause I were angry cross.

A Canine Ou are still skrikking and walking backwards while as I is walking more forwards.

'I've locked him back in the room.'

'Well, unlocked him in a room,' I charf, then when he don't do nothink, I go, 'Now!' and wave a gun like what a baddies in a movies do. It feeled quite cool holding a gun cause of I can check that a Canine Ou are so poeping hisself that he would of do whatever I do of charf him to.

We walk slow like to a room and a ou takes out a key. He starts to put it in a door then he do of stops.

'The police don't want to hurt you. They only want to take you back to your...'

'Shut up!' I charf. I don't not want this ou charfing me nothink cause of he are most likely lying like what all growed ups do and if I don't not rescue Zakes, then I may of do somethink dof like let a Canine Ou take me to a police.

'But...' A ou are now turning to face me.

'Unlock a door! Zakes, it are me, I did of comed to rescue you. Unlock a door!' I is screaming now, and don't not actually just says, 'Unlock a door,' like that, I also do of use a bad word cause of I do of got a gun and no growed ups are going to charf me nothink about a bad word or I will of shooted them one time.

A Canine Ou skriks and do of opened a door but he don't not stop checking me out. It are like as he now reckons I may of really shooted him. I haven't never shooted no one ever afore, but I don't not want a Canine Ou to knowed this, and maybe, just maybe, I would of shooted him if he had of not opened a door, or if he had of tried to get a gun from off of me.

But he did of opened a door so, like what Larry the Lithp do sometimes always say, 'it are epidemic.'

'Zakes,' I do of shout, but he didn't not come out. 'Zakes, it are me, come, we must go.'

I start to reckon that maybe a Canine Ou were lying and that a cops had of already comed and taked Zakes and that he were going to push me in a room and get a cops to come back for me. But then Zakes do of come to a door and he checks me out all funny like. It were as if he don't not want to come with me none.

'Come on Zakes,' I charf again cause of I is now skrikking that a cops will come soon while I is rescuing Zakes and they would reckon I were going to shooted a Canine Ou, so as they would of shooted me even though I weren't really not going to shooted no one.

Zakes checks up at a Canine Ou who like nods. It are as if he were of saying that it are okay for him to go with me. Bloody cheek! I should of have shooted him for that, but I don't not. I wait for Zakes to get out of a room then I charf a Canine Ou that he must of go in a room.

As I do of close and lock a door, he do shout, 'Zakes, remember what I told you.'

I like wonder what he are talking about, but there aren't not none time to ask.

'Let's go,' I charf and start to walk off. It are only when I do get to a main door that I check he aren't not following me none.

'Zakes,' I skrik cause of maybe a Canine Ou do of has a other key and did get out and grab him again. I is now like really going to shooted him if he are done this. But he didn't of. A door are still shut and Zakes are standing there like he do want to open it again.

'Come, Zakes,' I charf and like wave my hand with a gun in it. He checks me out, then starts to come. I is now worried that a Canine Ou has of done somethink to Zakes' brain what are making him want to stay, but I can't not think what.

All of a sudden like there are a lank loud bang what were like as a one when Zakes' brother did of shooted ouma and it do of feeled as if some ou had of hitted me in a arm but there are no one there. A bang do of makes Zakes catch a wake up and he do of starts to run. Shaka are outside and he are lank happy to see Zakes but we have to move quick like away from a Canine Ou's house.

I don't not knowed where are a best place to hide cause of we don't not want a cops to find us none. Zakes are not being too much helpful so as when I check that we is near a factory what we did visited earlier, I reckon we should of goed there. But I don't not goed to a gate where a scurity god are cause of I check a hole in a fence afore we get to there by him. There are a small building just on a other side of a fence what checks like no one are in it so as we go there and open a door. Cause of it are dark inside I reckon there are definitely no one around by this place.

It are nice to sit down after all a running and all and we don't not say nothink for a lank while. Zakes do of check me out funny though and I don't not like it none and do of want to ask him what a problem are, but I don't not charf nothink.

'Where'd you get the gun?' he do of ask me adventually. I can check that he aren't not happy that I did of got it.

'I did robbed it from a robber.'

He still don't not check so happy like, so I charf him a whole story of me being up a tree and all and a robber ou coming out. I did of thoughted that he would of have beed chuffed that I did do it so as to rescue him, so when he do still check me out funny I'm like, 'I only did it so as I could rescue you.'

He do smile then and I reckon we is sort of cool, but not proper cool like.

We is sitting on some sacks which is quite soft and it did of maked me want to go asleep.

'How long you reckon afore five o'clock?' I asks and yawn big time. I is a little bit worried that we would of miss a scurity god ou's friend what do knowed Zakes' grandparents.

'A few hours still, we'll hear the factory siren, so we will know when it's time.'

I like wonder why a factory would of have a siren, it are not like it do of have to go fast through a traffic none, but one think I have of learned are that Zakes are not dof, so as he must of knowed what he were talking about.

Shaka are sniffing round a room and I did of wished I had a peanut butter zarm to throw him with, but I do of stop thinkink this when it do make me lus for one myself too also and I don't not got much left in my rucksack. So I lie down on a sacks and start to go asleep.

'You need to get rid of it.' Zakes are not sleeping none.

'What?' I don't not sit up.

'The gun, you must get rid of it.'

'Why?' Now I do of sits up.

Zakes don't not check at me and he also don't not say nothink, so as I asks him howcomewhy again.

He still don't check at me none and he just charfs, 'Cause I don't like guns.'

'But what if I need to of rescue you again or somethink? I were lucky that a robber ou were there this time, but you can't not always aspect a robber with a gun to be there when you needs one, robbers is not like that.'

I start to laugh cause of what I did of said, but Zakes don't not even smile none and he were still not looking at me.

'Just get rid of it, please.'

I can check that he are serious and all, but I is now thinking about a gun and how it did of feeled when I were pointing it at a Canine Ou. It were quite lekker cause of he did of do what I did of told him to when I did point a gun. Maybe if I did point a gun at more growed ups then they would of do what I told them and I wouldn't not have to do anythink what they charf me to none more.

No, Miss Smit, I don't not want none homework today.

I won't not be in detention today Mr de Wit, my gun do of says I don't not got to be there.

Give me all a sweets what you did got, George.

Stop bouncing on my ma, Larry the Lithp.

Ja, I could call him Larry the Lithp to his face cause of I did got a gun and he couldn't not say nothink to me about it.

I start to charf Zakes all what we could do with a gun, but he do shout all of a sudden like, 'Just get rid of it, damn it!' and he are checking me out all weird like, like he do of want to donner me.

So I just shooted him, one shot atween a eyes like in a cop movie.

No, of course I don't not. Zakes are my friend. I wouldn't not never of shooted him none. But still I is like sad that Zakes did of shouted at me cause he never did of shouted at me afore.

'Just get rid of it, I'm serious,' he are not shouting now and it are like as he are sorry he did of shouted. 'We can't travel together if you want to keep the gun.'

Now I skrik cause of I don't not want to travel on my ace. I would of never find Zakes' grandparents on my alone cause of I don't not even knowed what they do of look like. So I charf, 'Okay, I'll chuck it in a veldt next door to a factory.'

Zakes smiles and charfs, 'Thanks.' He are a lot happier now.

I take a gun and check out a door first to make sure that no one are there, then run to a fence, but when I gets there, I check a gun out in my hand and it do maked me merember when pa were shooted and all and I starts to think of then, but I don't not like what I do of think so as I start to think again of all a thinks what I can make growed ups do if I keep a gun.

Zakes didn't not followed me so as I stick a gun down my pants and go back. Cause of it are so dark in a room, he can't not check that I did still got a gun.

Laterer, when he were sleeping, I put a gun right down at a bottom of my bag afore I go to sleep also as well. I don't not go to sleep straight away like cause of I is worried that Zakes may of find a gun and then leave me, but I do adventually fall asleep.

I were having a lekker dream about me and ma and Sally and ouma playing Go Fish, which are my favouritist card game, but then pa do of come in and he started to donner ma so as I start looking for a gun in my bag what are there in a dream. I can't not find it at first, but then I do and I do of point it at him and charf him to stop donnering ma cause of I can now cause of I did got a gun.

Pa do of just laughs at me and I are just about to shooted him when I heared a police sirens and skrik. Next think I knowed is that I are awake and a police sirens is still going, like right there by a factory.

TWENTY-EIGHT

Zakes did of laugh lank at me skrikking like what I did, and I aspose I would of have laughed too also if it had beed him what did of skrikked. Also, after him shouting at me like he did of done, I didn't not want to make him cross none more, so as I did of just laugh also as well. We can of laugh cause it weren't not a cops what were sirening, but it were a factory. You see, when it are time for a ou's what work in a factory to go home, they do of have a siren what tells them that. Zakes charfed me he did learnt that from his pa afore he died.

So, with a factory sirening, we did waked up. Zakes charfed that we should of move so as a ous didn't not check us coming out of a little building what we was in. We do goed to a fence, then walk like as we were always outside a fence to a gate. Even Shaka did of walked so as all a ous what was coming out of a factory couldn't not check that we had of beed sleeping in their building.

There are lank ous walking in a way what we was coming from, so as we had to dodge them. I were scared that I would of lose Zakes and Shaka. Not scared in like Pooh Pants scared, but scared in like worried. I is not a woosie like Pooh Pants du Plessis were.

Anyways, we do of get to a gate and a scurity god ou were just starting to leave. He checks us out and smiles. It were a nice smile what did of tell us that he had of merembered us and all.

'Those are the boys,' he charfs a other ou what were also a scurity god. Then he charfs us, 'Solomon is the man I told you about, he knows just about everyone in Mpumalanga.' He did of actually talk in black, but Zakes did of tell me in English what he saided.

A ou Solomon where really tall, so much that he had to of bend down to heard us. He did of speaked English which were nice so as I could of understand him.

Zakes telled him his grandparent's names and then he did stand up straight for a bit and I could check that he were thinking, cause of he were frowning and all, then he did of smile.

103

'I am not one hundred percent sure, but I think that your grandparents live near the town of Ermelo.'

'Ermelo? How can we get there,' Zakes asks.

'Get a taxi, the taxi rank is just along that road there,' and he do of points.

'We can't not get a taxi,' I charf, 'Cause of I is white and they don't not let none whites on a taxis.'

He checks me out skew for a bit, then do of laugh lank loud and charfs, 'If you have the money for your fare, they'll take you.'

'But Zakes charfed...' I check Zakes out, but he are not looking at me none. I is now angry cause of he did of lied to me.

'Oh, you must be from Gauteng. The taxis there don't take whites, but here in Mpumalanga,' and he like shows us his hands to show us it were in all of Mpumalanga, 'they don't mind who they take. Your friend Zakes must be thinking of the Gauteng taxis.'

I can check that he are looking at Zakes and Zakes are looking like a thank you, so as I reckon that maybe he had of just said this so as I weren't not cross with Zakes, but I didn't not care none.

We do walk off after thanking Solomon. I don't not say nothink to Zakes and he don't not say nothink to me neither and Shaka don't say nothink neither to both of us cause of he are a dogs and dogs can't not say nothink.

Adventually, when we is by a taxi rank, Zakes charfs me to wait with Shaka while he do of goes and checks out when a taxis is going to Ermelo. It are like as a last time when we did of meet a Mielie Lady and I did of have to wait. There are a lady selling mielies on a braai nearby to where I is standing, but she didn't not look at me none so as I didn't not talk to her none.

I were worried that a Canine Ou's lady friend would of drive by, or even that she had of let him out of a room and that they did of call a cops and all, so as I find a place that were quite far from a road so as no one can of seed me.

It are starting to get dark now and it are a little bit cold, but I don't not mind too much. I just stands there and check out all a ous what is coming to a taxi rank and a taxis what is driving out. There is lank lots of noise cause of a ous in a taxis is shouting and whistling what I reckon is acause so as to make people get in their taxis. Also a taxis are hooting lank as well. I is quite tired and do of want to sleep, but a taxis is so full so as I don't not reckon I could of sleeped in them none.

It weren't not too long after Zakes went to find a taxi to Ermelo when suddenly Shaka did of start to barking and running. I checked up and a taxi were going past with Zakes in it. I skrikked big time and shouted at a taxi to stop, but they didn't not of heard me and droved still so as I did of start running after it. Shaka were nearly by a taxi and I were ahind it shouting to Zakes to make a taxi stop. He didn't not even turn around and a taxi were going fasterer and fasterer now.

When it did get to a big road it just speeded off like, with Shaka running after it. I ranned and ranned, but couldn't not of even kept up with Shaka and adventually my legs were so sore that I couldn't not of ranned none more so as I just do of sits down by a side of a road and watched a taxi and Shaka disappear. I didn't not knowed what I were going to do, or how I were going to get to Ermelo now. I is not a cry baby, but I were about to start crying when I checked a cop car coming along a road.

TWENTY-NINE

I did of adventually find a cave where we had of sleeped last night. It weren't not easy cause of it were dark, but cause of a moon what were shining, it weren't not too dark so as I could of seed a little. I were lank, lank tired and did of lie down as soon as what I did got to a cave. I were too tired to of cry even though I had of beed thinkink all a time about howcomewhy Zakes would of have lefted me and Shaka ahind.

Shaka never did of comed back to me neither so as I reckon he were still running after a taxi. It must of have beed somethink what a Canine Ou had of said that did make Zakes go. He were really weird from since when I did of rescued him.

I were still thinkink when I did of goed to sleep and I must of have sleeped lots cause of a sun were shining when I did waked up. I were still itchy from a bush what I did of hide ahind so as a cops didn't not see me none and my one arm were of bleeded a little bit from me scratching it.

I don't not like seeing a blood cause of it merinds me of pa when he did get shooted. I shouldn't not of let Zakes' brother in a house, but he were bleeding and all and I did of only want to help him. I were going to get him a plaster cause of he were sore. If I only didn't not let Zakes' brother into a house, then I wouldn't not of...

Ag! I don't not want to talk about that none more. I do of need to think as to how I is going to get to Ermelo. A cops is looking for me, probably

105

so as I can charf them where Zakes are so as they can ask Zakes what his brother did of done and where he did of get a gun and all.

Cause of I is not a best Einstein in a world, I don't not want to talk to none cops cause of maybe I would of say a wrong think and then there would be kak in a land for me and Zakes and then we would maybe not be allowed to live with his grandpa and grandma in Ermelo.

I do of pick up a stone and throw a bird with it. A bird skriks and flies away quick like and then I are sorry I skrikked it cause of I is lonely and there are nobody there now, not even none birds. It are only then that I do of check that my shirt are tored. It must of have happened when I did hided in a bush. My pants is also lank dirty but at least my takkies is okay, even if they is making my feet sore a bit.

I meremer how lekker it did of felt to have a shower there by a Canine Ou's house and how lekker a towels was and I wished I were home with ma and Sally and could of shower whenever I did of want.

Then I did of meremer that there were a small waterfall not so far from a cave so as I check out a road first so as to make sure there is no cars cause of I have to walk from ahind a rocks to where ous on a road could check me, afore going ahind more rocks to a waterfall. There is none cars on a road so as I grab my bag and run over to a waterfall.

It are lekker to be clean again and it do of make a itchy stop, but I didn't not got none towel so as I do sit on a rocks to dry. I check a lizard sitting on a rocks too also like me and then I is also a lizard. I do of stick my tongue out and in really quick like what a lizard do and he charfs me 'hello' so I charf 'hello' too also.

'What is you doing out here?' a lizard asks.

I then tell him all what did of happened with ma and pa and ouma and Larry the Lithp and Zakes' brother and a policemen at a shop and a old toppie what lost his 'teef', a lizard do laugh at this. And then I charf him about Ted what had a wife Mildred what weren't not there and a Mielie Lady and Moses what were nice to us and did gave us a lift and his friend Joshua and Lizzy what was nice too also, but were going to call a cops, and a Canine Ou what did locked us in a room and did of called a cops and all and how I did of rescue Zakes and how he did of leave me by a taxi rank.

A lizard did listen to all this, then he did of bugger off without not saying nothink, cause of lizards don't not really talk none. I did still of tell him everythink, even though he didn't not really ask me.

After a lizard had of goned, I did sit for some more, but were feeling lonely. I didn't not knowed what to do so as I did start to think of how I could get to Ermelo. I checked in my bag to see what I did of have.

There weren't not too many much sweets left and Zakes did of have most of a money. I did only got two hundred rand left. But then I check that I still do of have a gun. That are when I do of merember how a Canine Ou did of done what I did of told him to done when I were pointing a gun at him. I do of then thinked that maybe if I did of pointed a gun at other growed ups, like say maybe a shopkeeper like George, then they will of have to gived me sweets and chips and all a lekker stuff what I do of told them to gived me so as I don't not need none money never again. I could of even make a taxi taked me to Ermelo, even if I are white or not.

I do of put a gun back in my bag and then starts to thinked how I can of get to Ermelo. Even though I could of maked a taxi taked me there if I do of use a gun, I don't not want to take none taxi, not without Zakes and also I can't not go out in a daytime cause of a cops is now looking for me and all. So, I reckon I must walk to Ermelo in a night time and reckon too also that I will of find a sign by a road what charfs Ermelo and go that way, even if it do of take me lank ages to get there.

Now that I have acided what to do, I don't not feel so lonely none more and I go back to a cave to sleep more so as I are not so tired to walk in a night.

It are dark when I do waked up. Not dark, dark as in I can't not see nothink, but dark as in like night time. At first I did of forgot that Zakes had of gone, but then when I do waked up proper like, I merember but I do start to walking so as I don't not get sad none. It aren't not so easy going down to a road in a dark and I do fall once and hurt my knee, but not too sore like.

When I get to a road I do walked away from a town where a Canine Ou lived and as I get futherer and furtherer away I do of feel betterer and betterer. There aren't not so much many cars on a road so as I don't not have to hide lots, but I didn't not see none signs for Ermelo for lank ages and it are nearly almost morning time when I did of adventually find one what charfed me I must of turn left at a next road and that it were 312 kimolitres away. I did of reckon that maybe if I do of walk 200 kimolitres a next night then I would of beed there in two nights if my maths were right.

I don't not reckon I would of have feeled so happy that night if I had of knowed how far 312 kimolitres were, but still I were happy that I had of seed a sign what said Ermelo.

Acause it were getting lighterer, I did start checking round for a place to of sleep and then I did of seed that I were near a town. I acided not to go and see a town cause of maybe a cops were about, so as when I check a lank tall tree by a picnic spot by a side of a road, I did of climbed up it and founded a lekker branch where I could of sleep without not falling out none.

I were lank tired from all a walking and even though my feets was sore, I did of goed to asleep quick like. When I do of adventually waked and checked down from a tree, there is two small boys on a ground checking me out and pointing. Next think is their ma and pa is there, checking me out.

'Get the kids away, Joan,' a pa suddenly charfs after he has checked me out lekker skew for a bit. 'It's him!'

THIRTY

I don't know why a pa charfed, 'it's him,' cause of I are not him, I is me. But I aspose that a pa couldn't not of charfed, 'it's me' cause of a pa is him. He should have charfed, 'you is me and I are him.'

No, that would of also have beed dof. Maybe if he had of charfed, 'I are my him and you is my me and you is your him and I are your me', that would of have beed right.

No, hang on, it are a other way round, 'I are my me and you is my him and you is your me and I is your him.' Of course it must of be a Pa Ou what charfs this otherwise it are a different me and a different him what are his and mine.

Ag! I dunno. It are all lank confusing and all and I don't not have a cat's clue what I are talking about, but I didn't not neither have a cat's clue how a Pa Ou did of knowed that I were 'him' whoever 'him' were.

A Joan Ma checks me out and charfs, 'What him?'

I is also confused and want to ask a Pa Ou, 'What him?' too also as well, but I don't not. Instead I just shout at a Pa Ou and a Joan Ma, 'I is not a him, him's is what you sing in a church.'

No I don't not. I would of have if I did of had thinked of it then, but I did of only thinked of it much more laterer.

'Joan, just get the kids away, quickly. Go back to the car with them and call the police.'

I skrik and so do a Joan Ma, but I reckon she does of skrik cause of she did now knowed what 'him' I is asposed to be. I skrik cause of a Joan Ma are going to call a cops. I can't not let her call a cops none, but I is up a tree with no place to go and I can't not charf a Pa Ou to move so as I can run away. Suddenly I do of merember a gun and that growed ups will of do what you tell them if you did got a gun.

So quick like, afore a Joan Ma, who are still realising what 'him' I are, do go call a cops, I grab a gun and point it at a Pa Ou and charf, 'Don't nobody move,' like what a robbers do in a fillums what I did of have checked.

Now there are like a whole big skrik party going on by a bottom of a tree. A Joan Ma are trying to get a two boys to come to her and a Pa Ou are like handsupping and all and going, 'Don't shoot, don't shoot.'

'I won't not shoot if you don't not call a cops,' I charf a Pa Ou.

He checks me out skew for a bit, then charfs, 'Okay, okay, just stay calm. We won't call the police, just let us go.'

I think for a bit, but I don't not trust growed ups nothink none more, so as I go, 'Where are your cell phone.'

'In my pocket,' he charfs and do of starts to go for his pocket.

'Hold it,' I charf loud like and he do of skrik and stop going for his pocket none more while a Joan Ma do like go, 'Please don't shoot,' and she are just about crying and all. I do of feel a bit sorry for a Joan Ma cause of she didn't not knowed that I weren't not going to shoot no one none cause of I don't not shooted people, but I couldn't not of let her knowed this otherwise a Pa Ou would of not do what I charf him to.

I did of only charf him to hold it so as to make sure he didn't not have none gun in his pocket. I did of also seen this in a fillum as well.

'Slow like,' I charf a Pa Ou, 'get your phone out real slow like.'

A Pa Ou do of nod and do of take out his phone and all.

'Put it down there,' I charf and point at a picnic table what had a picnic basket on what I hadn't not of seen afore.

A Pa Ou do what I charf him and while he are doing this I become Einstein cause of I do suddenly think that maybe a Joan Ma did also got a cell phone. My own ma and pa did of each got a cell phone so as they do probably got one each as well also.

But now that I had of thinked of ma and pa, I do suddenly not like pointing a gun none cause of I do keep checking pa getting shooted in front of me in my brain like. I do of just want to chuck a gun far away and run, but I can't not so as I do keep pointing a gun even though I don't not like it none. I can of now understand howcomewhy Zakes don't not like guns cause of it were a gun what did of killed my pa.

'What about your phone, Joan?' I charf and then want to laugh cause I had of called a growed up Joan and not Aunty Joan or nothink, but I can of call her that cause of I do got a gun and not she or not a Pa Ou can't do nothink like maybe smack me for not calling her aunty.

I also do of want to laugh cause of I did make a rhyme. 'What about your phone, Joan?' I is a poet and I know it.

'It's...it's in the car,' she charfs and do of starts to go to a car.

'Wait!' I charf loudly again and point a gun at her now. I don't not trust her neither even if she are a ma. 'Aunty must send one of a kids to get it.' I are a Einstein again cause of I reckon if I had of let a Joan Ma go get a phone she would of have called a cops quick like afore bringing it back, or maybe she would of have just drived off.

A Joan Ma checks me out for a bit and then says to one of a lighties, 'Go get mommy's phone, honey, it's in my handbag by my seat.'

She then do kiss a lightie on his head and I do of want to cry cause of I merember that my ma did of sometimes kissed me on a head like that and I do miss her so much now. It are hard to keep pointing a gun and merember that my ma are deaded. So I do think of a cops what a Pa Ou would of call if I didn't not of keep holding a gun and do charf myself to merember my ma laterer when I have of sorted these ous out.

A little kid do run to a car and come back quick like with a phone and I charf him to put it on a picnic table like a other one too also.

'Ok, now bugger off,' I charf, 'And don't not come back cause of I will shooted yous all if you do.' I won't not really shooted them none, but I do of charf this so as they will do what I do of charf them to.

A Pa Ou checks out a Joan Ma and a kids do check at their ma and pa and I can check that a kids is scared cause of their ma and pa is scared and I do of feel bad and want to charf them that it are going to be okay, but I don't not.

'Go!' I charf loud like now and they do of goed. A Pa Ou do like make a kids go first, then a Joan Ma, then him. He do of keep checking back at me till of he do got in a car. Then they do drive off and I check them all a way down a road afore I put a gun in my bag and climb down a tree quick like.

I check down a road proper like and there is no cars or nothink, but I reckon I do of have to skedaddle cause of a Pa Ou will of probably go straight to a cops when he do of get to a town. I then check a picnic basket and a cell phones. I is quite hungry so I do of open a basket and grab all a stuff what I can and shove it in my bag, and do of pick up a cell phone. Pa did of never let me touch a cell phones cause he did of said that he didn't not want me phoning London none. I do reckon I can now use a cell phone to phoning London, but then I do think that I don't not knowed nobody in London, so as pa were a bit dof charfing that I would of phoned there. But I don't not want to think about pa. I don't not also knowed Zakes' grandparents number to of phoned them, so as I just leave a phones and bugger off big time fast.

I did of walked as far away from a road as what I could across a lank big veldt. I were skrikking all a time that a cops would of seed me and I did of wish that Zakes were here cause of he would of have thinked of somethink so as we wouldn't not have to worry about them none.

When I did of heared a sirens I couldn't not check a road none more which were good cause of if I couldn't not check a road, then a cops couldn't not of check me. Still, I reckon I need to move more quickerer, so as I run as fast like as what I can with a rucksack on.

Not so long later, I do of heared a dog what do bark and I reckon it are Shaka so as I stop, but then I do hear it bark again and I knowed it are not Shaka, it are a cop dog. Now I do pooh my pants big time. If a cops do got dogs, I is in serious trouble. At least, I scheme, pa are not here to give me more kak as what I already did of got. I heared a dog bark again and it are even closerer now so as I run fasterer, even if my legs do of hurt, I is running for my life.

THIRTY-ONE

Sometimes a ou can of be really lucky and today that were me. I were Lucky Luke. Not like a cowboy what were in a cartoon book what I did of got at home, but Lucky Luke cause I were Lucky, even though my real name aren't not Luke.

But when I did of watched a cops going back to a road, I did sit by a rocks I were hiding ahind and charfed myself that I were big time lucky.

Let me charf yous what all happened. A dog were getting like really close and all and then I did of check a river in front of me. It weren't not such a big river, but it were big enough and as I did of get nearerer to a river I did merember a other fillum what I did of seed once where a ou were being chased by a cop dogs and he did of goed into a river and run up a bit and did gotted out on a same side of a river. When a cop dogs and cops did of got there, they reckoned a ou had of crossed a river, so as they did of go over to a other side and carry on looking for him there, but they never did of finded him.

So I reckon that a only way I can of get rid of a dog were to do a same think. There were a rocks what I already did of said I were hiding ahind what I seed so I did of run to them and they was far enough away from where I had of goed into a water so as a cops wouldn't not seed me none.

I were just sitting down ahind a rocks when I did of heard a dog coming up to a river so as I did peek through a rocks and trees what were helping to of hide me and I sawed a dog. It were big like Shaka, but it weren't not a library door and I didn't not knowed what kind it were. Anyways, I were checking a dog out and it were sniffing round by a river to check where I did of goed when all of a sudden like I check this crocodile what jumps out of a river and it do of have a dog in its mouth afore a poor dog can of do nothink.

It did of maked a horrible bark noise what maked me feel lank sorry for it, but I can't not do nothink. A dog's legs were still of kicking when I check a cops arrive. There was three of them and they did stop running really quick like when they do check a dog in a croc's mouth. They do stand there for a bit, just checking, then one of a cops do of try and shooted a croc, but he do of miss and a croc do of go under a water.

A cops stand there more, then adventually they do of start to walk back to a road. That are when I do have a brain wave what do of make even Einstein check dof.

Let me first asplain to yous about a river. A rocks what I were hiding ahind were nearby a bend so as from where a cop dog did get chowed, you couldn't not seed round a corner too lekker.

Cause of a cops did of turned around to go back to a road, they couldn't not check me none so as I did of taked my shirt off and go round a bend. Then I did of goed to just next to a river and really quick like throwed my shirt in and did of start screaming, 'Help! Help!' and did run super fast like to ahind some bushes what were there.

A cops did of comed quick like, but all they could of check were my shirt what were starting to of float down a river. They do check this out and they are skrikked big time. One of them do start running by a river a bit. He did of even runned right by where I were, but didn't not seed me none. He didn't not run for too long afore he did goed back to a other cops and they do talk and point for a bit while I is trying not to laugh too much. Adventually they do of walk off back to a road.

I do wait for a little bit, then do start walking up a river, away from my shirt. I didn't not knowed if they was going to come back so as I do think I must skedaddle quick like, but also I don't not walk too near a river none cause of I now knowed that there was crocs.

I do walk for lank ages. A sun were hot to start with, but did of get colderer as a night did of come closerer. That were when I did of start to think that I were a bit dof to of throwed my shirt in a river like what I did cause of I were now did of got colderer. I weren't not sure now if a cops would of still be looking for me and I also didn't not of knowed if I were going to a direction of Ermelo or not.

So when it did of start getting darkerer, I did of go to a direction what I did think a road were. It were nearly almost totally dark by when I did of get to a road and did start walking back a way what I were walking afore. I were cross that I did of have to walk this bit again once more, but, I did charf myself it were worth it if a cops did of now thinked I were deaded and living in a croc's tummy. When I did thinked this I did of laughed cause I did of merember a cops face's when they did thinked I were eated.

I were still far away from a tree what I did get caughted in by a Pa Ou and a Joan Ma when I could of seed a lights. They was lank bright and all and I could of check that there was lots of ous and cars there by a tree. There was also a cops blue lights what were flashing and all.

That were when I acided to go to a other side of a road. I did of want to get to a town what were furtherer on so as I could maybe of finded a shirt and a place to sleep what were warmerer.

When I did of get really close to a tree and a lights, I could of check that there were like TV cameras and all and TV ous what were talking to a Pa Ou and a Joan Ma.

I did of stayed quite far on a other side of a road where it were darkerer and no one could of have seed me. There was also lank cops under a tree. I didn't not knowed why a cops were there cause of I were in a croc's tummy floating down a river, a other cops what did of seed me get chowed must of have told them that.

I did of want to shouted to them, 'I is not here, go look for a croc what ated me,' but I don't not charf nothink cause of I is not dof merember. So I do just keep walking really quiet like past all a cops and TV ous.

Then I check a bakkie what were parked next to a road. There were a ou standing outside it and he were checking out all what were happening. Acause a bakkie are pointing to a town, I reckon he must of beed going there when he are finished watching what were going on, so, really quiet and quick like, I do run to a bakkie and climb into a back. There are some partaulins there what I did of hide under. It were a bit stinky, but it weren't not so cold as outside and also it were only till we did of get to a town I did of thinked.

Some ous can of watch nothink happening for lank ages. I don't know what this ou were wanting to check cause of even if they did of catch that croc what ated me, I wouldn't not be inside it none.

I do almost want to stick my head up from under a partaulins and charf a ou this and charf him to get moving to town cause of I do of need to find a shirt. But I don't not.

Adventually a ou did of at last get in a bakkie and start to drive and we were in a town chop chop. I could of feeled that we was there cause of a bakkie did slowed down and stop, then drive, then stop. You don't not do this on a long roads atween towns.

I were so chuffed with myself for of getting a lift that I weren't not ready for when a ou did of stop proper like and turn off a bakkie. He did of getted out and come to a back and pull up a partaulin.

THIRTY-TWO

A shirt did of fitted me quite lekker and so also did a pants. I did of feel a bit bad taking them, but seen as how my shirt were gone down a river and my pants were dirty and torn like, I did of really needed them lots. It were aspecially bad to of have tooked them from a Bakkie Ou cause he did of gived me a lift even if he didn't not knowed that he had of. If he had of pulled a partaulin back more furtherer, then he would of have knowed, but he didn't not. He did of only pulled it back far enough to of take out a toolbox what were there.

I did of wait lank ages afore getting out a back of a bakkie, mostly cause of I had skrikked so much when a ou did of lifted a partaulin that my legs wouldn't not of never moved till next Sunday if my brain hadn't not of keep telling them to.

A bakkie were parked in a garage and a garage door were shut, but cause of there were a window and a light from a house could comed in by a window, I could of seed a bit of what I were doing.

There were a door what I reckoned did of goed into a house and a other one what did of goed outside. By a house door there were a basket what did of have clothes in and that were where a shirt and pants was what I were now wearing.

There were also a fridge what did of mostly have cokes and fantas and I did of drink some and chucked some more in my bag. I did still have a

114

picnic food from a Pa Ou and Joan Ma, but even though I were hungry I did of thinked that I had better not sit in a garage and chow it in cause of in case a Bakkie Ou camed back.

I were just getting ready to skedaddle when I checked a newspaper on a pile by a outside door. It were acause of there were a picture of me in a paper what did of maked me looked. There were big writing what charfed, '11, ARMED AND DANGEROUS.' There were also a small-erer picture of a Canine Ou and also one of ma and pa. I did thinked back to a time when Jaapie had of charfed me about his uncle what did of commit sewerage pipe, but what weren't not in a newspapers none. I aspose maybe I had of committed sewerage pipe cause of I had of maded a cops think that I were in a croc's tummy so as I maded myself deaded without not deading myself none. But a newspaper wouldn't not of knowed it were only pretend sewerage pipe so as that were howcomewhy maybe they did of got me in there.

It also do of maked me thing that even though pa didn't not of had his gun, I reckon he would of have killed us all that night, ma, ouma, Sally and me too also if Zakes' brother hadn't not of brought a gun and all what happened then.

There were lots of writings next to a picture, but apart from a big letters what charfed that I did of had arms and were dangerous, a rest were all small and I couldn't not be asked to try and read it cause of I don't not read so lekker. Miss Smit at school could of charfed yous that.

Still, I chuck a newspaper into a bag and then go really quiet like out of a garage. There weren't not anyone around on a outside of a garage and a road were lekker quiet and all so as I could of walk without nobody not seeing me none.

When I did of got to a big street I checked round for signs till I did of seed one what did of have a arrow what pointed and charfed Ermelo.

So now I were walking again, but cause of all a cops and everythink, I were even more carefuller as afore even though I were asposed to be deaded. It were lekker walking cause of it weren't not too cold none and I did of got a shirt and all. Also cause of there weren't not lots of cars on a road, I didn't not have to of hided all a time. And also I were going to Ermelo where Zakes and his grandparents was so I did of feel quite happy.

But then, acause of there weren't not nothink else to do but walked, I did of started to think. At first it were lekker thinks like as when we did once goed to Durban by a sea and pa did of buyed ice creams and we did of swimmed and builded sand castles and all. Pa didn't not of even shout too much or donner ma none neither, accept sometimes in a night when I were asposed to be asleep, then I did of heared pa slapping ma, but it were like a time when Larry the Lithp did of 'do it' with ma so as I do now reckon pa were 'doing it' with ma there in Durbs and weren't not hitting her none.

This do then make me think of Larry the Lithp and I did of wonder if Sally were okay there by him. I do of merember one time when ma were in a hopstibal and pa made me and Sally go and stay with Uncle Francois and Aunty Suzanne. It weren't not lekker there none. Sally didn't not like it, aspecially when she did of have to go and bath. I didn't not knowed whycome she did of cry when it were bath time. Uncle Francois were cool to go bath with cause of he did tickle me and all and did of make me laugh in a bath. Maybe it were cause of uncle Francois didn't not tickle Sally that she were crying. I dunno.

Anyways, I did of hoped that Larry the Lithp did tickle her so as she do like to bath there by him.

I did then started to thinked of that night what I took Sally to Larry's place. I merembered that I had of seed Zakes' brother there by George's shop and how there were blood and all. Then I did merember how, as I did of got nearerer to my home, he comed to me and charfed me that he did of need to lie down and he did of asked me if he could of lied on my bed. Cause of ma were at home, I did maded him to climb through a window of my bedroom. I did of thinked that he could do it no probs cause of he were not old like ouma, but he did of really struggle big time to get in a room.

I did of goed in by a door so as ma could knowed I were home and all, but when I did of get to my room, Zakes' brother were already asleep on my bed. I could of check now that he were bleeding by his soldier and that some of a blood were gone down his arm from his soldier, so as I reckoned he did of needed a plaster.

Ma were in a kitchen with ouma making supper, so as I did go really quick like to a bathroom and get a plasters. When I did of got back and started to trying to put them onto Zakes' brother's, he did of waked up, but not proper like.

'Hey boss,' he charfed and did of sort of smile, 'can you look after this for me.' Then he do of takes out pa's gun and gives it to me.

No, hang on, I can't not be merembering proper like cause of if he had of gived me a gun, then he couldn't not of shooted pa none. Maybe it were after he had of shooted pa that he did of gived me a gun. Ja, that must of beed what did of happen. I just can't not merember it so good.

I do of definitely merember Zakes' brother on my bed though. He must of have comed out of a room when he did of heard ouma shouting at pa. Ja, that must of beed what did of happened. He did comed out of my room with a gun what he did of give to me laterer, after he did shooted pa. I can't not merember what I did of do with a gun though.

I didn't not merember all this when I did of telled you about it. I are only now merembering it what I thinks is proper like.

Anyways, I do adventually stop thinking and check that it are nearly almost day time. What are weird are that I are standing in a middle of a road and crying like a big fat cry baby, but I didn't not knowed how-comewhy.

THIRTY-THREE

A numbers what are next to Ermelo on a signs is getting smallerer and smallerer which did of meaned that I were getting closerer to there, but they is still big numbers. I had of beed walking every night and finding a place to hide and sleep in a day time so as people can't not seed me.

My feets is lank sore from all a walking and my takkies is beginning to get holes in. I did of finish a picnic food, and did of scale some bread from one shop when a ou weren't not looking and did of also find a apple tree outside one house and did of load up.

Sometimes I do of find some food in a rubbish bins by a picnic spots. It are not always too lekker, but cause of I is so hungry I do still eated it. Like my pa did of sometimes said, 'big guys can't be choosers.'

At one place there were a newspaper in a bin what did of had a other picture of me and it did said, 'WANTED BOY TAKEN BY CROC'. I didn't not read all a small words again, but it were good to check that they did of really thinked that I were eated cause of now they wouldn't not be lookink for me none.

I did of thinked that I sawed Shaka a other night. First there were a bark what did of sounded like it were his, so I did of goed to where a bark were, but when I did of seed a dog, I knowed it weren't Shaka cause of it were a black dog and Shaka were a yellow one.

I did of feel lank sad when I sawed it weren't not Shaka cause of I did of missed him. I did of missed Zakes too also as well. Also Sally and ma and even ouma and her very cross veins, but I can't not do nothink cause of ma are deaded and so are ouma too as well. I do of want to seed Sally again, but I don't not want to go to Larry the Lithp's. Even if I had of wanted to go, I don't not have a cat's clue as to how to get there, so as I reckon I can't not check Sally never again none more.

So I did of just walked and walked and walked. One night I did of seed a Zebra what were really cool, but he did of skrikked and runned away even afore I could charf him it were okay, I wouldn't not hurt him none.

After lank days of walking, I did of find it harderer and harderer to find food. There weren't not nothink in a bins by a picnic spots and when I did of seed shops, they was closed or there were too many ous there so as I didn't not want to go try and scale some bread or nothink just in case I did of get caughted.

Then one night I were of walking, but were so tired. My feets were lank sore that I couldn't hardly not even walk none neither. I were so lank hungry and thirsty too also and I had of not seed a sign for Ermelo for lots of a long time. I were hardly not even thinkink none neither cause of all I could of thinked of were to keep walking. I weren't not checking where I were going or nothink and when I did of trip and fall over, I did of just laid there on a path and cause of I were too tired to even get up none, I did of just fall asleep there.

A path were not too near to a road cause of I still didn't not want nobody to seed me none, but when I did of adventually waked up a sun were shining and there were these three ous what were checking me out. At first I did of think that it were Zakes what I were of checking three times, but then I did of blink and seed that they did of all looked a little bit differenter to Zakes and differenter to each other.

Still, when I did of start to think proper like, I did of thinked that maybe I were in Ermelo cause I had of walked so much.

A ous were talking in black and checking me out really skew like, aspecially now as I did of open my eyes.

'Are this Ermelo?' I charfed, but I did of feeled too tired to stand up. A ous jumped back and checked me out even more skewerer while they did of laugh lank lots and talk more black.

I did of tried to sit up, but feeled sick so as I did of lied down some more afore trying again to sit. This time I did sit. My mouth were so lank dry so as I could hardly not even talk none and when I did of ask if this were Ermelo, it did of sounded like it were someone else what were talking.

My bag were there next to me so as I did picked it up. There weren't not nothink left in it cause I had of chowed all a food and drinks what I did of have had. There were now only a gun and my old pants left. Cause of it were now daytime I did thinked that I must of find some place to sleep, but then I merembered that there are these ous there so as I can't not hide none cause of they would of seed me and all.

Still, I reckon that maybe if I did of walked away they wouldn't not follow me none. So I did of tried to stand up, but had of only walked a little bit afore I falled over again and didn't not knowed where I were.

I don't meremer too much from then till laterer. I do of thinked that maybe a ous what was checking me out did of helped me to walk by carrying me atween them. I do of also meremer a little bit of coming to this place where there were of some small houses. That are all what I meremer till I did of waked again which might of beed lank ages after a ous did of helped me, but I don't have a cat's clue how long it actually were.

When I did of waked there were a lady what were sitting there by me what at first I did of thinked were a Mielie Lady, but then I could check that it weren't not her none.

She didn't not say nothink, but when she did of seed that I were awake, she did maked me to drink some water. Then she did of gived me some soup. It were really lekker, but I had of only just eated a little bit then did of feeled sick like I were going to hurl, but did of managed to stopped myself and lied back down. A lady were nice. She tooked a soup and put it by a bed, then she did of brush my hair out of my eyes like what ma did of done when I were sick. It were like this lady were my black ma.

She still did of sayed nothink and after a bit, she gaved me a soup again so as I could of eated some more. It did take lank long to eat all a soup, but I did feeled betterer and betterer each time what I had some.

When a soup were finished, a Black Ma did of get a dish with warm water and washted my feets, really careful like. They was lank sore and I could check that they had of beed bleeding. A water did sting, but not too much. It were more nice than stingy.

I must of have goed asleep again while a Black Ma were cleaning my feets, cause of when I did of waked up, she were not there, but there were a black girl who were small like Sally. She did of goed out a room when she checked that I were awaked.

A Black Ma camed back and gaved me some more soup. I did of tried to asked her if this were Ermelo cause of I did now meremer where it where what I wanted to be, but she just charfed, 'Tula, tula,' which I knowed were black for 'Shhh', but a nice 'Shhh', not a shouted 'Shhh'.

I were feeling quite good now cause of a soup and water and cleaned feets and all, so as I did of sit up slow like in a bed. That were when a Black Ma did of leaved and I did of heared her talking to a man in a next room. Then I did of get a huge skrik cause of a ou what comed into a room were witch doctor!

THIRTY-FOUR

It must of checked funny, me skrikking and screaming and trying to of climb up a wall ahind a bed and a Black Ma running back in a room and her eyes was like eyeball sweets like what Zakes sometimes did and she were going 'Tula, Tula,' again and there were also these other lighties what were smallerer as Zakes what were checking me out and laughing and all and then there were a Witch Doctor Ou what were of charfing, 'It's okay, it's okay, I'm not going to hurt you.'

It did of take my brain lank ages to realise that a Witch Doctor Ou weren't not even talking black and that also he weren't not attacking me none neither. But even so, it did of take longerer for my legs to make a realise so that they could of stopped shaking.

A Witch Doctor Ou weren't not a real witch doctor, he were just a ou what were wearing a Basotho blanket what maked him check like a witch doctors what were on TV sometimes. He did of laugh big time when I did calmed down and charfed him that I had of thinked he were a witch doctor, but when he were finished laughing he did of give me a serious look and charfed, 'But it is good that you are afraid of the sangomas,' sangomas are a black name for witch doctors, 'Some of them can be dangerous.'

Now that we had of sorted out that he weren't not a sangoma, he did of asked me what I were doing there, where I were comed from, why I were so hungry, howcomewhy my clothes were of torn and where was my ma and pa?

I didn't not like him asking about ma and pa, and did of just want to charf that I weren't not even there in a room with him cause of I were actually in a belly of a crocodile. But I couldn't not of sayed that cause of then a Not A Witch Doctor Ou would of have knowed that I were a lightie what a cops were looking for and that I weren't not really eated and all and then he would of taked me to a cops and then I don't knowed what would of have happened. But I also don't now knowed what to answer him cause of if I did charf that ma and pa were dead, then a Not

120

A Witch Doctor Ou would of taked me to stay with a horrible people what Zakes did of charf me about.

So I just charfed that my ma and pa did lived in Mbombela and that I were going to see my ouma and oupa in Ermelo and that I did of falled off a back of a bakkie what my uncle were of driving and that he didn't not checked that I had of falled off and all and he had of just droved away and I did of runned after a bakkie, but I couldn't not catch up and then I did of start walking after him, but did of get lost and that were it. I were quite chuffed with myself cause of I did maked this all up without not lying none.

A Not A Witch Doctor Ou did of check me out a whole time what I were talking and did of shake his head and say, 'Sorry, sorry,' lots like as it were his fault that I did of falled off a bakkie. He would of have beed even more sorrier if I had of charfed him that I were actually eated by that croc. Then I did of realise that he were not sorry cause of it were his fault, but he were sorry cause of this did of happened to me, which it didn't not really.

After I had of finished my story and he had of finished saying his, 'sorry, sorry,' he checks me out for a bit and I can see that he are thinkink. Adventually he do charf, 'This is very unfortunate. As soon as you have got your strength back, I will take you into town. The police will sort you out.'

It were a way what he did said it that maked me check that he didn't not knowed that a cops were after me anyways and that I couldn't not go to a cop shop. So instead of showing him that I were skrikking, which I were, I did of just nodded my head. Anyways, I did think, I didn't not knowed where I had of left my strength so as it could of take me forever to find it and also I didn't even not knowed what it did of looked like so as if he had of brought it to me I would of have charfed that it weren't not mine and then he wouldn't not take me to a cops.

Still, I reckon as soon as I did of feel better I would have to skedaddle, so I did of hoped I did felt betterer afore I did of got my strength back.

A Black Ma did of maked me stay in a bed for lank ages and did of feeded me mostly soup, and then some rice and tomato gravy. I were then allowed to get up and walk around a little bit. Sometimes there were some meat in a gravy too also. Soon I were allowed to play soccer with a lighties what had of finded me when I did of falled over and sleep on a path.

They didn't not have a proper ball, just a plastic bag ball like what Ben did of had there by Joshua and Lizzy's place. I didn't not seed a Not A Witch Doctor Ou much which were a pity cause of he were a only ou there what did of spoked English. But when I did of started to play soccer, I began to reckon that he were out looking for my strength and so I had of better skedaddle out of there afore he did of comed back with it.

I did of feeled bad that I had to leave a Black Ma cause of she were really nice to me and did of looked after me good and all, but I couldn't not go to a cops cause of they did wanted to send me to a horrible people.

I weren't not sleeping in a bedroom none more, but did of now sleeped in a room with a other kids. My bag were hunged on a back of a door what were never locked so when a night did of comed, I waited till I reckoned that everyone were asleep, then I, really quiet like, did of grabbed my bag and go out of a house.

There were a dog what did lived there by a house, but he weren't nothink like Shaka. When I did of get outside, he comed and sniffed at me but didn't not charf nothink so as I could of walked off no problems.

I felt lank sad cause of a Black Ma were a bestest ma what I did of had ever, accept for my real ma of course. I weren't not too sure which way I did of had to go cause of it were lank dark. There weren't not even none moon so as I did of tripped sometimes, but adventually I finded a path and goed in a direction what I thinked were where a road were. I did of hoped like mad that it were a right way cause of when I had of tried to walk one way on a path when I were playing soccer with a light-ies, they had of stopped me and I could of checked that they were scared to go that way, but in a dark I couldn't not merember which way a scary way were.

THIRTY-FIVE

Cause of it weren't not so cold and after I did of adventually get used to walking in a dark, it were lekker to be walking again. But then I did of start to thinkink of ma. At first it were nice thinks what I did of think of, like a time she did of tooked Sally and me to a zoo. We did of have a picnic then. I merember ma were laughing and bought us ice creams and cokes and all.

I merember also that she did of charf us to keep quiet when we did go out a house. It were a Saturday cause of there weren't not none school and pa weren't not going to work none neither, but he were sleeping. Ma

122

charfed that he were tired which Jaapie did of charf me once that that did of mean he were babalas cause of he did drink too much whiskey. I merember once ouma did charf that pa weren't not tired, he did got hung over. Cause of ma and pa weren't not in a kitchen that time, I did of charf ouma that I thought Pa were just babalas.

Ouma had of smiled and charfed, 'Hung over, babalas, same thing.'

Anyways, pa were 'tired' that morning and so we did of goed to a zoo without not him coming also. It were a really lekker day, but when we did of get ready to of goed home, ma did of stopped laughing and playing with us. It were like as she were scared. Then, when we was getting in a car, she did of charf me and Sally that we mustn't not to tell pa that we had of gone to a zoo none cause of he would be sad that he didn't not also come. We must only charf him that we did of go to Aunty Trudy's. Pa don't not ever comed when we go see Aunty Trudy.

When we did getted home, pa never did of asked where were had of goned. He were sitting in a lounge, drinking whiskey and he didn't not say nothink, not even hello.

Ma charfed us to go play in our rooms even if we did of have done nothink wrong. It were only when we did of goed out of a lounge that I hearded pa talk, and it were only cause of I didn't not go to my room that I could of heard, but I did stay quiet like outside a door. At first he did of speaked really quiet like which were strange cause of I did thinked that, cause of a way ma were, that he were lank cross and would of beed shouting, so as I did of thinked that maybe he weren't not cross that we did of goed to a zoo without not him. But it weren't not long afore he were shouting and then I did of heard him hit ma, a proper hit, not a 'doing it' hit, and she did of start crying and he did of hit her more and she did cry more and it were horrible. I had of never heared pa hit ma so much.

I did of want to go into a lounge and tell pa to of stop donnering ma and all, but I were just a lightie. Pa would of have donnered me into next week if I had of. So I did just goed to my room and put my pillow over my head so as I couldn't not hear ma crying none. I were also crying, not being hit crying, only woosies cry when they is hit, I were sad crying.

After a bit I did of stopped crying and taked a pillow off of my head. I couldn't not hear pa shouting or ma crying none more and did of skrik a bit that maybe pa had of donnered ma so as she were now waiting for us in next Saturday already. A house were really quiet like and so I did of tiptoe to a lounge but there weren't not nobody there. Then I did of go to a kitchen. Ma were standing by a sink and washing her face. She didn't not seed me none and it were only when I charfed, 'Ma?' that she did of turned round. At first I did of thinked that she were crying blood cause of there were lots under her one eye, but I couldn't not tell proper like as she did of cover it with her hand and shouted at me to bugger off to my room.

I couldn't not understand why she were angry cross with me and did of start crying again, but only after I had of left a kitchen. I didn't not go to my room, cause of I did have a brain wave. If ma were bleeding she would of need a plaster. So I did of goed to a bathroom and getted a plasters what I did taked back to a kitchen. When ma did of turn round this time I showed her a plasters and she did of start crying proper like and then did give me a big girlie hug and charfed that she were sorry she did of shouted at me, then she did smile at me, but it weren't not like a proper happy smile.

I did want to cry more then cause of ma were lank happy afore we camed home and pa had donnered her so as she did bleed. I did of really want to kill pa then cause of he had of stoled ma's happiness. But I were just a lightie, I couldn't not do nothink to pa cause of he were lank biggerer as me.

After ma did of stopped hugging me, I did go to Sally's room to check if she were okay.

'Are ma alright?' she did of asked me and I did of nod, but I were still lank cross with pa.

That were when I did of said, 'If only I did of had a gun, then I wouldn't not let pa hit ma none more.'

THIRTY-SIX

My legs was getting lank tired, but I did make them to keep walking cause of I knewed that I must get far away from a Not A Witch Doctor Ou's place as what I can so as they couldn't not find me and take to a cops.

I still weren't not sure if I were walking in a right way cause of it were still dark and all, but it were too late to go a other way now. I did of reckon that I must find a place to hide afore it got to daytime, but must of keep walking till then.

I is not happy walking now cause of my legs is lank sore and it were so lekker there by a Black Ma's house and now, cause of I is only walking, I is thinkink thinks what I don't not like. It are about a night when pa were deaded what I are merembering, but I are not merembering it proper cause of I don't not reckon it could of have happen like that. But it are bugging me that I can't not merember proper like. So as not to think about it I do of sing to myself and that do make me feel bettererer.

I do of reckon that I have walked lank far when it do start to get light and I do find a lekker spot to sleep. It are a little bit away from a path under a big tree. There are some soft grass there and, cause I is so tired it don't not take long afore I are asleeping.

It are sunshining when I do of waked up and I do of waked up cause I do heared someone what are calling, 'Samuel! Samuel!'

Cause of Samuel aren't not my name, I reckon that a ou what are shouting are not looking for me, but then I do of merember that Samuel were a name what I charfed a Not A Witch Doctor Ou were my name and then I check through a grass that it are him what are calling.

But I just sit quiet like cause of I reckon he are looking for Samuel and I are not Samuel. He do of stop on a path and shout a name some more, then he do of shout, 'Samuel, come back, it is dangerous out here.' Then he do walk on some more, but I can check that he are not too happy walking this way cause of he are looking round all a time and it are not just for me that he are looking.

At first I skrik cause of it are dangerous, but then I do want to laugh cause of I can tell that that are what growed ups always do to make lighties do what they want. They do charf somethink like, 'it are dangerous,' when it aren't not really, but it do of make a lightie skrik so as they do what they is told. But not this lightie. I is too much of a Einstein for a Not A Witch Doctor Ou to catch me out.

Anyways, he do of carry on walking till I can't not see him none more, but it aren't not too long afore he do of come back and walk off in a way what he did comed.

I is now wide awake and my legs is not so tired so as I acide to walk more as soon as I can't not check a Not A Witch Doctor Ou none more.

It are late in a arvie when I do start walking and it aren't not too hot which are good. There aren't not nobody to be seed anywhere, it were just me and a path and a bush which are lekker cause of I is tired of people. People just give me trouble. I reckon I don't not want to check a people none more never again.

A sun were starting to go down and it were making a sky all lekker colours, red and orange and yellow. It were like a pictures what Sally do of drawed. Sally are a good drawerer, I do of always liked her pictures, but I never do of told her this cause of she are a girl and I can't not say nothink nice to a girl, I is not a woosie. I do of reckon though that Sally would of have drawed a lekker sunset if she had of checked this one.

I do stop to check out a sunset and then I do of heared a noise which do make me skrik. There were somethink in a bushes nearby. At first I reckon that maybe a Not A Witch Doctor Ou had of comed back and were going to take me to a cops, so I is just about to hide when I check this warthog what come sniffing on a path not so far away close from me. It do of stop sniffing when it checks me.

'Hello, Mr Warthog,' I do of charf, but I do of make my voice nice so as he could check that I were a friend.

Mr Warthog do sniff a air, maybe to check if I do of smelled friendly, then he charfs, 'Hello young man, what you doing here so far away from everyone?'

'I is tired of people, I just want to be on my ace for always.' I don't not tell him that I is running away from a Not A Witch Doctor Ou cause of he were going to take me to a cops cause of I is worried that maybe Mr Warthog would of taked me to a warthog cops.

'I see,' Mr Warthog charfs, and he do of start sniffing a ground and then eating some of a grass. I do wish I were a warthog cause of they do eat grass and there were lank plenty grass so as I wouldn't not never be hungry none. Also I reckon that a warthog pa wouldn't not drink whiskey neither, so if I were a warthog lightie, my warthog pa wouldn't not donner me or my warthog ma none.

'So, you don't want to see Zakes again, or his grandparents? Or even Sally?' Mr Warthog do of chew a grass and check me out more.

'Yes, I do of want to see them,' I charf, 'they is people what I are not tired of.'

Mr Warthog do of sneeze so as I do say, 'Bless you,' then he do of eated some more grass and do looks at me again.

'Well, you're not going to see them walking this way. There are only wild animals for miles in this direction.'

I do of want to charf Mr Warthog that it are rude to talk with food in your mouth cause of that are what my ma had of charfed me lank, but then I do of think that maybe in warthog world it are not rude. How lekker would it be to be a warthog and to talk with food in my mouth and not have no one moan at me never, unless maybe you check a person what do of charf you it are rude. But it would have to be a dof person that are not a Einstein like me cause of I do knowed that it are not rude for a warthog to talk with food in his mouth.

Still, I aspose that Mr Warthog are right and that I must of go back past a Not A Witch Doctor Ou's place so as I can get back to a road.

But afore I do turn around, I charf Mr Warthog, 'Do you want a whiskey?' I don't not got none to give him, but I do of just want to check.

'Don't be silly, warthogs don't drink whiskey. We drink water and coke and fanta.'

'That are good,' I charf, 'don't never start drinking whiskey cause of then you will become like my pa and I will of have to shooted you.'

'Don't worry,' Mr Warthog do says, 'I will never be like your pa.'

Of course a warthog did of never charf me nothink, they can't not talk, but I do of talk to Mr Warthog and he do of anwered in my brain. I had of already reckoned I were going a wrong way to get to Ermelo so now I do turn around after I charf Mr Warthog goodbye.

A sun are almost down proper like and it are beginning to get darkerer which are good cause of I reckon that it will be proper dark when I do of go past a Not A Witch Doctor Ou's house.

As I do walk, I think of what I did of charf Mr Warthog about that I would of shooted him if he did of drink whiskey like pa. I are sorry I did of said this cause of I didn't not really mean it none. I would never of shooted Mr Warthog accept maybe if I were a warthog lightie and Mr Warthog were donnering my Warthog Ma.

But I don't not like to think about it cause of someone did of shooted my real pa deaded.

It were good that I did of stopped thinking then cause of I do suddenly check a hyena what are standing in a pathway and it are checking me out like I are a hamburger and chips.

THIRTY-SEVEN

A more what I do thinked about a night when ma were donnered dead and ouma were pushed dead and pa were shooted dead, a more I don't not want to think about it none.

All a time now I is merembering it different. I do of wished that ma were here so as she could of telled me proper like what did of really happened, but she were deaded and in a ambalance afore pa were shooted, so even if she hadn't not of beed deaded, she weren't not there to check what did of happened, at least that are how I merember it.

I do of merember a night again differently after a hyena are sorted and I is walking again. But I haven't not charfed yous yet what did of happened with a hyena. Yous are going laugh at this. Hyenas is poep scared of warthogs. True's Bob. I did of seed it with mine own eyes. Maybe a hyena what I did seed were a woosie hyena, or maybe Mr Warthog did of go and drink whiskey so as a hyena did of reckon that he were going to get donnered. I dunno, but a hyena were checking me out like I were chops on a braai and I were poeping myself so much so as to make old Pooh Pants check like a ou what weren't scared of nothink. Then I do of heard a noise ahind me and I do of break a skrikometer. But afore I can of even think of poohing my pants proper like for real, Mr Warthog do of come charging by me and if a hyena had of beed wearing pants, there would of beed some hyena poohing going on. But cause of he don't not wear pants none, he just skedaddles fasterer as a cheetah and I'm like having a chortle attack big time.

Mr Warthog do of make sure that a hyena has of buggered off proper like afore he do of come back and check me out and charfs, 'You still here? You'd better get moving before he comes back,' and I scheme he are right. I wished I had of got somethink what I could of gived to Mr Warthog to say thanks, but I did of only got a gun and my pants in my rucksack so as I can only charf, thanks. I do also charf him that if I do of ever come back here I will bring him some lekker warthog food to chow.

I is a bit more worrieder when I do of start walking again, so as I do walk fasterer, checking round all a time for a hyena, but Mr Warthog must of have skrikked him off proper like cause of I don't check none more aminals. But then maybe it are cause it are getting darkerer that I can't not check nothink.

It are full on dark when I do of adventually go past a Not A Witch Doctor Ou and a Black Ma's house and I do of have to go off a path for a bit cause of there are a small fire outside and ous what I can't check too lekker sitting there by a fire. I know they is ous sitting there cause of I can seed their funny hats moving round and I can of also heared them talking, but it are like as they is talking into a pillow like what Sally sometimes did of done cause of I can't not heared them proper like. But this are fine cause of if I could of heared them proper, then I would of knowed I were too close.

I did of also feel saferer now cause of I weren't not there where a hyena did of lived. Then I merember that a Not A Witch Doctor Ou Were going to take me to a cops so as I do walk fasterer past a house and it are not too long afore I check a car's lights on a road far away ahead.

As I walk awards a road, I do of telled myself that I must make sure I do of find some food and some drink every day now. I don't not want to fall over again. Even if it do of take me longerer to get to Ermelo, it will of take me even more longerer if I do of fall over again and if maybe a other Not A Witch Doctor Ou do of pick me up and take me to a cops. I do of laugh when I thinked this cause of I do of start to thinked, what if a Not A Witch Doctor Ou did of have taked me to a cops?

A cops would be like, 'Aren't not you a lightie what a croc did of eated?'

And I can go, 'Ja, a croc did of eated me, but I donnered it's tummy so much that it did of spitted me out.'

Then a cops would of be lank scared of me cause of I is a ou what donnered my way out of a croc.

I do of laugh so much now and I is boxing a air like it are a croc's tummy, then I do of jump like I are being spitted out of a croc's mouth. I also do of reckon that a hyena were actually running away from me and not Mr Warthog cause of a hyena could of smelled that I had of donnered a croc's tummy so much that it had of spitted me out.

I is feeling much more happier now and are not so sad that I did of leave a Not A Witch Doctor Ou's place. It are not acause I were sad there, he were nice to me and all, and so were a Black Ma and all a lighties, but it were nice to be going to Ermelo to see Zakes and his grandparents. I did still of wonder if a Not A Witch Doctor Ou would of goed to a cops anyway to charf them that there were a lightie what had of falled off a back of a bakkie and all. I did of hoped that he hadn't not of, but did thinked that if he did of have and a cops did come looking for me, and there weren't not a croc nearby to pretend to be eated by, then I would of just have to make that bridge cross when I did comed to it, like what ouma used to of said.

By a time I had of stopped all this thinkink, I were by a road and it were beginning to start to get light. There was some cars on a road, but not lank lots so I didn't not goed to close and did of start to check for places where I could of kip.

I check there are a bridge like a bit down a road what do of go over a river what don't got none water in it. It are lank sandy there and I can of crawl right up under a bridge so as no one can of seed me.

Once I are there I do of lied down and closed my eyes. I is feeling hungry and thirsty and wished I had of tooked some food and water from a Not A Witch Doctor Ou's place, but I couldn't not of had acause I would of waked a people.

So I acide not to think about peanut butter zarms like what I were thinkink, but then I do start to thinkink of ouma cause of I are under a bridge and I don't not want to make it cross like what she did of used to say.

I knowed that pa did of definitely pushed her over cause of every time I merember that night, I do of seed pa what are pushing her. I don't not really seed it with my eyes, but in my brain like. I reckon if my brain do of say every time that pa did of pushed ouma deaded, then that were what did of really must of have happened. I just can't not merember proper like if it were afore he donnered ma deaded what he pushed ouma or after. Anyways, here are how I do of merember it afore I do of go to sleep under a bridge.

Zakes' brother do of come up to me afore I did getted home and charfs me he do need to hide so as I take him to my room. This are how I merember it most times now, but sometimes he do of just appear there in a passage without not me knowing how he did of gotted inside.

This time I merember me taking him to a room and all and trying to get a plaster for him, but afore I do of get a plaster, I do hear pa shouting so as I goed to check in a lounge, even though I don't not want to cause of pa don't not like me checking him donnering ma. I do of check in a door and pa are shouting, 'Slut! Slut! Slut!' at ma and ouma are standing in atween ma and pa and she are trying to push pa back and ma are checking lank scared.

Ouma checks real small next to pa. I don't not merember her checking so small and I reckon maybe her very cross veins did of make her go smallerer. But even though she are small, she are not too skrikked of pa so as to push him. I do of want to go into a lounge to charf ouma to not push pa cause of he will donner her, but I is only a lightie so I just check through a door still. Ouma do of push pa more and he is like still shouting at ma over a top of ouma's head like he don't not even feeled her pushing, but then that are when he do of push ouma deaded. This are how I merember it this time. Ouma are like a fly what I did of sometimes see that did of bothered Shaka. It were like as Shaka didn't never check a fly till all of a sudden like he would of try to donner it with his pause. And that are what pa did do. He don't not check ouma till all of a sudden like, then he do of donner her, accept pa don't got none pause, he do of only got a big hand what he do use to shove ouma. She bliksems her head big time on a floor and pa don't even not check her. He do of just step over her and donner ma who are too skrikked at ouma being deaded to check that pa are coming for her now.

I do of try to shout to ma to be careful, but pa are quickerer as my voice and he are donnering ma afore I can of charf nothink. I do of only look again after it have of gone quiet and pa have of stopped shouting and ma have of stopped screaming and crying. It aren't not lekker what I do of see cause ma are lying on a floor and there are lank blood coming from her head and all. Pa are sitting and checking out ma and ouma and he do look skrikked big time.

A way I merember it this time are that when I check all what had of happened and that pa aren't not doing nothink, I reckon ma and ouma do of need a doctor, so as I go quick like to a phone. Ma had of showed us how to call a ambalance if ever we do of need one so this are what I do.

But afore anyone on a phone can answer I do of heared pa charfing me to put it down. He are talking quiet like what he did that time after we did of went to a zoo without not him, and afore he did of donner ma somethink chronic. Maybe I did of merembered a ambalance that time when I tolded you earlier about what happened cause of I did try and called one. This time I don't not merember actually seeing none, only trying to call it.

Anyways, I don't not call one cause of pa do of start coming at me to donner me and I do of skrik and put a phone down and I'm like charfing, 'But pa, ma do of need a doctor.' I is poohing my pants nearly like for real, like what old Pooh Pants du Plessis did, cause of I can check that pa are going to donner me deaded and all what I can think of is about Jaapie's oom what did of killed all his fambily and all and I start shouting to Sally to like run out of a house. And that are when Zakes' brother do of shooted pa. BLAM!

I do of then take a gun back to my room and chuck it on to a bed where Zakes' brother are lying deaded. I knowed this do of sound funny cause of how can I have of taken a gun to a room when Zakes' brother were already deaded cause of if he were deaded how could he have of just shootted pa? But like I did of said, I don't not merember it all too good.

THIRTY-EIGHT

I must of have sleeped lank under a bridge cause of it were nearly almost dark by a time I did of waked up. I were feeling lank hungry and lank thirsty too also as well and I did of merember what I did of told me that I did of got to have food and drink so as I don't not falled over again. I acide that that were a first think I must do afore I do of go look for signs to Ermelo on a road.

I do of seed a sign to Ermelo afore I can of find nothink to eat or drink, but it aren't not too long afore I do of seed a town. When I getted there I check a petrol station what had of got a shop so as I go first to a toilets and have a lank big drink of water and fill up a empty coke bottle what I did of find. Then, cause there are nobody around, I acide to go into a ladies toilets and put all a toilet seats up. This do of merinds me of Zakes and I are a bit sad that he aren't not there to laugh with.

I still don't not knowed howcomewhy he did of goed off in a taxi without not me. Maybe there weren't not enough space in a taxi, I dunno.

I check a shop by a petrol station and there is a few ous inside. Some are shopping and some are ahind a tills. There is too many ous for me to rob a place with a gun, but I reckon I can of zick some stuff and a ous ahind a tills won't not see nothink.

I is in and out of a shop so quick that a ous don't even of knowed I exist. I did of get some bread, some chips, some milk and even five rolls of Toff-o-lux what I did of shove in a bag while no one were looking. I move quick like up a road and down a other small road where there are not nobody around afore I do of count all a stuff. I is just about to chuck a Toff-o-lux into my mouth when a ou comes out of a door there what I didn't of seed afore. He are so quick that I don't not even have time to skrik.

'Hey,' a ou charfs. Even though it are dark, I can check that he are a bit skrikked to check me, but he don't not skrik long cause of he are much biggerer as me. He are not old like pa, but are older like as a ous what are in high school.

'What you doing back here?' he do of asks and do of lights a cigarette. He are like not charfing me I must go, he are just asking.

'Nothink,' I charf. There are a really lekker smell what do of come from a door what a ou did of comed out. It do smell like a braai.

A ou do check me out, not skew like, but more like he did of knowed me and I do of start to worry cause of I reckon that maybe he didn't not knowed that I were eated by a croc and that a cops were still of looking for me.

But then he do of smiled and charf, 'You know, for a moment there, I thought you were my baby brother.'

I don't not like that he do of call me a baby, but I don't not say nothink.

'But he'd be a lot older now. Want a drag?'

I don't know what a drag are, but acause of he are holding a cigarette out to me, I reckon that maybe he do mean a smoke. I are about to charf no cause of pa would donner me if he did of catched me, but then I do of merember that he are deaded.

It do take like about ten hours to of stop coughing and a other ten hours for a ou to of stop laughing at me.

'First time?' he asks when I do of adventually stop coughing and I do of nods so as he do smile, nice like.

'I'm James,' he charfs and like shakes hands with me, then takes a drag on a cigarette. I can charf that cause of I do of now knowed what a drag are, accept he don't not cough like I did of, he do just blow out a smoke real slow like. Then he checks me out.

'You got a name?'

I do nodded and then cause of he are still checking me out I do of realised that he do wants me to charf him what my name are.

'Samuel,' I charf.

'Nice to meet you Sammo,' he do charf and shake my hand again. I do of like James, he do talk nice with me.

'So what you doing out so late? Where your parents?'

He were just asking, not like checking up on me. I don't not knowed why, maybe it were acause of he did of gived me a drag that I did said, 'My pa were donnering my ma, so as I did of just go out for a walk.'

'Bummer,' he do charf and do of hold out a cigarette for me to drag again.

I start to laughing cause of he did said 'bum' and do take a cigarette but don't not suck so hard this time, only a little bit. It still do make me cough, but not for ten hours like a last time.

'My pa used to donner my ma,' James do charf. 'He doesn't anymore.'

Even though I is shy I do ask, 'Why not?' cause of I do want to knowed what would of stop a pa from donnering a ma.

'He died. Got drunk one night and wrapped the car around a lamppost. Your dad drink?'

'Ja, lots. That are mostly when he donners ma, but sometimes he do donner her when he have not of drinked. He do of also bliksem me sometimes.'

'Bastard!'

It are weird, James don't not even knowed my pa, but he are angry with him for donnering ma and me. He do of take a other drag and holds out a cigarette again. I do of shaked my head and he do of nods.

'My pa donnered me as well,' he charfs after a bit.

I are interested that James' pa had of donnered him. I didn't not knowed no one else what had a pa what donnered them. I mean Jaapie's pa did of smacked him when he were naughty, but that weren't not donnering. I do of also meremember one time hearing old Theresa Dern charfing that her pa neither her ma did of never even smacked her, even

133

if she were of naughty. So I had of reckoned it were only my pa what donnered people. But now I knowed it were only my pa and James' pa what donnered people and they were both of them deaded, even if James didn't not knowed that my pa were deaded. Then I reckons that maybe if you donner people, you get deaded, so as I acide then never to not donner no one ever.

I did of want to ask James lank questions about his pa and all, but didn't not have a cat's clue what to ask and afore I can of say nothink, he do of stand up and stomp a cigarette flat.

'Well, Sammo, I've got to get back to work. Nice to have met you.'

I check him out and nod, but I do of feel sad that he are going and I must of looked like I were sad cause of he did stop by a door and it checked like he didn't not want to go neither.

'Hey, you hungry?' he do of suddenly asks and I nods big time.

'Wait here.' He like goed inside and it are not long afore he are back with a packet.

'Here, leftovers. You know, some people just don't appreciate good food.' He do give me a packet and then charfs, 'Don't be home too late, if your pa catches you...' He then do of rub my hair like ma did of sometimes done.

'Keep safe,' he charfs and then goes inside and shuts a door.

In a packet there are some hot chips and a lekkerest piece of steak what I have of ever did chow. It were even lekkerer as a one time when pa did of taked us to a larny restaurant and he did of asked for a Gordon Blue steak for us all. It don't not take too long to chow it all finished. I do of want to go and ask James if there are more, but I can't not. So I sits there and try to work out what to do. I knowed that I should of goed on walking, but cause of James were so nice to me, I do of want to talk more to him. I is worried that he may adventually see that I are a ou what a cops is looking for even if they do of thinked that I were in a croc's tummy.

I are still trying to acide what to do, which have of taken me lank ages to acide nothink, when a door do open again and James did comed out.

'You still here?'

I do of nod. Howcomewhy can't I not say nothink? I must of look dof, but it are just acause I is shy.

Anyways, James do of laugh, then charf, 'Don't want to go home? You need somewhere to sleep tonight?'

I do nod again and smile.

'Okay, give me a few minutes to finish up, then you can come over to my place. It's not much, but I like to call it home.' He do then chuck some stuff in a bins and go back to inside.

At least now I don't not have to acide what to do. I is not so tired as to need to sleep, but it are lank late at night so as maybe James reckons I do of needs to sleep even though I don't not.

It are not too long afore he do of comed out again and do chuck out some more stuff, then he do of close and lock a door.

'C'mon, Sammo, it's not far.'

We do of walked down a road and into a other road, then we do of cross over and go down a small road to a other big one what we do of also cross over, then we do stop at a gate what he do unlock. We go up a stairs, past some doors then James do stop by one and unlock it. It are a small flat what are a bit like a place where my Aunty Margie did of lived.

'Want some hot chocolate?' James do of charfs and puts his keys on a table in a lounge.

Steak, chips, hot chocolate! James are a bestest friend in a world what I ever did of have.

'Ja, please,' I do charf, but I is talking lank quiet and just checking round a place. It are like as I are aspecting a cops or pa to of jump out of a other room. No one had of ever beed this nice to me never. Accept maybe, Joshua and Lizzy and Moses and a Black Ma, but none of them did of ever have gived me hot chocolate afore. Ted did of gived me tea and scones, but they weren't not there so as that don't not count.

'Make yourself comfortable,' James charfs and points like to a sofa, then he do go into a room what I reckon are a kitchen cause of I can of heared cups and a kettle. I do of almost want to ask if I can of have a peanut butter zarm, but I reckon I mustn't not push my luck none.

I check round a lounge. There are a sofa and a other small chair and a TV and a table. On a one wall there are a picture of a girl what are wearing a red bikini, but only a bottom so as her boobies is showing. I knowed pa did of said it were a sin to check a lady with no clothes on, but he are deaded, so as I reckon that I will acide what are and aren't not a sin now and looking at a lady in a picture's boobies are not a sin today cause of I is now beginning to understand why Zakes were of so interested in boobies.

'I see you've met Charlene,' James charfs as he brings in a hot chocolate.

'I weren't not lookink at her,' I charf and are now lookink at a floor.

'Of course you weren't,' he do of say, but a way he charfs it, it are like as he were really saying, 'of course you were.' And I were, but I didn't not want him to think I were a sinner.

'You can look at her if you like, I don't mind. She doesn't bite, do you Charlene?' He do then look at Charlene for a long time so as I do adventually also look. She are a beautifulest girl what I did of ever seed with no clothes on, even more beautifuller as ma.

James puts a hot chocolate in front of me, then charfs, 'So, croc didn't really get you then.'

THIRTY-NINE

I have of acided that when I adventually do of have to have a girlfriend, I wants one that do look like Charlene. I can't not have Charlene for my girlfriend cause of she are James' and I don't not want a girlfriend now anyways cause of I still don't not like girls none, but last night James did of charf me that I definitely will of want a girlfriend when I do growed up. I do of asked if Charlene would of beed my girlfriend when I did got to have one but James do laughed and charfs that I can't not have Charlene cause of she are his.

Anyways, cause of James are still asleeping and I were awaked in a morning, I were looking at Charlene and thinkink what kind of a girlfriend I did of want to have when I growed up.

I had of sleeped on a sofa after me and James did talked lank lots last night. Of course I did of skrik when he charfed that stuff about a croc. I did of at first reckon that he were going to take me to a cops and all, but he were cool. A first think what he did of want to knowed were how-comewhy a cops did of thinked I were eated by a croc when I weren't not and he did of laugh lank lots when I did charf him what I had of done.

I weren't not looking at him, when I did of talked cause of I were reckoning I were in trouble so as I did of check at my takkies and did of telled them what I had of done with my shirt and all. I would of have made up a story, even have of charfed that I weren't not a Croc Boy none, but I couldn't not think of none story to say, so as I just charfed him what really did of happened.

'Genius!' he did of say when I were finished telling a story. I is not sure what 'genius' do mean, but I reckon that maybe James do of says this cause of he don't not knowed of Einstein. But he do laugh when he charfs 'genius' so as I knowed that he do reckoned I had of done a good think.

'So what you going to do now? You going to keep on running, or have you got a plan?' he do of asks.

'You not going to take me to a cops?' I do charfs.

'What! You're joking. Why would I help the pigs?'

I is not sure why taking me to a cops would of helped a pigs cause of they do live on a farm with old MacDonald, unless maybe old MacDonald are also a cop and were of shouting at a pigs cause of he can't not catch me.

'No, you're safe here. I won't tell anyone.'

I do of feel betterer, but still do worry about a pigs a little bit, I don't not want them to be shouted at none.

But cause of James are not going to a cops, I do reckon I can of telled him that I are going to find Zakes and his grandparents in Ermelo.

'Ermelo? Geez, that's quite a way away. You planning on walking there?'

'Ja,' I charf, but it are not good that it are still so far.

'I'd give you a lift if I had a car, but unfortunately I don't. They don't pay me enough at that restaurant. Still it's a job I suppose.'

We do of talk lank more, mostly it are James what talk and he do of told me all about his pa what did of donner him and his ma and his brother till of he did adventually runned away. He were lank sorry for his ma cause of he did leave her and all, but he were a lightie then and he couldn't not do nothink to stop his pa from donnering them.

'Why don't you not go home to your ma now that your pa are dead?'

He do of check me out sad like and charfs, 'After I read about my dad killing himself in that accident, I tried to find my ma and my brother, but they had moved and no one knows where they went.'

We don't not say nothink for a bit, then he do of get out his wallet and do showed me a picture of his ma and brother and him. There are also a man in a picture, but a face were tored out. I didn't not have to of ask, I knowed a man with a tored face were his pa. James do of check like a lightie in a picture.

'That was five years ago, I was fifteen then. Ran away about a year after that was taken.'

I do of wished I had a picture of me and ma and Sally, but I don't not have a wallet to put it in none. I also do think that if I did of have a picture and pa were in a picture I wouldn't not of tored his face like what James did of done. Maybe James' pa were so ugly that he didn't not want to scare people with a picture of him. I reckon that must of have beed a problem.

I charf James that if I do of ever seed his ma, I will of tell her that he are okay and all.

James do smile now.

'You're a good kid you know, Sammo.' He do still call me Sammo even though he do of knowed my proper name which he had of readed in a newspapers.

I were getting lank tired now so as he did charf that I could of sleep on a sofa and he did fetched me a blanket. Afore he did of turned off a light, he charfs, 'Sammo, you've done nothing wrong, don't let anyone tell you otherwise.'

I do of now wonder what he did of meaned by that. I can't not ask Charlene cause of I is too shy still to talk to a lady what did got none clothes on, but at least she don't not seem to mind if I do of look.

Cause of James are still asleeping a next morning, I goes to a kitchen and check round till I do of find a peanut butter and make a zarm with a bread what I did of zicked a other day. It are a lekkerest peanut butter zarm what I ever did of tasted. I are still chowing it when James do of come in and check me out. But he don't not moan or nothink, he just do of smile and asks me if I did of sleeped good.

Then he do charf, 'Want some coffee?'

Yous merember I did charf that pa did of never let me have none coffee when a Mielie Lady did gived us some and also that she did gived us drugged coffee, but this are different. This are James what are asking, so as I do of course charf, 'Ja, please.'

I still don't not like a coffee, but acause I did of asked for it, I do drinked it all anyhow.

'Do Charlene ever come and visit yous?' I asks while I is chowing a zarm.

'Charlene?'

'Ja, your girlfriend.' I do of have to say, 'your girlfriend,' cause of it are like he do of forgot who Charlene are.

He still do of look at me skew for a bit and then he do laugh, 'Oh, Charlene. Come visit? I wish.'

'But she are your girlfriend, she must of come visit sometimes,' I is now confused.

James do of shake his head and laugh again. 'I suppose she's not really my girlfriend as in we are seeing each other, she's more like, I dunno, I suppose she's more like a dream girlfriend. It's like I sometimes just imagine that she's my girlfriend and that she's come to visit.'

'So she are not real then,' I are sad cause of I were hoping that she would of come visit James, not so as I could of seed her boobies, but cause of she do look friendly.

'Oh, she's real, but she's a model. Some lucky guy got to take her photograph and it ended up in a magazine.'

I chow more of my zarm while I do of think. 'So do yous have a real girlfriend?' I do ask, then do of merember that I are chowing and I shouldn't not of speaked with my mouth full.

But James don't not charf nothink about me speaking with my mouth full. Instead, he do of just shakes his head and charfs, 'No. There is a girl that I like, but she doesn't seem interested in me.'

'Why?'

'I dunno. Women are funny creatures. You'll see when you grow up. You never know where you stand with them.'

I do of then ask, 'Do this girl what you like ever show you her boobies, like what Charlene do?'

James do of laugh lank then, and charfs, 'I should be so lucky. Maybe if she was really my girlfriend I'd get to see them.'

This girlfriend think were acoming complimicated. You could of have a girlfriend what are not really a girlfriend, but are a picture and she will of showed you her boobies cause of she are a model, but if a girl are real, then then she will of only showed you her boobies if she were a girlfriend, but afore that, you don't not even knowed where you is standing. I did of wonder if someone like Miss Smit at school who are got no boobies could of ever be a girlfriend, not a girlfriend for me, I would of never want a teacher as a girlfriend.

'Zakes would of like Charlene,' I do charf so as I don't not check like I is confused.

'Yeah? Why?'

'Cause of she do got big boobies.'

James do laugh again and charf, 'Yes, she does have a nice pair.'

We do of finish breakfast, then James do charf me that I should of go shower and then he would of cut my hair so as people can't not recognise me as a Croc Boy. 'We may also dye your hair,' he charfs and then cause of I must of checked skrikked, he do charf, 'No, that's d-y-e not d-i-e. I'm not going to kill your hair, just change its colour,' and I do give a sigh of belief.

When I are showered and James do of go showered, I do check out Charlene again. James are wrong, it were a apple what she are eating, not a pear. Maybe it are a dream pear what he were talking about. Anyways, as I do of sit and looking at Charlene, I do of wonder if maybe I can of stay with James. He are really nice to me and maybe Zakes didn't not want me there by his grandparents in Ermelo. Maybe that are why he did of goed in a taxi without not me.

FORTY

James do of cutted my hair lank short, then he do of beach it. That do mean that he did of stick stuff in it what do make it go from a dark brown colour what it were to a yellow colour of a beach. It are lank weird when I check me in a mirror, it are like as I are checking out a other lightie what I don't not knowed.

'Maybe you should grow a moustache,' James do of charf.

I do of nod okay, even though I don't not how to.

'If anyone asks, you're my younger brother, is that okay, Sammo?' James do charf when he are finished. A funny looking lightie in a mirror do of nod and then do of smile cause he do thinked it are cool to of have a brother. He do of only got a sister afore, so as now it are lekker for him to have a brother, aspecially one like James.

'Okay, let's take you for a test drive,' he do charf.

'But you did of said that you didn't not got none car.' I is confused again.

'No, I don't have one, I just mean we'll take you out and see if anyone recognises you as the Croc Boy. I reckon you'll be okay, but we should test things out first. We'll go for a short walk and see.'

There is quite lank ous on a street, but they do of all walked past us. Some do of say, 'howzit' to James and one ou did of stop and talked to him, but only for a little bit and he didn't not even look at me none.

'Looks like your disguise is working,' James do of charf after a ou leaves and I do of smile. 'Come, I need to do some shopping.'

We do of go into a Pick 'n' Pay and James do start putting stuff like bread and milk and juice and cornflakes and tomatoes and carrots and a tin of spaghetti and some cheese into a basket. I had of goned shopping with my ma lank afore, so as I do of knowed that I can't not chuck stuff like chips and Nutella and sweets in a basket even if I do of really want to, but while James are paying, I do of quickly grab some Cherrols, a Tex Bar and some Toff-o-lux and shove them in my pocket.

When we do of get outside, James do of becomed a coolest growed up what I ever did of knowed cause of he do charf me, 'Okay, what did you steal?' and I reckon I are in a doggy doo cause of I did stealed, but when

I do of showed him, he do charf, 'Well, I don't like Cherrols, so you can have those, but we go halves on a Tex Bar and a Toff-o-lux.'

That are cool with me. No growed up what did catched me zicking sweets did ever want to share, they did of always take everythink.

We do of go sit in a park what are nearby and chow all a sweets and while we is there, James do of point to a girl what are walking down a street.

'That's Debbie, she the one that I want to have as a real girlfriend.'

I do of check Debbie out and she do of look okay, but I reckon I wouldn't not of maked her my own girlfriend if I were olderer cause of she don't not check like Charlene none. Debbie do of walked right past us on a other side of a street, but don't not seed us none.

'Why don't you go charf her hello?' I do of asked James and he do just go dunno with his soldiers and do of finished a Tex Bar what he are eating.

'Come on,' he charfs, 'I've got to go to work soon.'

We do take a shopping home, then James do change so as he can go to work. Afore he do go, he shows me how to turn on a TV then charfs, 'Come round the back of the restaurant later and we'll see what leftovers we can feed you.'

I do of watch TV, sleep and look at Charlene till it have of beed dark for lank ages, then I do turn off a TV and go out. While I is walking to a restaurant, I do of check Debbie. I don't not knowed howcomewhy, but I acide to follow her. She do go down a big road for a bit, then she do of turn into a small road like where a back of James' restaurant are, accept this are a differenter one, but it do of also got a door what she do of open and go in without not even checking me none cause I do of hide ahind a rubbish bin.

When a door are closed again, I do of go and open it quiet like so as I can check inside. There are not no one there so as I do of go inside quick like. There are a passage what do got some doors on a sides of a passage. I can of heared girls what talk in a room. At a end of a passage there is some stairs what do of go up and there are music what I can heared.

I are just checking around when I do of heared a toilet what are flushing and just after I had of hided ahind a box I seed a really huge ou what did comed out of one of a doors. He are still pulling up his zip and he do of walked down a passage to a door to a outside and stand by it. He are facing a door and not me so as I can move up a passage more, but then I do of heared someone what are coming down. So real quick like I duck into a toilet room, what a ou did of just comed out of, till a person did gone past.

I are just about to come out of a toilet room when I seed Debbie what have of comed out of a other room. She are wearing different clothes like a bikini and do go up a stairs what I go up after her. I did of have acided that I is going to ask her if she do wants to be James' girlfriend, but she don't not wait for me and goed through a curtains at a top of a stairs and when I do of check round a curtain a little I check she are dancing and there is lots of lights so as I can't not check nothink of a room, but I do of hear ous what are shouting and whistling.

I reckon a ous are all shouting cause of Debbie are pretending to be a fireman and are sliding on a fireman's pole what are in a room. I is a bit worried that maybe if a real firemen do of have to use a pole they might of bump Debbie off it cause of they wouldn't not be aspecting her to of be there on a pole. But Debbie are lucky cause of there are not none fire nowhere.

After she did of finish pretending to be a fireman, she did of do a weird think. She did of start to taking off her clothes, but she were still dancing. I is like should I go stop her cause of there are ous in a room what can of seed her and it would of be a sin for all a ous if she did of take all her clothes off. But a ous, what I can't not see cause of a lights, were of shouting and cheering so as I do think that maybe they do of really want to sin. I do of want to sin too also but aren't not sure if I should of, but after thinkink of it for a little bit, I acide that cause of there is no growed ups there to charf me I were sinning I can't not be, so as I do of just keep checking Debbie out.

It do of taked Debbie lank ages to of take all her clothes off cause of she would take off somethink, then she do dance more, then do of take off another think, then dance more. I do of think that if she did of want to dance with no clothes on, then howcomewhy didn't she not just of stop dancing, take off all a clothes, then dance more. But she do of rather want to dance and take off and dance and take off. But when she were completely with no clothes no, a music did of stop and I'm like, 'See, you should of stopped dancing and taked off all your clothes, then you could of had more time to dance with nothink on, but now a music are finished.'

I don't not get none time to of thinked much though, cause all of a sudden like Debbie are almost running to a curtain and I do of skrik and tried to runned down a stairs quick like. But then I do of do somethink real dof. I are just by a bottom of a stairs and I check round to see if Debbie are going to seed me and I do of trip and fall over and donner my head.

Afore I can of do nothink, Debbie do of check me and she do charf, 'What the...' and a bad word. I do of try and sit up but do check some blood and when I put my hand on where I did of donner my head, I can feel that I are bleeding.

It must of beed acause of a blood that Debbie are not cross with me. Like ma when I did of hurted myself so as I did bleed sometimes, she would of beed all skrikked till she had of fixed up a sore, then she would of beed cross. So Debbie are like ma cause of she do get a ou at a end of a passage to of carry me into a room where there are a other girl what do leave and after she do of put on a dressing gown, Debbie do of sort out me with a plaster and all.

It are only when she did of finished sorting a plaster out that she did said, 'So, what were you up to on the stairs? Were you being a little pervert?' I don't not know what a purr-vert are none and I do of thinks that maybe she reckons I were trying to be like a cat climbing a stairs cause of cats do purr, but anyways I do charf her, 'No, I did of just wanted to talked to you.' I says this but I are talking to my takkies cause of I don't not want to look at her face none just in case of if she are cross with me.

'Talk to me? Why?' She don't not sound so cross now.

'I did of only want to ask if yous would of be James' girlfriend.'

'Who's James?' I do of look at her now and can check that she are confused.

'James are my friend, I mean my big brother. He did of said that he did of wanted you to be his girlfriend, but he don't not know how he is standing and he won't not ask you hisself so as I did of thinked that maybe if I did of asked you for him then maybe he could of knowed how to stand you.'

Debbie do of check me out now like she don't not knowed what I were charfing her and I do of think that maybe she are dof and that I do of need to tell James that she are not cleverer enough to be his girlfriend. But then she do smile, but not too nice like.

'I see,' she do charf, 'James is one of those creeps out front I suppose. How much did he pay you to come back here?'

'No, James didn't not paid me nothink, he don't even knowed that I are here talking to you. We did of just checked you this arvie walking by a park and James had of charfed me afore then even that he would of like you to be his girlfriend, but when he did of seed you he did of charf, "There are Debbie what I want to be my girlfriend," and so when I did of seed you now, I did of followed you to here. James are my frien...my big brother and I do of just want to help him, so please will you be his girlfriend, please?' I do of pull a face what I sometimes had of used on ma when I did of wanted somethink really lank much. It did of worked

143

with ma and I were of hoping it would of worked with Debbie and I do of look at her properly now.

She do of thinked for a bit, then do say, 'I don't even know James. I can't be his girlfriend if I don't know him.'

'But you must knowed James. He do work at a restaurant there down a street.'

'You mean that steak place?'

'Ja, I think so, they do of cooked steaks there.'

Debbie do of thinked some more, then she do go, 'I think I know who you are talking about, he's kinda cute. You say he's your brother?'

I do of nods even though James are not really my brother. Nodding are not lying.

'And he wants me to be his girlfriend?'

I do of nods more and Debbie do of thinks more, then she do of say, 'Okay, I'm not promising anything, but I'll meet with him and we can see what happens.'

Now my head are not hurting so much none more cause of I is happy big time.

'Come, I will of take you to him,' I do charf and grab her hand.

'Woah tiger, I need to get dressed first,' she charfs so as I do nod. Debbie do of check me out for a bit, then she charfs, 'Well aren't you going to give me some privacy to change?'

I is confused cause of she did of just taked her clothes off in front of all those ous in a other room, but now she don't not want to put all her clothes on when it are just me, but I don't not say nothink and do of just go wait in a passage.

I do of rub a plaster what Debbie did of put on my head and check out a ou by a door, but he don't not check me.

Adventually Debbie do of come out of a room and she do take my hand so as I can of lead her. But when we do of comed to a small road to where a door are what James do work ahind, she don't not want to go none furtherer.

'I'm not meeting a strange man down a dark alley. He must come out here,' Debbie charfs and she do of stay on a big road even though I charf her that James are not strange.

I are not too happy now cause of I reckon that she are going to bugger off as soon as what I do of go and see if James are there.

'Promise me you will of wait,' I charf her and she do nods. 'Cross your heart and hope to die?' She do nods again.

Now she can't not go cause of she did of promised and also did of crossed her heart too as well. So I do go knock on a door and James do of adventually open it.

'Sorry, Sammo, I nearly forgot your leftovers, it's been hectic tonight. Wait here I'll grab you some now.' He do of not even letted me speaked.

When he do of comed back with some steak and chips, I do charf him afore he can say nothink that he must come seed a surprise what I did of find for him.

'A surprise?' he do of charf and I can check that he did got no diarrhoea that Debbie are waiting in a big street to be his girlfriend.

'Ja,' I charf, 'a big surprise, but you must come now.' I are so acited I don't not even have opened a packet with a steak and chips in.

'Now?'

'Ja, now.'

James do of check round, then charfs, 'Okay, but I must be quick.'

He do of follow me to a big road and I are chuffed to see Debbie what are still waiting there.

'This are my brother James,' I do of charf her. I don't not need to charf James who Debbie are, cause of I knowed that he do of already knowed, but now I check that he do of looks scared of her.

FORTY-ONE

I do of make myself a peanut butter zarm what I put lank lots on and also do of make some tea what I taked back to a lounge and sits on a sofa so as I can look at Charlene. My throats are a bit sore cause of a cigarettes what I did of drag on last night so as a tea do taste even lekkerer, but I can of now drag without not coughing none.

I chow my zarm and some chips from what I did keeped of a food what James did of gotted me last night. Cold chips are not so lekker. I did of also drinked some beer last night, but it did of tasted horrible so as I didn't not have none more an two sips.

At first Debbie had of charfed James that I shouldn't not smoke or drink a beer none, but she didn't not of say it like as she did of meant it so as James did of carry on to let me drag and taste a beer.

After he had of stopped skrikking when he did check Debbie, they did talked and adventually James did of charf me and her to wait while he did

145

of finished his work, which didn't not take too long. Then we did of goed to a shop what sold milkshakes and I did of haved a banana one and James did haved Vanilla and Debbie did of haved strawberry. Debbie and James talked lots and laughed lots. When a milkshakes were finished, James do of asked Debbie if she do of wants to come back to his place for coffee. That were when we did of drinked beer and drag cigarettes and all.

I were happy now that Debbie were James' girlfriend so as I could of have Charlene as my girlfriend. I must of have gone to asleep afore Debbie and James cause of I didn't not meramber her going and James going to bed. But then I do of get a surprised when Debbie do of comed out of James' room, just afore I were about to tell Charlene that she could of now be my girlfriend. Debbie do of check lank happy.

'Ah, there you are you little matchmaker,' she do charf.

I don't not knowed howcomewhy she did called me a matchmaker cause of pa had of told me not to never play with matches none so as I did of never not even played with them so as I can't not make them none. Still I do of just smile and asks Debbie if she do of want some chips.

'Chips! For breakfast! Yuck!' Then she do go into a kitchen and I do of check out a chips. They is a bit yuck, but I do of still eated some more anyways and also did of finish a peanut butter zarm.

Debbie did of comed out of a kitchen with two cups and go back into a bedroom. I do of watch some TV till of adventually James and Debbie do of comed out and James do of kiss her afore she buggers off.

As soon as Debbie are gone, James do look at me and charf, 'You!' It are like as he are trying to be cross, but he do of got a huge smile on his face so as I can't not belief that he are cross with me so as I just do laugh cause of I is happy that he are happy.

I do of stayed with James then for lank ages. Every night he do go to work then do meet Debbie afterwards and we do of go to his place and drag cigarettes and drink beer, accept I don't not drink it cause of I don't not like it none.

James checks real happy most of a time now. He do of buy me lekker thinks like some new pants and shorts and undies and even some new takkies. We do of go have milkshakes and sometimes he do of buy hamburgers and hotdogs.

Debbie do of also buy me sweets and lekker stuff and I haven't not of ever beed so happier as of now. I do of want to go see Debbie dance with no clothes on again, but she charfs no when I do of asked.

'Howcomewhy?' I do of want to knowed.

'Because you're too young, you shouldn't be seeing that sort of thing at your age.'

I do think for a bit, then do of ask her why she do do it.

'It's a job,' she charfs. 'It pays good money.'

There are somethink that are not right about this, but I don't not charf nothink cause of I can't not say what it are that I don't not think are right and if it don't not bother Debbie and James, then it don't not bother me none neither.

What do of bother me after a bit are that James do sometimes always drink too much beer when he do of get home with Debbie and one time he did of shouted at me when he had of drinked too much.

I didn't not see Debbie for some days after that and did of adventually go to a place where Debbie did dance to of seed her, but a big ou by a door wouldn't not let me in so as I had to of wait till she did adventually comed out. I did of start to asked her howcomewhy she don't not come to see James none more and she did of smile sad like and charfed, 'Let's go for a milkshake and I'll tell you.'

'I'm scared of James when he drinks too much,' she do charf me while we is busy drinking our milkshakes. 'He gets this look in his eyes, like he's going to do some violence.' She do start crying a little bit then and I don't not knowed what to of say.

'His pa did of drink too much and then donner him when he were a lightie.' Nor me, nor James neither had of charfed her this afore and it do of stop her crying, but she still do look sad.

'He's such a nice guy when he's sober, but give him a few drinks and...' She do of stops and sluck on her milkshake. 'It's probably only going to get worse, it looks like it's in his genes.'

That night James do of donner me cause of he are cross that Debbie aren't not there none and he did of drinked too much. He were lank drunk and did of fall over afore I had of stopped a blood on my eye.

Cause of he were now sleeping I did of goed into his room and check in his jeans, in a pockets and everywhere, but all I could of find were two hundred rands, a handkerchief and keys, but I couldn't not find what it were what Debbie did of charf me were a problem. I did of taked a money then go back into a kitchen and maked lank peanut butter zarms what I did of put in a plastic bag. Then I did of grab some chips and cokes and go put them in my rucksack. After this I did of get all a beers what I could of find and pour them all down a sink.

In a lounge, James were still asleeping so as I do take a picture of Charlene off a wall and put it in my rucksack. She were mine now, I did reckon and also I didn't not want James to of donner her neither. Last of all I did of grab his cigarettes and matches and also put them in my bag.

It are dark outside cause of it are late in a night and I do of closed a door ahind me. I are feeling lank sad and are nearly crying, not cause of it are sore where James did of donner me, even though that were sore, but cause of I are sad that I are leaving. But I couldn't not stay with James and his jeans none more cause of if he had of donnered me again I would of had to shooted him, like pa. I don't not mean like I shooted pa, but like pa were shooted.

At first I do of thinked that maybe I could of go lived with Debbie, but then I reckon that James would of finded me there and donner me for leaving him so as I do of go where I knowed there were a sign what said Ermelo on it and do of go out of a town in a way what a sign says.

My hair were still short and beached so as I didn't not have to worry that ous will of think I were a Croc Boy, but still didn't not want no one to of check me just in case now someone did of charf James where I were.

Cause of I hadn't not walked for lank ages, I did get tired quite soon quickly, but still did of walked more. I can't not understand howcome-why James did of goed from being a coolest growed up in a world to one what just needed to be shooted.

What are it with growed ups that they must of donner people? I reckon I don't never want to be a growed up cause of I don't not want to donner people. But then I do of merember what Debbie did of said that you did got to have jeans afore you can donner people and I never did of have none jeans so then maybe I are alright. I reckon now that I will of shooted anyone what do of try to give me jeans so as I don't not have to donner people none.

I do of light a cigarette as I walk and do drag on it. I is getting good at dragging cigarettes now. I couldn't not walk too far cause of my legs weren't not used to walking so as I did find a place to doss and do fall asleep quick like, but I do of dreamed about a night that ma were deaded what I hadn't not of thinked of for lank long. This dream were a worstest merembery of that night what I ever did of have had.

FORTY-TWO

I didn't of have sleeped too good cause of my head were sore where James did of donner me, but also cause of a merem-bering, but I don't not want to think of that none.

It are late arvie and I can check that I hadn't not of walked too far cause of I can still check James' town. I did found a old house what were like Ted's place, you merember, a place what didn't not have none roof, but only walls? And it are cause of a walls that I didn't not seed him till he are there already.

'Thought I might find you here, Sammo.'

He do of smile, but it are not a happy one. Even though he were smiling, I do of visit skrik city and grab my bag so as if he do of try donner me again I can of get a gun, but he don't not come no closerer.

'Hey look, I'm really sorry. I mean that. I of all people should have known better, but I guess I've ended up like my dad. I thought I might do, but last night just confirmed it.' He do of check out his shoes now for a bit and cause of I don't not knowed what he are charfing, I do of still carry on feeling in my bag for a gun.

'How's the head?' He do asks after a bit when he did check at me and stop checking his shoes.

I still do of say nothink cause of I don't not knowed what are happening.

'Come back, Sammo. I promise I won't hit you again.'

I do of check at him like as to charf that I weren't not never going back cause of I knowed that pa did of so often charf ma that he wouldn't not never hit her again none and then it were hardly almost no time afore he were donnering her again. Growed ups is all bleddy liars.

I reckon James do of check what I are thinking cause of he do charf, 'No, I guess you're right, Sammo. You're not safe until I've sorted myself out. And I will, I promise you that. I'll do it for you. You're my hero you know.'

I do of stop trying to find a gun cause of I do think that I are okay from being donnered cause of I can check that James are really sorry and all, acides, no one has never called me a hero ever afore.

'Stay safe, Sammo, and if you ever feel like some left over steak and chips, you know where to find me.' He do of hold out his hand for me

149

to shake and I do of think a bit afore I do. And then James do of walk away back to a town. I check him go till I can't not seed him none more, then I do of picked up my bag and walk in a other way to Ermelo.

Cause of I are only walking now and there are not much happening, I may as well charf yous what I did of dreamed about that night.

Zakes' brother weren't not even by a house is what I do of have dreamed. I do of check him by George's shop and he do gived me a gun and charf me to look after it for him. I knowed this are a wrong merembering as I did of seed Zakes' brother there by a house when I did go back after I did meet with Zakes in a veldt, but maybe in this merembery, Zakes' brother do of go to a house after I did of left.

Anyways, in my dream I do of got home and go into a kitchen so as to make a peanut butter zarm. Ouma were in a kitchen with her very cross veins and tea and all and she did of told me I can't not have a peanut butter zarm. I get a moer in really suddenly like, just like pa do sometimes when he are okay, maybe even happy, and then all of a suddenly he would of be lank cross and shouting and donnering and all.

So in a dream I do of do a pa and go from being fine to being lank cross and a moer in and I do of push ouma so as she do fall and donner her head on a sink. Ma do of come into a kitchen and she do start crying when she checks ouma and then she do of try to donner me, but I donner her back till she do of fall over and all and are deaded and then when pa do of come into a kitchen I do of shooted him too also deaded.

Like I did of said, it were a dreamed so as it can't not be a proper merembery of what did of really have of happened, and anyways, I would of never have of pushed ouma over unless it were by an accident, and I never ever would of donnered ma, so this dream can't not have beed what really did of happened can it?

FORTY-THREE

I were a bit worried that James would of maybe called a cops or maybe even Debbie would of, so as I did of try to walking fasterer. Even though I were going to Ermelo, I weren't not so happy to be going there none more cause of I didn't not knowed if Zakes did of wanted me there none. My brain were of beginning to told me that if he did of, then he wouldn't not of have left me ahind.

I do of walk for long but mostly on a road cause of there aren't not lots of cars. Whenever I do of heard a car, I did hided by a side of a road. I can't not stop thinkink about a dream cause of it do of feel like that are what really did of happened, but I knowed it couldn't not of so as I do think harderer and harderer to of make my brain merember proper like what did of really actually happen. But this do of maked me think more and more that it were me what did of deaded ouma and ma so as I do of stopped thinkink about that and do of try to thinked more of Charlene what are in my rucksack and this do of make me feel happier.

I still don't not knowed if Zakes will of be happy when I do get to Ermelo, but I just do of charf myself that even if he aren't not happy, I do of want to knowed homcomewhy he did of just left me and Shaka there that time he did of went off in a taxi. But I also don't not want to think about that none more neither.

It must of have beed about two nights after I did of left James, I don't not merember too good, but it weren't not long after that I did of finded him. I were walking in a night by a side of a road and cause of it were dark, I did of nearly almost falled over him. In a light what a moon did of maked, I couldn't not tell proper like what it were I did of kicked, but when a car do of come soon, I check in a car light from where I were hiding and I do skrik.

I acided to waited there till it are daytime light to check out for sure proper like so as I do of find a place to doss nearby. When I do of waked up, I check first for a cars and then when there is none, I go and check thinks out proper for myself.

It were definitely Shaka what were there deaded by a side of a road. A car must of have donnered him dead, but I can of also check that there are blood on his pause what I reckon are from walking on a road too much, seen as how he don't not got none dog takkies. There is lank flies what do of buzzing round him and that are how I knowed he were proper deaded cause of if he weren't not deaded, he would of have eated at a flies.

I do of feel so lank sad as I check him out that I nearly don't not heared a car coming and do of just about hided in time. I then do go back and check him out again. He can't not of beed deaded too long cause of he don't not have holes in him what I have of checked in other dead dogs what I had of seed.

Anyways, I can't not just leave him there so as I do reckon I do need to funeral him. I do of find a sharp stick what I can of use to dig a hole with and there are a bush not so far away what I can of dig ahind without not a cars checking me none.

It do of taked me lank ages to make a hole big enough so as Shaka can fit in and also he are really heavier as what I had of aspected so as I do of have to drag him by his pause. I had of seen a funeral once on a TV show and I knowed that if a ou wanted to be funeraled proper like, someone do of have to said a special words which I do of merember. So I do charf, 'In a name of a father and of a sun and into a hole he goes,' and I do of drag Shaka into a hole as I do of said this so as he can be funeraled proper like.

Then I do of cover him with a sand what I had of taked out of a hole. Suddenly I are lank cross with Zakes cause of it are all his fault. If he hadn't not of left me and Shaka there with a taxi, then Shaka wouldn't not of runned after him and he wouldn't not of got deaded by a car. I don't not want to go to Ermelo none more to check Zakes.

'You can keep your bleddy Ermelo and you bleddy grandparents,' I do of shout. 'I wish you had of died when you did of jumped off a third floor there by school.'

It don't not maked me feel none betterer and it don't not make Shaka alive again neither also so as I do of picked up a stone and chuck it as hard as what I can into a veldt. I do of imagine as if it were hitting Zakes on a head so as he do of bleed, then I do of just sit there by Shaka and feel sad.

Then I do start to of wonder if ouma and ma did of have beed funeraled proper, like what I did of seed on a TV. In a one what I did of seed, there were a little girl whose pa were a cop and he were deaded by a baddies. She were there at a funeral and I do of think that I should of have beed there for my ouma and ma's funeraling and are now even more sadderer cause of I were asposed to of have beed there, but I weren't not.

I do of then start to thinked about a school and how Zakes did of jumped from a third floor cause of he did of wanted to commit sewerage pipe and all. When he did of done it, I didn't not understand howcome-why a ou would of want to be deaded, but as I do of sit there I do of feeled that I do want to be deaded cause of my ouma and ma are deaded and I don't not think Zakes are my friend none more cause of he did make Shaka get deaded, and James did of donner me so as he weren't not my friend none more and all a other ous what I did of meet did of either donner me or did of want to take me to a cops. No one do of want me around so maybe I should of be deaded.

Cause of I aren't not in a school none more, I can't not jump off of a third floor, and even if I did of, then maybe I wouldn't not of get deaded and would of have to go to a hopstibal and then seed a psycho the rapist like what Zakes did of have to. I then do of merember a gun what I did of have. A ou can commit sewerage pipe with a gun cause of that are what Jaapie's uncle did of done. While I are sitting there by a road, I do of take a gun out of a bag and check it out. It are lank heavy for somethink what are small, but my heart which are also small do of feel lank heavy too also.

I didn't not knowed what it are like to be deaded. I do of merember Miss Smit by school that did of said that Pooh Pants du Plessis' pa were with Jesus in heaven after he had of beed shooted dead. I do of think about Jesus and consume that he are a growed up cause of a growed up like Pooh Pants' pa won't not go stay with a lightie, lighties don't not have a house, only growed ups do.

Maybe there are a lightie Jesus what dead lighties do of go stay with. Maybe there are a special lightie heaven. Miss Smit did of never charf us that there weren't not one and she did of maked it to sound like heaven were a lekker place where no one donners no one and no one are not nice to no one nothing, so as I scheme that maybe it would of be lekker to go there. Maybe if I do of shooted myself and go deaded, then I would of go stay there by a lightie Jesus in heaven. I do of put a gun to my head.

BOOK II

ONE

I had nearly forgotten about the case. The media hype died down soon after the boy was supposedly taken by that crocodile. I say supposedly as I was never quite convinced. They found his shirt, but never any remains, even though they got the one that swallowed that poor police dog. Those pictures have done their rounds on the internet, and I suppose in a gruesome sort of way they were interesting. It's not something you see every day, an almost whole dog being sliced out of the belly of a freshly dead crocodile in some sort of macabre caesarean section.

I guess saying I had forgotten about the case is not quite right, it was more like I had given up on it, what with the mother in a coma, the little girl, Sally if I recall correctly, wouldn't say anything except that she wanted her mother back. And then there was the young lad and his friend. How they had managed to evade us for so long still amazes me. I suppose we adults are not good at noticing children, especially if they want to remain unnoticed.

I did try and follow up on the black kid. They said he had tried to commit suicide a few months before all this happened, but we have no idea why, what with his psychologists file being confidential and all. He seemed to have slipped the net as well. We tracked down his grandparents in Ermelo, but they said they had not seen him. We never followed that up and maybe we should have, especially after that apparent spotting of him in a taxi heading to Ermelo.

It was a mess that case. The mother beaten almost to a pulp, how she survived is anyone's guess. The grandmother was pushed over, knocking her head on a coffee table which resulted in a snapped neck and the father shot through the heart. It seemed at first that that tsotsi they found in the kid's bedroom did it, but the coroner's report refuted that theory.

The tsotsi was probably dead by the time the neighbour heard the shot and, even if he had been alive, he would have most likely been unconscious and too weak to pull the trigger due to the amount of blood he would have lost.

The bullet they pulled from him matched the police sergeant's gun, proving what we suspected – he *had* been hit during that shootout. The other bullets from the house matched those from the recent spate of murders as well as from that attack where the guy survived. These also match the one we took from the father. Conclusion, someone had taken from, or had been given the gun by the tsotsi after he had been shot and then used it to kill the father.

The strange thing was that the murder weapon, which we found at the scene, was registered to the father. How the tsotsi got hold of it is anyone's guess. It had never been reported stolen, yet it was used to perpetrate those earlier crimes. There was no sign of forced entry to the gun safe so it was filed next to my Loch Ness Monster and Abominable Snowman files.

We were pretty sure the father was abusive. The neighbours talked of hearing him yelling and the mother crying. Also her medical records show a series of injuries that, although other explanations were given – walked into a door, tripped and fell – the doctor suspected abuse, but couldn't prove anything.

The grandmother's records also indicated some abuse, but at a much lower level and the daughter showed signs of sexual abuse, but nothing recent.

The worrying thing was that there had been indicators of abuse of the young lad, but no one picked up on them. I won't go into that though, you must have read all the reports in the papers about the recriminations and sackings in the social services department.

Now, that young lad, there was the big question mark. He had a history of violence at school, apparently throwing a cricket ball at another kid's head quite unprovoked. Then there was that whole fiasco of him falsely accusing the father of the girl who he threw the ball at of beating him up. What was the name again? Dern, that was it, a respecttable businessman. Boy, did we get hauled over the coals for arresting him all on the strength of the young lad's accusation. Not a nice chap, Dern. I imagine though if it had been his daughter doing the accusing, we would have been hauled over the coals for not carrying out the death penalty on the accused there and then. Still, not an experience I'd like to repeat thank you very much.

So, we knew that the tsotsi hadn't shot the father because he was unconscious or dead at the time. The fingerprints on the band aid that we found matched those we took off the young lad's toothbrush, so we assume it was him who tried to play doctor. A rather pathetic attempt the coroner declared, although I had thought it was rather touching in a strange way that he had made the effort. He probably reasoned that his mother had always put a plaster on him whenever he was bleeding.

But with the tsotsi out of the frame as the killer of the father, we tested the mother and the grandmother for gunshot residue. Both came back negative which only left the young lad. His fleeing the scene didn't really help prove his innocence. Neither did his prints all over the gun. The only question mark about this was that there seemed to be another set of prints on the gun, but they had been practically wiped off by the young lad's. It is possible that these smudged prints were the tsotsi's, although I had a theory that they belonged to that other kid, Zakes, that was his name.

Turned out that this Zakes kid was the younger brother of the tsotsi so I reasoned that Zakes possibly had found his brother dead at the house, assumed that the father had done it and shot him out of revenge, but that theory didn't rest easy with me. I didn't wholly dismiss it though, just a gut feeling you could say, but you must never dismiss evidence.

The other strange piece of this puzzle is the teacher with the lisp. He seems a genuine character, but there is something about him. He appeared far too eager to take responsibility for Sally, even fighting off attempts by the social services and the kid's uncle for custody. Given the social services' track record about the young lad, the courts seemed reluctant to release him into their custody and as the girl was petrified of going to the uncle (possible source of the abuse, but no evidence), and made it clear that she wished to stay with the teacher, she is still with him and the case continues to trundle through the courts at a pensioner snail on valium pace.

I'm still not convinced that this teacher's not involved somehow. He's been visiting the mother every day in hospital, always taking little Sally with, but I get the impression that he's using her as an excuse. I've seen the way he looks at the mother, holding her hand and trying to talk her out of the coma. There is, or should I say was, something going on between them. It's possible that they were having an affair which the father found out about and this precipitated the savage beating the mother got.

We're pretty sure it was the father who put the mother in hospital. Her bruises matched his fist size. He could have been responsible for the grandmother's death too, perhaps she stepped in to try and protect her daughter, but this is all speculation, it would never stand up in court.

The grandfather was too far gone with Alzheimer's to really take on board the news that his wife was dead. Sort of a blessing in disguise I suppose, you can't mourn for someone if you don't remember them.

We keep on coming back to the young lad as the prime suspect. The team's always been divided on this with some saying that it was self defence, that the father came after him once he had beaten the mother and killed the grandmother, others think that given the lad's violent history at school that this was premeditated, a revenge for the beating he had taken and possibly those that his mother had endured. I'm not sure myself, both arguments have merit, but I feel we'll never be able to prove beyond reasonable doubt either way, even if the lad is still alive and did turn up, we would only have his word to go on.

I was rather devastated when the news came though that he had been taken by that crocodile. I would have liked to have heard his account of what happened and judged for myself if he was telling the truth or not, I'm usually quite good at gauging people. I do hold out some hope that he may still be alive, but as time passes and there have been no reported sightings, it's beginning to look more and more like he had been croc lunch.

As new crimes came across my desk, this case sank further down the pile, the news that the young lad was dead proved to be its iceberg. I had not revisited it for a long time until one morning. I was at my desk going over a new assault case when the phone rang. It was the hospital. The mother had regained consciousness.

TWO

The teacher, the one looking after little Sally, he was there holding her hand. There's was no doubt in my mind that there was something going on between them, although she seemed a little confused and hesitant. Not surprising really given that her memory was still hazy at best. The doctor was noncommittal about whether she would ever recall everything. 'Too soon to tell,' he said, although he did go on to add that even if the lack of memory wasn't physical, the psychological scaring of the events that night could well have blocked out the memory. I hate psychology.

I nearly had to have the teacher physically removed from the room when I wanted to question the mother. He didn't want to leave, especially when Sally started crying about leaving. 'Police brutality,' he had shouted and I nearly did oblige him with some, but managed to keep my cool. I've been on the force too long to be baited by that, but there are still times when you do want to put some of those combat skills we learned during training into practice.

He eventually moved off, I guess my threat to mention to the courts that he was being uncooperative with the police helped him to decide.

None of this really helped as the mother couldn't recall much, or if she did remember anything, she wasn't prepared to say. I did get the feeling that her husband, despite being dead and unable to hurt her anymore, still threatened from the grave.

The doctor had warned about over exciting the patient, so it wasn't easy work questioning her, especially about her mother and son. I was under strict instructions from the doctor, not to mention that both were dead, they didn't think she could handle the distress at the moment. The problem was the more I avoided her questions about them, the more she began to panic, so I was forced to bring the interview to an end, none the wiser as to what had happened.

'You just concentrate on getting better,' I said and felt like a real fraud as I left the room.

The lisping teacher was back in there as soon as I left which irritated me and I decide to do a little bit of checking up on him. My first thought was to ask the young daughter of that businessman fellow, Dern, but decided I couldn't face him after the false arrest incident. Besides I never liked his attitude when we had done our original questioning. He had been quite scathing of the family, practically accusing the young lad of beating up his mother, then killing his grandmother and father before fleeing. He had even called after that incident where that chap, Shyler had been threatened at gunpoint by the youngster. Shyler was an idiot, he had tried to hold the boys captive and was busy trying to negotiate a reward (despite there not being one) when the young lad escaped, returning with a gun to rescue his mate. Shyler kept on going on about his dog and how it had been killed, like it was our fault. I had been tempted to suggest that the dog had committed suicide rather than live with an idiot owner, but held my tongue.

Anyway, this Dern guy rang up after that story hit the press demanding to know what we were doing to apprehend that young thug, going on and on about it being our duty to keep scum like that off the streets. It's amazing how money can turn one into an arsehole. What pious bullshit.

He wouldn't have survived a day in that family, let alone have stayed alive on the run, avoiding the cops like that young lad had. No, the Dern girl was not an option.

Neither was the young du Plessis lad. They had moved away after his father had been killed and I doubted I would get the sign off for the expenses to go and see them. That left the young lad's friend, Jaapie. His parents had seemed genuinely concern-ed about the young lad, said he was a bit mischievous, but nothing more sinister than the usual nonsense that boys get up to. The mother did, however, say that the last time she saw the lad, and this was a little while before all this happened, she thought that he might have had a gun in the packet he was carrying. At the time she just thought it had been a toy one.

She was a pleasant lady and, if my memory served me correctly, made the most delicious choc chip cookies. It did make going to see them all the more pleasant, helped one cope with the 'get well soon card' decor in the house.

'He's okay,' Jaapie had said when I asked him about Larry van Staaden. I guess at that age I wouldn't have been prepared to admit much more than that about a teacher, and that really summed up the impression of Larry that I left with, he's okay. I did have to refrain from laughing when Jaapie accidently let slip that the kids called him Larry the Lithp.

'Jaapie, that's not nice,' his mother chided without any force.

He didn't know if Larry the Lithp (now I'm even calling him that) knew the mother outside of school, but he had heard talk that the young lad had spoken of seeing the mother 'doing it' with Larry the Lithp.

'Jaapie, you shouldn't be talking about that.'

Boy, this kid had it tough if that was the strictest tone she could muster.

It was only when I asked about the incident with the cricket ball being thrown that I got an answer I wasn't expecting.

'He never threw the ball and besides it was only a tennis ball. It was an accident, the ous were playing cricket and Petrus Buthalezi hit the ball that donnered Theresa Dern by mistake. That's what happened.'

Again Jaapie's mother got involved. 'Why didn't you say so at the time, darling? There was all that trouble over it and it was only an accident. You should have said.'

Jaapie just shrugged, but I could image the scene if someone had accused the lad, peer pressure and mob mentality would have con-demned him. Still it was rather annoying that some stupid playground jealousies had ended up with me getting an earful because of that false arrest. I was not best pleased but, after further questioning, I came away with the opinion that the young lad was not as prone to violence as was suggested, more likely he was prone to false accusations.

This cast a different shade of light on the case and made me lean a little towards the self defence theory, although there was still a lot to prove and it would still probably come down to the word of the young lad, if he was still alive. I decided to visit Larry the Lithp again and see what we could find out there.

I asked him outright if he had been having an affair.

'No.' It was a blunt, almost insolent answer.

'That's not what I heard.'

Some soiling of underwear took place.

'Come on, Mr van Staaden, there are no jealous husbands or wives in the picture. You're both consenting adults and the way you've behaved since the incident does tend suggest more than just a parent-teacher relationship.'

It turned out to be easier than I had expected because he admitted to having started the affair not long before that fateful night. I was pleased to have got the confession without having to revert to the mentioning of an eye witness.

Larry's main concern was the school and his reputation, that's why he had never said anything before.

'It would look unprofessional if the school found out that I was having an affair with a married mother of one of the pupils. Please don't tell them.'

If it wasn't pertinent to the case, then there was no reason for me so say anything, but I did have to ascertain that the affair had not been the cause of the killings. It's amazing how much more cooperative people can be when you know a little bit of dirt about them. Larry swore blindly that he had had nothing to do with the killing. He was only just finding out about the father's abusive nature and was trying to persuade the mother to leave him. Larry had started to put in place plans to move the whole family (minus the husband of course) down to the Cape where he would join them soon afterwards and hopefully put all the abuse behind them. But the mother had been too scared to go.

'If only she had agreed, we would have been long gone and none of this would have happened.'

He gave me the name of an estate agent that he had been dealing with to try and find a place to rent and this strengthened his case when a quick phone call confirmed his story. I suppose I should have done all this investigating at the time, but we were so focussed on finding the boy that we overlooked things. Fortunately so far, nothing that we have subsequently discover-ed would have changed the course of the investigation.

I dismissed Larry with a conditional promise to remain silent about the affair, but given that he was practically screaming about it from the hospital room, I didn't think it was really a secret.

I decided to return to the files and see if there was anything I had missed. The bullet that they took from that idiot Shyler's place matched those from other crimes, but these dated to a time when the youngster was still at school, so I believe that he had acquired the gun, who knows how, at some point along the way. Shyler claimed that the lad had taken a pot shot at him, but given that the bullet was taken from the ceiling it indicated that (a) Shyler was on top of him and he was defending himself, (b) it was a warning shot or (c) it was an accidental shot. The chances of it having been aimed and fired deliberately at a completely innocent Shyler seemed remote.

This further strengthened my belief that if the lad had shot his father, it was either a last resort to stop him beating the mother, or in self defence as the father prepared to repeat the treatment on his son. I was busy contemplating this when Larry the Lithp rang. The mother wanted to talk.

THREE

She looked more relaxed this time and I let Larry sit in on the conversation. She had been informed of her husband, mother and son's deaths and her eyes were red from crying, although she was in that state of quiet exhaustion one reaches after giving vent to one's grief. Her ordeal was over, her husband couldn't hurt her anymore.

I began gently, expressing sympathy for her loss, then explained that we were still trying to put together the pieces of what happened that night. I refrained from mentioning that her son was one of the prime suspects in the killing of her husband.

Larry the Lithp held her hand as she began to tell her version of what happened that evening as far as she could remember.

'My husband came home earlier than usual that evening and I could tell that something were not right. I got to know the signs when there were trouble brewing. He acted as though every-thing were fine, but then he started on the whiskey. This were not unusual, except for the speed what he were drinking them at, it were frightening.

'Well, I knew not to say nothing so as I just kept quiet and carried on making supper. But then he called me into the lounge and said that he had heard that I were having an affair with Larry,' here she squeezed his hand, 'I said that I weren't, but I were never able to lie to him too good. "It's all over the school," he then shouted, "Your son watched you guys fucking from the bedroom cupboard." I didn't not know what to say.'

She began to sob and I let her get this out of her system while I mused on how easily the expletive had fallen from her lips. It no longer seemed to be a bad word these days.

Once she had calmed herself, I quietly asked if she knew how he had heard of the affair.

'He said that one of the other parents from the school had heard it from their kid and phoned him at work. He was really cross that not only were I having an affair, but that the whole bleddy school knew and that he had had to hear it from another parent.'

'Do you know which parent it was?' I asked, not that it really mattered. She shook her head, then winced slightly.

'Then what?' I prompted.

'He punched me a few times.' The tone was neutral. She could easily have been saying, 'he gave me a peck on the cheek.' The violence was an everyday occurrence.

I nodded for her to go on, but she started sobbing again.

'Take your time.' It has always amazed me how gentle I could be, even when I feel like shaking someone to get the truth out of them.

She smeared the tears away with a flat hand, swallowed hard and said, 'Then he just left.'

'What?'

'He left. It were like he knew that if he stayed he would kill me, he always did know when to stop.'

This was not what I had been expecting to hear.

'Did he return?'

'I don't know. I went to the kitchen to wash my eye, then I heard a noise in the lounge, so went back. It were better if I just went because he would be more angry if he had to call me. But he weren't there in the lounge. I didn't see nobody there, but then suddenly someone donnered me from behind.'

Again the tears came while I tried to figure out where this was going. I had assumed that the husband had returned without her hearing and attacked her when she went back into the lounge. Rule number one in detective work – never assume.

'Your husband was in the lounge then?' I prompted when she had calmed herself.

She sniffed then said, 'No, that weren't my husband, it were someone else.'

'Did you see who?'

'No, he hit me from behind and then started donnering me something chronic. All I saw were that he were wearing a baklava.'

I tried not to smile at the image of a man wearing those syrupy cakes on his head, which had jumped into my mind.

'Are you sure it wasn't your husband?'

'No, I know how he beat me, this guy beat me different. He weren't as strong as my husband, it were definitely someone else.'

FOUR

I've always likened solving crimes to Tarzan swinging through the jungle. Each pertinent clue is a vine that you grab and swing on, hopefully taking you closer to your goal. And yes, there have been times when a particular clue has excited me enough to want to puff out my chest and beat it while emitting that primal yodel, but so far, all I have managed in reality is to give the air a little punch and hiss, 'Yes!'

The Tarzan analogy does rather fall down when he grabs that final vine and swings to his goal, Jane's tree house. I've never really pictured Jane as being the criminal sort, and I can't forsee Tarzan arresting her but, I suppose, it's about reaching a goal, and in my case the goal is solving the crime.

Sitting listening to the mother, I was forced to remember the old schoolboy joke about Tarzan's last words being, 'Hey! Who greased that vine?' I sat on the floor of the jungle looking and feeling quite stupid, with a bruised backside to boot.

Aside from the bombshell, the mother remembered little else. She thought she vaguely recalled this masked figure pushing her mother over, but her memory was 'frosty', by which I think she meant fuzzy.

I thanked her for the information and left Larry the Lovebird to soothe the sharp pain the memories had stoked up. I was quite impressed with the mother's strength to continue after all that had happened. There was a real sense that she wanted justice for her family, even her husband. I will never understand what keeps a woman loyal to a monster who would beat her up for fun.

I returned to the case files to see what we had missed. If there had been someone else in the house that night, we needed to find out who they were and what they had done. I had cast a quick glance over at Larry the Leather Jacket to see what his reaction to this revelation was, but he remained Larry the Lamb. Either he had been privy to this information already or, if he was involved, he was a cold bastard to show no emotion, but my doubt that he had anything to do with it was strengthening.

I studied the notes on the case till my head began to hurt. If someone else had been in the house, there must be some trace of him, or her, somewhere. I was beginning to give up hope when I noted that there had been an update to the report on the gun used to kill the father. The small bit of thread that the forensic guys had found caught in the trigger had now been identified as being from a rather expensive glove. No wonder there were no prints on the gun other than the young lads, and a smeared print which was still a mystery.

I decided to visit the crime scene again and took a young forensic lad called Phil with me. I wanted to check the outside of the house and surrounds for the balaclava. With a bit of luck, the intruder had thrown it off as he made his getaway.

It was nearly a block away that Phil spotted it shoved into a thick hedge. Give that boy a raise, I thought as he examined it, then pulled a hair out of the inside of it.

'Will we be able to get DNA off that?' I asked.

Phil nodded and carefully placed the balaclava and hair into evidence envelopes. I was tempted to say, 'Don't let the boys eat the evidence, but Phil had not been privy to the baklava comment, so I just smiled quietly to myself and we returned to the station. I was swinging from tree to tree again.

The next morning I decided to get a DNA sample from Larry the Lab Rat so that we could rule him out as a suspect. Even though my gut was telling me that he wasn't involved, it's always good to dot your i's and cross your t's.

We were directed to the playground where he was conducting a P.E. class. It was a warm morning and we found him leading an exercise session. He had taken his t-shirt off and was wearing trainers and a pair of ridiculous, luminous green short that went out of fashion in the 80s.

Despite his lack of taste in clothes, his tanned torso and well toned body was what probably attracted the mother, I mused.

I had Phil with me again and we stood in his line of vision till he finished a session of star jumps.

'Take over for a minute, Petrus,' he commanded a young lad who started, rather nervously, to direct the class in sit ups. Larry the Louse was hardly out of breath as he came up to us. Bastard.

'How can I help?' he asked.

I explained that we had found a clue and that we wished to obtain a DNA sample from him to rule him out as a suspect. He was a little taken aback, but nodded.

'Just not in front of the kids,' he requested.

After informing the class that he'll only be a minute, Larry the Loin-cloth led us into his office where he, thankfully, put a t-shirt on, then opened his mouth for Phil to take the necessary swab.

As I suspected, his DNA didn't match that found on the hair in the baklava (sorry, I can't help it) so I went back to the case file again. I felt sure we were missing something.

After a good few hours of poring over the file, I was about to give up for a while and look at another case as a distraction when my eye caught something. We had picked up that the boys were leaving a trail of lifted ladies toilet seats, mostly at petrol stations, so we had put out a request to all the garages in the province to report any such prank. I stared at the date of the latest report. It was only a week ago, long after the lad had supposedly been taken by that crocodile.

FIVE

'Let me at least go investigate,' the chief was being an arse, 'look, the toilet seat thing stopped just before the crocodile was supposed to have taken that boy and yet here is a new report. Why would it start again if it wasn't one of the two boys?'

The chief sighed, but fortunately he was too close to retirement to put up much of a fight. He'll probably claim all the credit if anything comes of this, I thought. Still, I was excited. This was the first real breakthrough that we had had since the boy was supposed to have been killed, maybe, just maybe he was still alive.

I decided not to mention anything to the mother and raise hopes that may well be dashed. It was, despite my excitement, a bit of a straw to clutch at and even if my gut was clutching, I had to remain calm and professional.

It was about a two hour drive out to the town, not a large place, it had a petrol station, a road house, a shopping mall, a steak house and a rather seedy hotel which also served as the local strip joint.

I started at the petrol station which had report the prank. They hadn't seen the kid and, other than the toilet seats, there hadn't been anything unusual to report. I decided to stick around the town for the night to see if anything turned up.

One or two people I showed the lad's photo to did seem to take slightly longer than usual looking at it, as though they had seen the face before, but couldn't quite place it with enough confidence to say they had seen him. It may well have been due to the news stories that I was getting this reaction, but I got a sense that it was a more recent memory that the picture was evoking.

By evening though, I was still no closer to confirming that the lad was still alive and had been in town. I had the choice of eating at the hotel and watching the striptease or heading off to try the local steak place.

I'd been in enough strip joints in my time, which I had regarded as a perk of the job when I was younger, but now those sort of places left me depressed so I thought I'd see what culinary delights were to be had at the local steak emporium.

I was distracted, however as I left the hotel by a stunning blonde, who turned up the side road next to the hotel. I wondered if she was one of the performers and, momentarily regretted my decision to go for a steak. Still, I hurried my step and called after her just as she was opening the side door.

'Police, mam,' I said, flashing the badge. 'We're looking for a youngster who we believe was here in the last couple of weeks or so.' I had to get to the point quickly, strippers always think you are out to get them. 'Have you seen him?'

She took the photo and studied it in the light that came from the open door. After a moment, she looked up, then at the photo again.

'This is that boy that was taken by the crocodile isn't it?' she asked.

I nodded and she studied the photo some more.

Eventually she said, 'I can't say for sure, but,' she paused, contemplating whether she should say or not.

'Please, mam, it's very important if you have seen him. His mother has just come out of a coma after being beaten up and she thinks that he is dead. I don't know if you followed the whole story, but the boy ran off when his father was killed and mother beaten. I'm sure that you'll agree the best thing for them is to be reunited.'

Even strippers have maternal instincts.

'I'm not one hundred percent certain, but he does look a bit like James' younger brother. If you give him shorter hair and make him bleach blonde.' She seemed almost reluctant to hand the photo back.

'James?' I asked

'Oh, some loser who I dated briefly. He's a dishwasher at the steak restaurant just up there.'

So steak it was then.

A word of advice, if you ever have something to hide from the police and you see a couple of guys approaching, who look like they could be plain clothes detectives, put down the tray of dishes you're carrying before they get to you and start asking their questions.

It took him a couple of minutes to sweep up what looked like a day's wages worth of broken plates and he was a nervous wreck by the time we managed to get him to sit down and show him the photo. At first he denied seeing the boy, but he was so transparent in his guilt that it only took a tiny bit of leaning on him to get him to talk. Kept calling the lad Sammo, although I'm not sure why.

There was no point in heading out that evening as we would never spot him in the dark, so we enjoyed a very good steak Cordon Bleu and then caught that nice young stripper's act, at my partner's request, I must add.

We headed out at first light, driving slowly and keeping our eyes peeled on either side of the road. The boy was not at the ruined house where the nervous waiter had last seen him, but that was to be expected. I did a rough calculation as to how far he could have walked since then and we slowed down even further when we got to where I thought he might be. We would stop and check under bridges and inside any other abandoned houses we saw, but without success.

Then I saw it. Not an obvious clue and to be honest I did think it was nothing, but the day was still young and we hadn't yet been disheartened into dismissing long shots, which was just as well. There were some strange drag marks in the dirt at the side of the road that led behind a large bush.

We pulled over and I quietly went to go see if there was anything of note behind the bush. I have never, in all my years of service, been faced with a ten year old holding a gun to his head and looking very much like he was about to pull the trigger.

BOOK III

ONE

Geez, don't cops not knowed it are dangerous to skrik a ou when he are trying to commit sewerage pipe. This ou what did of comed round a bush skrikked me so much that I nearly did of shooted myself by accident mistake. Now that would of have been dof. Still I reckon he were as skrikked as what I were.

I didn't not knowed he were a cop then, I only did of finded that out laterer, so I weren't not sure what sort of a ou he were and I did of stopped pointing a gun at my head and did of point it at him real quick like and he were all hands up and everythink, but he were too cool so as I did of thinked even then that maybe he were perhaps a cop cause of on TV cops don't not never get scared none when a ou points a gun at them. Ous what is not cops do of pooh their pants and all, but cops, they do of just talk to a ou with a gun. Most times a ou with a gun do of adventually not shooted, but sometimes on TV a ou with a gun do try and shoot and then they is shooted by a cop or sometimes someone else what are there.

So when a cop do of start talking to me, I have to acide if I are going to try and shooted him, or if I are going to not shooted. I can't not see no one nearby so as they could of shooted if I do of shooted a cop and also a cop don't not got none gun out so as he can't not shooted me none neither. I reckon that maybe I should of shooted this ou.

But then I do of start to listened to what he were charfing me. He did of knowed my name what he did of said a few times. He did of asked if I could put a gun down. He weren't not going to do nothink to me, he charfed, but I don't not believe growed ups none more. They is all liars so as I do of shake my head to charf him that I weren't not putting a gun down for no one.

'Okay,' he charfs, 'can we just talk for a bit?'

I do of think, then I do nodded even though I knowed that cops talking do of make ous put down a gun.

'Mind if I sit?' he do asked me all nice like and I do of nodded again so as he do sit on a rock what are there, then looks at a veldt.

'It's really beautiful round here,' he charfs, checking around. I hadn't not of noticed acause I had of been busy funeraling Shaka, so I don't not say nothink.

He do then check where I had of digged so as to funeral Shaka and I check that he do skrik a bit.

'You been digging, I see,' he charfs, but he are like worried about somethink what I don't knowed what. I is still saying nothink so I do nod and he do nod.

'You burying something?' he do of ask after a bit.

'Ja, I did of funeral Shaka, my dog.' My mouth do of say this afore my brain can charf me to not say nothink. But he do of now check not so worried none more.

'I see. What happened to Shaka?'

'He got donnered by a car. It were Zakes' fault cause of he did of leaved us when he did go in a taxi.' Now that my mouth are working it don't not want to stop.

'So, Zakes left you? Where did he go?'

'Ermelo. He did of goed there to find his grandma and grandpa.' I did of hoped now that a cops what had of caughted me would of also caughted Zakes so as they can take him to a horrible people cause of he were horrible to me and did lefted me ahind.

But a cop didn't not do nothink about Zakes. Then I do of realise he can't not do nothink cause of I is pointing a gun at him. I do of want to charf him to bugger off and leave me alone and go and catch Zakes and take him to a horrible people and all, but afore I can of say nothink, he do charf, 'I know you never threw that ball at Theresa Dern.'

I do of nearly shooted him then, not cause of what he did of said, but acause I were so surprised that he did of sayed it. He were a first growed up what did ever believed me about that.

'Your friend Jaapie told me.' He didn't not check that I had of nearly almost shooted him.

'Jaapie are not my friend,' I charf, but then I do of thinked that Jaapie weren't not my friend none more cause of he didn't not charf that it weren't not me what hitted Theresa bleddy Dern with a ball, but now seen as how he had of charfed this cop ou that it weren't not me what done it, then maybe he could of be my friend again.

'I see,' he charfs. This cop ou do seed a lot.

'Do you want to put that gun down, please? It's making me nervous.'

I do of check a gun and it are like as it are somebody else what are holding it, it are like as if it are not me what are pointing a gun.

'Look, I'll stay sitting here, I promise. It's just that I've got something to tell you and I don't want you getting such a shock that you end up shooting me by mistake.'

I could of have charfed that I don't not shooted people none, but I didn't not want him to of knowed and also, from what my merembery of that night were charfing me, I did of shooted my own pa. I don't not want to shooted this ou, even though he were a cop and all and he were probably going to take me to a horrible people. So, cause I don't want to shooted him, I put a gun down next to me, but not so far away so as I can of picked it up quick like if I do of need to.

A cop do check this out and he do of stop checking so much worried. But he don't not move from where he are sitting and all which are good.

He then do of said, 'Your mother has got better and she want to see you.'

TWO

If there's one thing in life that I never want to do again, it is to talk a ten year old, wild child down, especially from pointing a gun, firstly at his head, and then mine. His time out of parental care had given him a hardened look to the eye and the short cropped, bleached hair made him appear quite threatening.

To be perfectly honest, I did not know for sure that he wouldn't take a pot shot at me, either by accident from me making the wrong move and startling him, or with the malice aforethought that his eyes suggested.

My initial shock at seeing him with the gun to his head was only matched by his shock at seeing me. How he didn't accidently blast his brains out just from the way he jumped when he saw me is anyone's guess.

Despite my fears, I knew that I had to remain calm and, I hope, managed to convey this outwardly, even though I was a mess inside. Looking out over the veldt helped. It was a beautiful place to die, if that was what was to happen, I remember thinking.

Thank goodness for the police training on how to cope with these situations. It seemed to take forever, but in reality it was probably only a minute or two before I finally got him to put the gun down. But then he reached for it again when I told him that his mother wanted to see him.

'My ma are dead.' It was a matter of fact statement that indicated he firmly believed this and I realised that I would have my work cut out to convince him otherwise. He had grown to mistrust adults.

'Why do you say your ma is dead?' I asked, watching him carefully as his hand hovered over the gun.

'Cause of pa donnered her dead.' He then realised that he had implicated his father, but it was too late for him to retract it.

'Did you see your pa beating your ma?' I asked, noting that my partner had moved in around the other side of the bush, his weapon ready. I gave the slightest signal for him to hold his fire.

'Ja. No. I dunno.' He seemed frustrated at his own answer.

'You don't know? What do you remember seeing?'

It was difficult to try and coax the story out of him without prompting in any way and, I realised, I could also upset him and cause him to pick up the gun again.

Instead he decided to surprise me by starting to cry.

'I don't not knowed what to merember. It are different every time I do try. Sometimes it are me what do donner ma and deaded ouma and did shooted pa, and sometimes it are Zakes' brother and the other times ma and ouma and pa are deaded, but I can't not see who it are what deaded them.' He stopped to take a huge gasp of air, drawing in all he could so that he could expel his admission with as much force as he could muster, perhaps hoping to exorcise himself of the burden he had been carrying around with him. 'I think I did of shooted my pa.'

I nearly wept myself then because the anguish of this little lad was so heart wrenching. But I maintained my composure and took the opportunity to move over to him and hug him. He didn't resist, but cried long and hard into my chest, leaving dark tear patches and a shining sliver of snot. The things one does to uphold the law.

I let him cry for a while, patting him gently and saying, 'It's okay, it's okay.'

Eventually, the last shuddering sob left him and he looked at me.

'Are my ma really not dead?' he asked.

'She's not. She was beaten up quite badly and was in a coma, that's like a very long sleep. But she woke up the other day and the doctors say she's going to be okay.'

'And ouma? Are she dead?'

Never lie to youngsters, especially if you need them to trust you. 'I'm afraid she is.'

He nodded, then stared out at the veldt for a while. 'She had very cross veins, you know,' he told the veldt.

'My ouma also had varicose veins.' She didn't, but it was something I thought I could say to help him identify with me.

'And pa and Zakes' brother were shooted too also, weren't they?'

'Yes. Zakes' brother wasn't a good person. He shot your friend David du Plessis' father.'

'Pooh Pants were never my friend,' he said with some venom, as I recalled that according to Jaapie, the du Plessis kid had been the first to point the finger at the young lad in that 'ball throwing' incident. I was caught between cursing myself for the *faux pas*, or laughing at the nick name. I chose the latter.

'Pooh Pants? Why do you call him that?' It was a good call because he relaxed then and laughed too.

'I do of call him Pooh Pants cause of he did pooh his pants when Zakes did of jumped off a third floor there by school.'

'It's a good thing I wasn't there, otherwise you would be calling me Inspector Pooh Pants now.' I laughed again, noting that my partner had sensed that things were going to be okay and had moved quietly out of sight behind the bush, not wanting to cause any complications.

I let the laughter die down and we stared out at the veldt together for a bit.

'Your ma told me that someone else beat her up, and it wasn't your pa,' I said eventually.

The lad nodded, eager to believe me. Then his mood changed quickly.

'And pa? Did she said if I had of shooted pa?'

'She doesn't know if you shot your pa because she had been hit too much.'

His eyes asked the question and I wished I could have told him with certainty, but I knew this was too important to lie about.

'I don't know who shot your pa. It may have been you, but it also may have been the person who beat up your ma. It's my job to find out what happened, but I'm going to need your help. I know you can't remember things too well at the moment, but there are people who can help you to remember properly. Do you want to try?'

He thought for a bit then said, 'If I did of shooted pa, are I in trouble?'

'We'll have to see, but I don't think so.'

I let him digest this, hoping that I was right in that his need to properly recall what had happened would outweigh any fear of punishment if was found to have killed out of revenge rather than self defence.

He took his time deciding, but eventually he said, 'Okay, I will try but I do of want to see my ma first.'

'Of course you can. You ever driven in a police car before?'

His eyes lit up as he shook his head.

'Come on then,' I said and offered him my hand which he took. It was hard to believe that the media had portrayed this kid as some sort of demon child when he was so lamb-like as he took my hand. All he needs is a little love and a grown up he can trust, I thought and hoped like hell he was innocent of shooting his father, even if it had been self defence.

THREE

Cops aren't not so bad. I don't not knowed why I were scared of them afore, then I do of merember that it were Zakes what were scared, not me. This cop ou said I could of call him Inspector Nuts even though that weren't not his real name none, cause of he said he were nuts to of talked to me when I did of have a gun. I did of laughed and charf okay, but it aren't so much fun to called a growed up names what they said I could of called them. But then Inspector Nuts did of charf me that he had spoked to Larry the Lithp, ja, he actually did of charf 'Larry the Lithp', so I reckoned he were cool.

'Don't tell him I call him that, otherwise I'll say I learned the name from you,' he charfed and did of winked at me. I did of nodded to charf him that this were our secret.

Larry were looking after Sally really good, Inspector Nuts did of tolded me and I were happy to of heared this. He were also making sure ma were okay. I weren't not so sure if I were happy to of heared this, but I did of aspose that someone did of had to look after ma seen as how I weren't not there none. I wish I hadn't not of left now cause of ma weren't not dead, but I were proper sure that she had beed donnered dead.

It were lekker being drived in a cop car and Inspector Nuts did of push a button to of make a siren go and all, but only when there weren't not none other cars on a road cause of we didn't not want to skrik people so as they drived off of a road.

Even though I were happy to be going to see ma and Sally, I were still worried about not being able to merember proper like what did of happen. Inspector Nuts charfed that it weren't not pa what did of donner ma so as it must of beed Zakes' brother what did cause of I can't not merember no one else what were in a house.

We did of stop at a Wimpy on a way home and did of had toasted zarms and a milkshake and I were also allowed some chips, but Inspector Nuts didn't not have none cause of he did have a collects-a-roll problem which I did of seed cause of none rolls did of come with his toasted zarm,

It were then a lank long trip what we did of have to take to get back home and I did of goed asleep, but I didn't not dream nothink. When I did of waked up, Inspector Nuts charfed me that we was almost nearly home.

I did of started to worry now cause of I didn't not knowed if ma were going to be cross with me cause of I did of runned away. And maybe even Larry the Lithp would also be cross too also cause of I did leaved Sally with him and all and that maybe he will of maked me do more P.E. Then I did of also worry that Mr de Wit there by a school would of also be cross too and that he would of make me stay in attention after school. That were one nice think about having runned away were that I didn't not of had to go to school. I were going to have to be nice to ma so as she would write a letter to a school what did of said I were sick for a long time.

I did of wondered if Zakes would of have to get his grandparents to write a letter for him too also, but I did of aspose it wouldn't not be easy for him to get from Ermelo to school in time so as maybe he would of go to school there in Ermelo if they did of have got schools there.

Inspector Nuts did of charf that afore I can of go seed ma, that I must of get clean so as we did of goed to his house. It were a nice house what weren't not too different to my house. Mrs Inspector Nuts were there and she did of maked sure I did of wash ahind my ears and everywhere which weren't not so lekker, but she did of kept saying that I did of have to look a bestest for ma, so I aspose it weren't not so bad.

A other cop what were with Inspector Nuts weren't not as cool as him. He did of tried to be nice, but he were only growed up nice where as Inspector Nuts were lightie nice. A other cop were of having coffee in a lounge and talking growed up to Inspector Nuts when Mrs Inspector Nuts did of showed me there. I were wearing some of a clothes what were in my bag that James did of buyed me cause of they weren't not dirty none.

'Looking very smart,' Inspector Nuts did of said and then Mrs Inspector Nuts did of bring some juice and bicscits for me. They were lekker, but I did of want to go seed my ma more an eating bicscits, but acause

175

of he were nice to me, I couldn't not charf Inspector Nuts that. So I did of eated a bicscits and dranked a juice quick like.

Why do growed ups take so lank long to of drink coffee? I were ready to go long afore a cops were finished their coffee so as Mrs Inspector Nuts did of bringed me more juice and bicscits. I did of eated and drinked these more slowerer so as a cops were finished their coffee when I were finished.

'Are Sally going to be there by my ma?' I did of asked when a cops did of stopped talking. I did want to seed her, but didn't not really want Inspector Nuts to of thinked it were important or nothink, so I did of tried to asked in a way what said it weren't not important none, but I do of just want to knowed.

'I'm sure she will be,' Inspector Nuts did of said. 'Are you ready to go?'

Mrs Inspector Nuts did of comed to a door to of said goodbye and she charfed that she did of hoped my ma were betterer soon so as she can of comed home.

A hopstibal weren't not too far from Inspector Nuts' house and we was soon of walking down a long passage to where ma were. I were worried now cause of I did thinked I were going to cry when I did of seed her and Sally and I didn't not want Inspector Nuts to check me crying none.

FOUR

You'd think this job would have made me immune to sentimentality, but I really struggled to hold back the tears when that little tyke let go of my hand to run and hug his sister who came running out to meet him. And then all the tears of the mother when she was reunited with her son.

He seemed quite stoic about it all until I realised that it was my presence that was keeping him from expressing his emotions, so I left the room quietly and waited down the passage. It wasn't long before Larry the Lackey came to convey the mother's thanks, which I interpreted as him also realising that his place, like mine, was not in that room. Not yet for him just yet anyway.

I shared a cup of coffee with Larry the Loose End before we decided that we could join the reunited family. I stayed only long enough to ensure that the lad would be looked after. He was to stay with Larry the

Loco Parentis, something he didn't seem best pleased about, but it was the mother's wishes and I had to respect that. Besides, I had to return home to explain to my wife why she was now called Mrs Inspector Nuts, although I don't think I'll mention the gun.

Before going home though, I rang up the child psychologist we used, explaining the lad's memory problems, or selective amnesia as she liked to put it. She suggested play therapy. As opposed to real therapy? I thought. I hate psychology.

I did wonder how long it would take for this therapy to work, if it was going to work at all. The psychologist wasn't very reassuring on that front. If this, then maybe that, or perhaps. They should call it Maybeology.

Meanwhile, we had the press to deal with. How had we realised that the boy was still alive? How had we found him? What actually happened with the crocodile? (Genius if you ask me). How had he survived? Did he shoot his father? What star sign is he? What colour underwear does he prefer?

Okay, so they didn't ask the last two, but it did feel like they wanted to know every tiny detail. I felt exhausted after the news conference and, if the truth be told, was getting negative vibes from the chief. He had muttered something about being made to look like fools over the crocodile incident and it appeared that he also had a thing for slumbering canines remaining undisturb-ed. Seems he would have been happier if the boy really had been killed. Still, not long now till he retires.

I tried to concentrate on the case again, but was not having much luck. Something was bugging me about it, but I couldn't put my finger on it. This masked intruder was key. We had to find out who it was that had been in the house and, more importantly, were they responsible for the beatings and deaths?

I returned home that evening no further in my investigation. Mrs Inspector Nuts, God bless her, had to put up with me being a bit grumpy at my lack of progress. Even her delicious lasagne only managed to raise a quiet satisfied belch from me. It was while she was dishing the fruit salad that she hit the mail on the head.

'You were really good with that boy today.'

It wasn't so much what she said, but the look that followed. We had not been able to have kids of our own and, due to our hectic lifestyles, had never got round to doing the adoption paperwork necessary to go that route, and now we were a little past the age limit for adopting.

I think that Mrs Inspector Nuts had come to terms with this, but somehow she thought that I never got over the disappoint-ment, despite my assurances that I had.

I gave her my own look as if to say I had not made the connection between her remark and what she really meant, but she saw through me. She always has. Still, she changed the subject slightly asking where the Mrs Inspector Nuts had come from. I chuckled and began explaining, but my mind was still on the lad and the paternal feelings that his presence had stirred up in me. Despite my protests, I suppose I still would have liked a son. Perhaps not one that was as untamed as the young lad, but there was something about him that said there was potential. A bit of love and guidance from a good role model of a father and maybe things would have been different. I had to grudgingly admit that the lad could do a lot worse than having Larry the Latecomer as a step father.

I don't know if my face betrayed any of my thoughts or if my wife was as truthful as me about being at peace with our lack of offspring, but her laughter at my explanation of how she had become Mrs Inspector Nuts was touched with sadness. It could well have been that she was concerned that I had risked my life talking to the boy like I had (I ended up mentioning the gun, I had to didn't I?), but I convinced myself that it was due to the same reason that I felt melancholic.

Neither of us spoke our true feelings over the dinner table, but consoled each other in bed later. I pretended not to hear the slight sob that accompanied her climax, but held her close till I believed she was asleep, then rolled onto my back. I was not going lightly into this night. My mind was buzzing, not only with thoughts about fatherhood, but also about the case and how we could go about finding out who the mystery intruder had been. I stared at the gloomy ceiling.

I must have dozed off for a while before being rudely awoken. A ringing phone at late hours never brings good news, even more so when it's a cop's phone ringing.

FIVE

Larry the Lithp are a big fat woosie. Even a more biggerer woosie as what I did of thinked he were afore. But I will of told you how he did become a king of a woosies now now in a while.

First I do of need to charf yous all about ma and Sally and all. That bleddy Inspector Nuts and Larry the Lithping Woosie did of hanged around there in a room with ma after Sally did of come running out to me. I did of hugged her only cause of she are a girl and girls do of like hugs and all. Also there weren't not no one from school to check except Larry the Lithping Woosie, but he won't not charf nothink cause of growed ups like to check ous hugging girls. They don't not understand that boys aren't not asposed to hug girls.

I hadn't not really believed a cop none about ma being not deaded and all, but cause of I had hoped so much that she weren't, I did of goed with to a hopstibal with him, instead of running away, which I could of have done when I did of go to a toilet there by his house. I did of even put a toilet seat down for Mrs Inspector Nuts cause of she were nice to me.

But ma weren't not deaded. She were there by a hopstibal as a cop ou had of charfed, but even though it weren't not bed time, she were in bed. I did of want to cry when I did of seed her, but I couldn't not when Inspector Nuts and Larry the Lithping Woosie were there, and by a time they did of leaved, I had of forgot that I were asposed to of have cried.

Ma did cry lank. But then she are a girl and girls is asposed to of cry. She also did of hug me lots, but that were okay cause of even though they is girls, ma's is allowed to hug ous, they do of got special permission.

When she had of finished with all her snot and tears and Inspector Nuts and Larry the Woosie King had of left us, she did of asked me what I did of merember of what happened that night.

I didn't not knowed what to charf her cause of I couldn't not merember too proper like as I have of told yous already, and I couldn't not charf her that I did of shooted pa and maybe it were me what donnered her and deaded ouma. So I just charfed her what I had of heard Inspector Nuts charfing a other cop ou.

'I can't not merember too good ma, a cop said that I did of got selected ammonia.'

She did of check me out like I were talking dof, but then I aspose she aren't not a doctor so as she couldn't not of knowed what selected ammonia were. Seen how I also weren't not a doctor, I didn't not knowed as well neither.

Ma didn't not asked me too much more what did of happened that night and she maked me to told her about all a ous what we had of meeted when me and Zakes did of runned away. She did laughed lank about a ou with a false teef, but did of had to stopped quickly cause of where she had beed donnered were hurting. But I did of forgot not to make her laugh and she did of again when I tolded her about Ted with a wife Mildred what weren't not there.

'Serves me right for laughing. Your Oupa with his Alzheimer's are like Ted sometimes, can't not remember who I am sometimes,' ma charfed.

I did of wondered if Ted maybe did of also got Old Timers disease, but didn't charf nothink.

I never did of charf ma nor Sally neither that I did of missed them when I were away. A ou can't not charf that, it do of make him look like a woosie.

Oh ja, talking of woosies, I still do of got to charf yous about how-comewhy Larry the Lithp became a king of all a woosies in a world.

Well, after I had of told ma all about what I had of done, she did of said that I were going to sleep by Larry the Woosie's place. I weren't not too happy, but cause of ma did of look at me like as to say that she did of really wanted me to go there, I didn't not say nothink, but just did of thinked that at least Sally were going to be there too also.

I did of still asked ma if I could of sleep there by her in a hopstibal, but she did of laugh what made her sore again, and did said that a people at a hopstibal wouldn't not let me sleep there. I did of pulled a face at a nurse when she comed to charf us that we did of have to go, but not so as she could seed me. I did of reckon though that Larry the Woosie did of checked me making a face, but seen as how he didn't not say nothink, I schemed that maybe he hadn't not seed me none after all.

Larry the Lithp's place weren't not too bad and he did of gived me and Sally ice cream after supper. I did of reckon he were just doing it so as I would of liked him, but a ou can't not never like a teacher. There weren't not no one else what lived with Larry, so as he did of only have his room and another room what me and Sally did of have to sleep in. I weren't not too chuffed to have to sleep in a same room as Sally and even less chuffeder when, just as we was going to bed, Larry the Woosie did of realise that I didn't not got none pyjamas to sleep in.

'Sleep in your underpants tonight and we will get you some nice new pyjamas tomorrow,' he did of promised.

It didn't not bother me none to sleep in my undies, but I weren't not used to Larry the Lithp being nice to me.

Anyways, we did of adventually go to bed and I did of heard Larry the Woosie washing up a dishes and then he must of have watched some TV, but did of had a sound down low so as I couldn't not hear it too proper like. I were still awake when he did of adventually turn off a TV and a lights and go to bed, cause of I couldn't not sleep proper. There were too much stuff what were in my brain. It were like as I were going to waked up and I hadn't not of seed ma cause of she were really deaded that night, and cause of my merembry weren't not working proper, I did of only amagine that I had of seed her and that I were going to wake up a next morning and ma would of been deaded that night and Larry would of take me and Sally to a horrible people.

So, cause of all these thinks what were in my brain, I couldn't not sleep none and it were probably good cause of if I had of beed asleeped, then me and Sally and maybe even Larry the Woosie may of have been deaded now.

SIX

There were two different stories of what went down at Larry's place. Larry the Lionheart, if his claims are to be believed, singlehandedly fought off the intruder, while the young lad casts him as Larry the Loser who, 'poeped his broeks big time' and 'didn't not do nothink.'

I am probably biased, but I tend to believe the youngster. I was even tempted to check the laundry basket for soiled underwear to prove him right, but 'poeped his broeks' coming from someone who had dubbed a fellow pupil Pooh Pants du Plessis was, I knew, more a figure of speech than a literal interpretation of events.

Larry's recollection of events seemed to me a little rehearsed, like he had worked out a story to explain what had happened, a story that put him in a good light. Also, he didn't seem best pleased when I said that I wanted to interview the young lad about what had transpired. He hadn't banked on that.

'Hasn't he been through enough?' Larry the Lame had said.

I ignored him and interviewed the boy anyway.

For the record, here are the two versions of the events so you can make up your own minds. I will refrain from referring to Mr van Staaden as Larry the Liar so that I don't influence your judgement with my views.

According to Larry, he was just dozing off when he had heard a noise coming from the kids' room. He had gone to investigate and finding someone trying to climb in through the window, grabbed a golf club and swung, causing the intruder to fall back out and run off. Larry the Lightening (for he only strikes once) then checked that the kids were okay before trying to pursue the would be assailant, but the whoever it was had vanished.

The tyke said that he did of – sorry, it's difficult not to fall into his speech patterns if you are around him too much – he heard a noise outside the window and scrambled underneath the bed, dragging his sister and a golf club with him. 'It weren't not the right kind of noise,' he said when I asked him how he knew it wasn't Mr van Staaden. The person that had come into the room was wearing 'a pulled down beanie with holes for eyes', also known as a baklava in some circles. The intruder was just looking around when 'Larry the Big Fat Woosie' opened the door. Larry took one look at the intruder and started crying, 'please don't shoot' and was 'hands up and all' and was 'poeping his broeks big time'. That was when the young lad 'donnered' the intruder 'one shot in his sins'. I took the latter to be shins given the angle from which he would have been striking, it was too painful to think that he meant anything else.

The intruder got away as the young lad checked on his sister, then persuaded Larry to 'stop poeping your broeks and call Inspector Nuts.'

The common thread in the two stories is that there had been a masked intruder in the kid's room who had been frightened off by a blow from a golf club. Who delivered the blow and who poeped their broeks is still up for debate. One thing that was clear to me was that the return of the lad, which had been all over the news, had frightened someone, most likely the intruder in the initial crime, enough to make an attempt to keep the kid quiet. It was too much of a coincidence for it to have been a random house breaking.

I arranged for the house to be put under police guard and returned home to Mrs Inspector Nuts and to stare at the bedroom ceiling for the rest of the night.

By my third cup of coffee the next morning, I had resolved that I couldn't wait for the child psychologist and her play therapy. The kid was in danger as long as the intruder was at large so we needed to find him and fast.

There had been no match found in our databases to the DNA on the hair we extracted from the balaclava, but it had confirmed that we were looking for a male.

I decided to risk it and take the lad back to the crime scene in the hopes that it would trigger his memory and lead us to the killer.

I called ahead to the officer outside the house to make sure that all was okay, then headed over there. Larry the Late was in a tizz, wolfing down toast and trying to get the kids ready for school. Obviously not a trained parent. I informed him that the boy was needed for the investigation and that he had his psychologists appointment that afternoon so would not be going to school. Larry seemed relieved and the boy nearly hugged me on the spot. I didn't let Larry know what I planned to do, but told him that I would look after the lad for the day.

I took him to the station first so that I had some time to prime him on what my plan was. He seemed in two minds, wanting to try and remember things properly, but nervous as to what memories the visit may stir up, although he did do his best to disguise this with a brave face. I must admit I was nervous too as we set out in the car.

SEVEN

A house did of smelled like when you do of come back from holiday and, I aspose I had sort of beed on a holiday cause of I weren't not going to school none. I do of wished Inspector Nuts were my pa cause of he hadn't not never donnered me none, and cause of he didn't not make me go to school with Larry the Big Fat Woosie.

Inspector Nuts had of charfed that if I do goed back to a house, then maybe I might of merember what did of happen that night. I really did wanted to merember proper like acause it were bugging me lank that I can't not. Also I could of check that ma did of really want me to merember too also cause of I reckon that she were donnered so much that she don't not merember nothink herself.

Inspector Nuts did of also charf that I mustn't not feel none pressure cause of if I did of worry too much, my brain will of be so busy worrying that it did got none energy left to merember thinks with, so I do of try not to think of ma.

'Okay, now just relax. Close your eyes if you want and just let your thoughts flow,' Inspector Nuts do of charf.

I don't not want to close my eyes none cause of I reckon I would of look dof standing there like that. Asides which, I do of already had started meremboring thinks afore Inspector Nuts did of even charfed nothink.

'A ambalance what I did of checked, weren't not for ma, it didn't not of stopped by a house, it did of just drived past.' I do charf and I can of almost check a flashing red lights and all what do of go by, in my brain like.

'That's good,' Inspector Nuts charfs, 'There was an ambulance, but it was taking the policeman that Zakes' brother shot, to hospital.'

183

'Zakes' brother were here also too,' I do of merember now and do feel like it are a right merembery. 'I did checked him in a street when I were coming home and all. He were shooted and I could of checked a blood what were coming from his soldier. I didn't not seed him at first cause of he were hiding ahind a bushes over there.' I do of point out a window at a bushes what are near a end of a road.

'He did of skrik me big time I nearly did of pooh...I did of jumped.' I don't not want Inspector Nuts calling me Pooh Pants, but he don't not seemed too worried about my pants and what did of happened in them. He do of just nods and smile like so as I could of go on merembering.

'He did of asked me to help him, but I couldn't not heared him too good. He were talking like pa do of talked sometimes when he had of drinked too much lank whiskey, you know like when a ou do of talk like he do got too much spit in his mouth?'

'Slurring?' Inspector Nuts do of charf.

'Ja, he were slurping his words, but he hadn't not of been drinking none whiskey cause of I couldn't not smell it none.' I are now wondering if my merembery are working proper like.

'No, that's quite possible. If he had lost a lot of blood from his wounds, he may well have been, er...slurping his words.'

I check out Inspector Nuts now cause of I reckon that maybe he are just saying this so as to make me think I are merembering proper like, but then a other cop ou what are there do of also nods like as if Inspector Nuts is right and all and he aren't not even not checking me out, so I scheme that maybe Inspector Nuts weren't not just saying this.

'What happened next?'

I do of closed my eyes now, even if it do of make me check dof, but it do help.

'Zakes' brother are like bleeding and all so as I can't not take him through a front door cause of ma will of have a cadenza. She do of normally have a fit if me or Sally do of cut ourselves so as we do bleeded and there were so much blood on Zakes' brother so as I reckon she would of have freaked out big time if she had of seed it.'

My merembery are starting to work lank good now, but I are getting scared cause of a thinks what I are merembering. I don't not want to tell Inspector Nuts what I did of seed when I did gotted home with Zakes' brother, asides, I are still not sure if this are proper merembering or not, so I do of just start charfing that I can't not merember too good.

'Come, let's go outside to where you were with Zakes' brother. That may help,' Inspector Nuts charfs and we do all of us go out into a street.

He are right, cause of standing in a street I do of merember proper like what I did of check afore I did of taked Zakes' brother inside.

'Anything?' Inspector Nuts do asks. I reckon that he can of check that I are meremembering thinks proper. 'What is it? You must tell me whatever you remember, any little detail may help. You do want to help don't you?'

He are sneaky, old Inspector Nuts. He does of knowed that I don't not want to charf him what I can of merember. Growed ups, they are all bleddy sneaky. Still, I *do* of want to help and all, so I nod and take a big breath afore I charf him what I can check in my brain that did of happened.

'I were coming back to a house with Zakes' brother and when we was here, I do of check Larry the Big Woo...Larry the Lithp coming out of a yard quick like and he are busy putting his shirt on. He and ma must of been doing it, like I did of sawed then do once.' I then do laugh. Not cause of it are funny or nothink, but cause of I never did of have charfed 'doing it' to a growed up afore.

Meanwhile, old Inspector Nuts and a other cop ou are like checking at each other like what growed ups do when they do of knowed somethink what they don't not want to charf a lighties. So I do of stopped laughing now and do quickly charf that I did of hided in a bushes with Zakes' brother so as Larry can't not check us none. I is hoping like mad now that I didn't not of got Larry into none trouble cause of I knowed ma do of like him and all and I don't not want to upset ma.

When I do of stopped laughing and start charfing about Larry, then Inspector Nuts do nod so as I must go on.

'When Larry were gone, then I did of take Zakes' brother round a back of a house to my bedroom window and I did of charf him to wait there.'

We do of all walk round a house now to there by my window. I is checking all what happened clear like in my brain now. 'Zakes' brother were like nearly falling over and all, but I did of lefted him there and goed inside.

'Okay, let's go inside then.'

I do of follow Inspector Nuts into a house again.

'Pa were donnering...' I did of thinked that maybe I shouldn't not of charfed this, but then I merember that pa are deaded so as he can't not donner no one none more. 'Pa were donnering ma in a lounge which did of meant that I could of goed to my room and let Zakes' brother inside without not no one seeing me none, so I did of goed into my room.'

We do all now goed into my room. It do of smell really funny, then suddenly I merember that I did of left a peanut butter zarm in my undies drawer, but I don't not feel lus for it now cause of my room do of smell like vrot peanut butter.

'What is that smell?' A other cop ou do of charf and he are pulling a face what do says that he don't not like a smell none. I do of laugh cause of I knowed what it are.

I go to my cupboard and pick up some undies to of showed him but, instead of my zarm, there are a funny green think what do of stick to my undies. Inspector Nuts and a other cop ou do of check really skeef at this and I'm like wondering what did of happened to my zarm.

'Looks like a rather old sandwich,' a other cop ou charfs and do of hold his nose.

I check out a green think and it do of actually check like a zarm accept that it are green.

'I did of leaved a peanut butter zarm here, I charf and start to of look more for it, but Inspector Nuts do of stop me.

'I'm afraid that your peanut butter zarm is...um...deaded,' he do of charf.

I check him out, then a green think, then him again. He are not joking.

'Is that what do of happen to zarms what go deaded?' I asks.

Inspector Nuts do of nods, 'I'm afraid so.'

I do of thinks for a bit, then asks, 'Did pa have of gone all green like this when he were deaded?'

Now they do of really look at each other skeef and Inspector Nuts do of charf, 'Come on, we need to get on with what happened that night.'

Growed ups. They don't not knowed what are and aren't not important. I is still checking out my deaded zarm.

But then Inspector Nuts do go, 'I'll get Mrs Inspector Nuts to make you a nice fresh peanut butter zarm when we're finished okay?' Maybe growed ups aren't not as dof as what I did of thinked.

A other cop ou do of take a deaded zarm from me, but do of check like I were giving him a fresh egg zarm cause of his face are all like, 'I don't not want to touch *that* none.'

I check round a room now and start to try and merember again.

'I did of let Zakes' brother in through a window. It were difficult cause of he weren't not trying too hard to get in. I could of still heared pa shouting at ma in a lounge. I do of think I merembered wrong in that he weren't not donnering ma when I did of comed in a house. He were only shouting then. He did of only donnered her laterer. Ja, he were only shouting up till now.

I do check round my room and it are like as I can of almost check Zakes' brother there on a bed with a blood on his soldier and all and I can of almost heared pa shouting. I merember going to get a plaster and that were when I did heared pa donner ma. I are standing outside a bathroom with Inspector Nuts and a other cop ou and we is going back to my room, but I do of stop now like what I did of do that night cause of a sound what pa did maked when he hit ma weren't like a normal slapping sound and also I couldn't not heared ma crying like she normally did of done. I is not liking this merembery aspecially as it are now like it are all actually happening again.

'What is it, son?' Inspector Nuts asks even though I are not his son.

I don't not want to tell him and do of nearly go on walking into my room and charf, 'No, nothink,' but then I do of member that I must charf him everythink otherwise I is not helping.

'When pa donnered ma, I were standing here. It were like one shot what he donnered her and then there were no noise. Ma did of normally cry when pa donnered her, not that she were a woosie or nothink cause of pa could donner real sore, but she didn't not even cry this time. That were when I did of knowed that somethink weren't not right.'

All my merembering are coming back big time now. It weren't like when I were runned away, those were meremberies like dreams, this were real meremberies.

'I did of goed quickly to stick a plasters on Zakes' brother so as I could of go check to see if ma were okay. He didn't even charf nothink, not even thank you when I did of plaster him, but it did check as if he were sleeping so as I aspose it were okay.'

We don't not go back to my room to put a plaster on Zakes' brother now cause of I want to go quick like to a lounge afore my merembery do goes away again.

'Ma were lying on a floor and pa were standing over her and checking her out.'

We is now all in a lounge and Inspector Nuts and a other cop ou are checking out where ma were lying on a floor.

'Pa did of check like he were crying and all which did of skrik me cause of I did of never seed pa cry afore. He didn't not heared me come in a lounge and I did of stay really quiet. He were charfing my ma that he were sorry. That were when ouma did of come in. I think she must of have been in a kitchen cause of she did of like being there.

'She do of start shouting at pa and donnering him, but cause she did of got very cross veins, she can't not donner him so as he would of notice. So he just did of stand there letting her donner him, then all of a sudden like, he do of push her over and leave. He didn't even not seed me standing there by a door. Ouma did of fall over proper like when pa did of pushed her.'

I check round a lounge cause of in my merembery now, Ouma do of stand up after pa did of pushed her! This did never of happened afore. It were either me or pa in my merembery what had of pushed her and she did of never stood up again. But not she were stooding up in what did of feeled like a proper correct merembery.

I check at Inspector Nuts like as he could of helped, but he weren't not there that night, he can't not merember for me. He do of just nods like for me to go on, so I charf him what I had of merembered.

'Ouma were there helping ma. She weren't not deaded neither. Pa didn't of deaded ouma or ma.' This were news to me. I had of thinked it were pa what did of deaded them, now I are like really worried that it are me what did, but just as I are thinking this, I do of merember more and this do of skrik me somethink chronic cause of I knowed it are really a proper merembery and I knowed who did of donnered my ma and deaded ouma. But I can't not charf Inspector Nuts what I do of merember now, it would of cause much too much kak.

EIGHT

The poor tyke was so emotionally drained afterwards that he fell asleep with his peanut butter sandwich in his hand. Fortunately I caught it before it fell on Mrs Inspector Nuts' nice clean sofa.

Two things were worrying me about what the lad did, or didn't, remember. Firstly, had Larry the Lecherous really been there 'doing it' with the mother just before everything kicked off. If so, how much of the horror did his being there precipitate? It certainly seemed like he had been caught in the act and that the husband had punished the mother for her infidelity. But why hadn't he admitted to any of this?

Secondly, I think the lad remembered more than he let on. He started acting all strange just after the bit about his grandmother helping his mother up. He started crying, fake tears if ever I saw any, and saying he 'couldn't not merember nothing none more.'

Something that he remembered frightened him and he doesn't want to say what. Perhaps the psychologist will have some luck getting him to talk about it, that is if I haven't already totally messed things up by taking him back to the house.

I let him sleep till just before his appointment with the psychologist, then woke him with a fresh peanut butter sandwich which he wolfed down. There was something in his eyes when we arrived at the psychologist's office. Not reticence, it was stronger than that, almost fear, but not quite. I had to reassure him a few times before he went off with her while I waited in the reception room. I hate psychologist's reception rooms, they make me feel like I should be there for my own sake.

While waiting, I arranged to have Larry brought to the station so I could question him once we got back. Then I tried to relax while paging through an old magazine.

'There's a lot going on in his young mind. I can't give you all the details as you're not his guardian. I will say that you're going to struggle to get him to open up about that night. He seems to have remembered it all now,' the psychologist gave me a look when she said this, 'but whatever happened, he doesn't want people to know. I suggest you don't ask him too much about it, he'll just clam up more. Give him some space and he might tell you of his own accord.'

Space, schmace. This psychologist reminded me of my mum, but I couldn't tell her that, she'd set Freud on me.

The lad was pretty quiet in the car on the way back to the station, introspective, to use a slightly more psychological term. I didn't tell him that Larry was going to be there, I wanted to see the lad's reaction to The Lithp now that he had his memory back.

I had been expecting him to shy away from Larry the Love 'em and Leave 'em, suspecting that what the lad didn't want to remember had something to do with his mum's lover. But he seemed indifferent to Larry's presence and did seem a bit concerned when I said that I needed to ask Larry a few questions before they went home.

'He are not in none trouble, are he?' he asked, his young brow furrowing.

'No,' I lied, then feeling like I had been seen through, added, 'I don't think so.'

I left the lad and his sister, whom Larry had brought with, in the capable hands of a colleague and ushered Larry into an interview room. He looked nervous. And so he should have, the lying bastard.

'So, Mr van Staaden, please tell me exactly where you were the night of the murders. I'd like a full account of your movements.' I went in hard, annoyed at him for having withheld information.

It worked. He was a jabbering wreck within moments, thus reinforcing my view that it was the lad who dealt with the intruder.

Yes, he had been round the house just before it all happened. Yes, he had been in bed with the mother. Yes, the husband had come home early and caught them in bed together, but he already knew about the affair. No, he hadn't been threatened, just told to get out. Yes, he knew the husband was abusive. Yes, he was ashamed that he had deserted her, knowing that she would probably be beaten.

He broke down at this point and I couldn't find it within myself to even offer him a glass of water. I let him cry for a second or two, then pushed on.

'Did you see anybody else at the house?'

'No.'

'You sure?'

'No, it was just me and her.'

'What about her mother?'

'She was out. Visiting her husband, he's in care, but we knew she would be home soon. We were just...' he blushed and looked away.

'Just what?'

He shook his head.

'Just what damn it!' I hit the table hard. I always loved seeing the cops on TV do this and I know why they do, because it works. As the young lad would have said, 'Larry became Pooh Pants van Staaden.'

'We were just having a quickie.'

It was difficult not to laugh at Larry the Loser, but I kept my tough cop face on.

'We knew ouma would be home soon, and that the kids would be as well, but, well, you know how it is sometimes, you get passionate and you can't stop.'

He looked up, a male appealing to the understanding of another male and I wanted to nod and say, Oh, yes, I understand very well, I've been there often enough myself.' Instead, I just asked again, but in a slightly gentler tone, 'And you're sure there was no one else there?'

He shook his head. 'It was only the two of us till he came home. If there was someone else in the house, I wasn't aware of it.'

Did you check the cupboard in the bedroom? I nearly lost it as the thought flashed into my head, but managed to keep a straight face.

'So you just ran?'

'Yes, grabbed my clothes and got out of there.'

The hurried exit described by the kid seemed to tie in with what he was saying. It is unlikely that he would have been dressing himself as he left if he had been busy killing the father and grandmother.

'Anything else you might have forgotten to mention to us?' I just wanted him out of my sight now.

'No, I went home, hoping that she would call me later. It was only when Sally arrived on my doorstep that I knew something was wrong.'

The two kids were drawing on the back of some charge forms when I brought Larry to them. They didn't seem that interested in seeing him, but more importantly, neither showed any signs of being afraid of him, but the lad did seem pleased to see me.

I guess that my rapport with her brother was what gave Sally the courage to talk to me. Until then, she had been very reticent to communicate, but as I was walking them out the station, she tugged on my hand. I had to bend over to hear her because it was almost a whisper.

'Inspector Nuts, howcomewhy did of Theresa's pa donner ma?'

NINE

Bleddy girls! They is so stupid and all. Don't Sally not of merembered how much kak I were in when I did of said that Mr Dern did hitted me. Mr de Wit, Larry the Lithp and even old Miss Smit were all lank cross with me, although Miss Smit being cross did only meaned that she did of shake her head at me.

Still, I did of learned my lesson. You don't not charf no one it were Mr Dern what did of done somethink bad, even if this time he had of. It were while me and Inspector Nuts were there by a house that I did of have a proper merembery of seeing who did of donner ma. But you checked that I didn't not charf nobody cause of I knowed what happens. Maybe it were acause that she were a girl that Sally didn't not of thinked that she would get into none trouble for charfing Inspector Nuts what Mr Dern did of done. Girls never get into none kak.

After pa had of left, ouma were helping ma to stand up, I don't not knowed why I couldn't not merember this afore, but anyways, ouma helped ma up and then that were when I did of seed him. I didn't not knowed it were him straight away cause of he were wearing all black clothes and all, and did of had a beanie on his head what were pulled down over his face with just some holes for his eyes so as he can of seed.

This ou what were all in black had of been standing ahind a curtains, but I did of seed him stick his head out a little. Ouma did of also check him and she did of screamed which maked a ou skrik so as he did runned out from ahind a curtain and did of pushed ouma so as she did falled. This time she didn't not get up like what I were merembering afore. Even though ma weren't so lekker after pa did of donner her, she did of try to donner this ou in black.

That were when he did of donner ma somethink chronic so as I thought that she were deaded. I were just checking all this through a door what weren't not opened so proper so as a ou in black couldn't not seed me none. I did of wanted to go help ma, but had of learned that you don't not stop a growed up donnering another growed up unless you do wanted to get donnered good and proper yourself. I did of learned that from pa.

So I did of just goed to Sally's room to of seed if she were there. She had of gone to see oupa with ouma, so she were back now and were playing with her dolls, but she were also crying cause of she could heared ma being donnered.

I did of told her not to cry and that ma would of be okay cause ma were used to be donnered, but she weren't not too happy still. So when we did of heared that ma weren't not crying none more, we both went back to check through a door of a lounge. That were when we checked Mr Dern. He had of taked off a beanie and he did of kicked ma who were lying on a floor. I were now scared that he would of come donner me too also, cause of I did have of said that he donnered me after Theresa got hitted with a ball, so as I took Sally, really quiet like to her room and did of charf her not to never tell no one what she had of sawed.

We did of then heared Mr Dern walk down a passage so as I did of grab Sally and me and her did hided under her bed and we was just in time afore he opened a door to her room. All we could of check were his black shoes and his pants up to his knees cause of we were hiding and couldn't not check him proper like. He didn't not stand there for too long afore we did of heared him go to my room. I wished I had of been there to of seed his face cause of all I did of heard were Zakes' brother what did charf, 'Hey boss, I wouldn't come any closer if I were you.'

I could of almost heared Mr Dern poeping his broeks then. I merember thinking that I were going to charf Theresa at school a next day that her pa were a big fat pooh pants. And I would of have done accept that I didn't not goed to school again after that night. And also even if I had of goed to school, I wouldn't not of merembered it all so lekker anyways cause of it weren't till I did of adventually get home just now that I did of even merember that Mr Dern were there by a house.

Mr Dern were like, 'Don't shoot, don't shoot,' and all and I were wondering howcomewhy Zakes' brother didn't not shoot him. I would of have done even if just to shut him up.

I do want to go and check what were happening, but is also worried for Sally cause of I didn't not trust Mr Dern to not donner her if he did of seed her, so as we did of just stayed under a bed.

Then it did of sounded like Mr Dern and Zakes' brother were fighting and it weren't long afore there were a bang. I did of thinked that Zakes' brother had of shooted Mr Dern and did of charf Sally to stay under a bed while I do go check what had of have happened.

It didn't not check lekker. Mr Dern were standing with pa's gun pointed at Zakes' brother who I do of reckon were proper deaded now cause of he weren't not moving or nothink. I did of skrik big time, but not as big as what Mr Dern did of skrik when he did of first check Zakes' brother cause I aren't not a big fat woosie like what he are.

So I did of skrik without not poohing my pants, even more when Mr Dern did of turned around and seed me. I do of reckon now that he would of have shooted me too also if pa hadn't not of comed home then.

Mr Dern skrikked a huge big time then so as he did of pushed me out of a way and I did of falled down, but it weren't not too sore like and I did of check him put on his beanie afore he did of runned down a passage. I aspose he didn't not want pa to of checked who he are, but that didn't matter none cause of as he did runned out of a house, he did of shooted pa.

TEN

Adrian Bloody Dern. Why, oh why did it have to be him? Why not Larry the Lithp, or even that weedy headmaster de Wit? No, she had to go and point the finger at Dern.

I could tell straight away from the look on the tyke's face that she hadn't made that up. This was what he had remembered and wasn't prepared to talk about and I now understood why he had been reluctant to say anything. He must have felt that no one would believe him after what happened last time.

When pushed, he had reluctantly confirmed Sally's story while I was busy giving myself a darn good mental kicking up the backside for not questioning Sally at the time. That's the problem with small people, out of sight, out of mind. I guess that's how the young lad managed to stay uncaught the whole time he was on the run, he was too small to be noticed.

I let them go with Larry and warned them not to breathe a word of this to anyone, I would sort it all out. I sent a uniform along with them. Despite Larry the Lifeguard insisting that they would be okay, I was pretty sure that the attack last night was by the same masked figure of that fateful night and that masked figure was a certain Adrian Dern. My detective brain said that he was desperate to shut the kid up and would most certainly make another attempt.

I checked a few things which helped get the search warrant, then headed off to the Dern Estate. Okay, estate is a bit over the top, they're rich, they have a big house, and I'm not bitter.

He was not best pleased to see us. Nervous is a word I would use, but he's one of those guys who works on the 'attack is the best form of defence' principle. He started by asking if we had come to tell him that we had charged the kid with killing his father and that black tsotsi.

Our reply was, 'No, but we do have a warrant to search your place.'

Boy, did he hit the roof then. How dare we accuse him of anything? His family had been the victims of that horrid child. First his vicious attack on their precious Theresa, then the slanderous accusations against him. And now more slanderous accusations. Was it that kid again? He would see to it that I never worked in this town again. On and on he went.

I waited till he stopped to draw breath, then asked if he had called the father the afternoon of the murders.

Having a kniption fit like he had just had tends to bring a lot of blood to the face. My question had a rapid opposite effect.

'No.' But his voice was no longer angry and confident.

'Gosh,' I said, looking at the papers I had brought with me, 'these phone records can be very slanderous sometimes.'

He wasn't keen on sarcasm.

'Okay, so I called him. So what?'

'May I ask what you called him about?' Some arrogance returned to his face.

'I heard that his dirty slut of a wife...' and here Mrs Dern who was standing next to him tutted, only to be shut up quickly by a deadly glance.

'...that dirty slut of a wife,' now with more venom, 'was sleeping with one of the teachers.'

'And you felt it was your duty to inform him of this?'

'Yes.'

Mentally punching someone for smugness is not police brutality.

'Mr Dern, were you aware that he had a history of violence towards his wife?'

'No.'

Mentally punching someone for lying is not police brutality.

'But daddy, I told you that was why he hit me with the cricket ball, because his dad hits his mum, he thinks it's okay to hit girls.'

Mentally kissing Theresa Dern for saying the right thing at the right time is not paedophilic, glancing at your daughter as if you mentally want to slap her is not child abuse, well not something that would stand up in court, but it does lend an air of guilt to a person.

'I'd...I'd heard rumour to that extent, but that's their problem.'

'You didn't stop to think that perhaps by making that call, you were endangering the life of his wife. You didn't think that he would beat her to a pulp.'

Dern faltered only slightly, then repeated, 'That is their problem. All I know is that if my wife was cheating on me, I'd like to know about it. It's not my fault he nearly killed her.'

'But that's where you are wrong, Mr Dern. He didn't beat her, nor did he push his mother-in-law over and kill her. You see, I have a theory. I believe that you were so enraged by the accusation the kid made that you wanted revenge. You knew the father was the violent type and when you heard about the affair, you thought you had a way of getting back at the kid. You rang up the father and told him of the affair, then, wanting to see the fruits of your revenge first hand, broke into their place and hid behind the curtains in the lounge.

'You were disappointed when the father only punched his wife once and then left. But before you could do anything, the grandmother saw you and you panicked. You pushed her over, she hit her head on the coffee table and that killed her. You then had to deal with the wife, viciously beating her and leaving her for dead, hoping that it would be blamed on her husband.

'Then you went after the kid, again thinking it would look like the father did it, but instead you found that tsotsi in his room and, I allow you this, killed him in self defence, or should I rather say, finished him off in self defence as he was pretty far gone anyway. But the kid saw you shooting the tsotsi and you couldn't leave him as a witness. Unfortunately for you, the father came home just as you tried to silence the kid, so you ended up shooting the father as you fled.'

He shook his head to each accusation.

'Where were you the night of the murders?'

'At home with my wife.' He glanced over at her quickly.

'And she will vouch for you in court?'

'Of course,' he smiled, and she nodded her consent even if it appeared somewhat reluctantly.

'Tsk! Tsk!' I tutted pretending to consult my notebook. 'Perjury is a crime, do you know that, Mrs Dern. Before you officially support your husband's contention I should let you know that I have statements from at least eight women in your bridge club attesting to the fact that you were with them that night for a time period covering at least an hour before and after the murders.' I looked back at Mr Dern as I concluded.

Smug to mug in 0.3 seconds. I love it when I'm a step ahead of the bad guys.

I let him digest the news, then said, 'Oh, and talking of perjury, perhaps your daughter would like to tell you the truth about being hit on the playground, bear in mind Theresa, I've heard a different story to yours from a lot of your classmates.'

With a bit of coaxing from her mother, Theresa soon admitted that the young lad had never thrown the ball at her, but she hated him, 'he was poor and smelly and horrible.'

I left Dern staring at his daughter and went to liaise with my colleagues on what they had discovered during their search. I was feeling slightly nauseous that all this violence had been triggered by a petty playground prejudice.

ELEVEN

Larry the Lithp wouldn't not of leaved me alone with Sally so as I could of charfed her to be careful what she do of told growed up. You can't not trust them, but Sally are too small to knowed this so as I weren't not too cross with her, she were a girl and just needed to be learned proper like.

I were poeping my broeks that Theresa's pa were now going to come and donner Sally cause of she did charf it were him what did of hitted ma. I had of seed what he done when I did charf that he did donner me and my brain were now telling me that it were Mr Dern what had of comed into a house last night and what I had to have donnered with a golf club to of frighten him away and my brain were also charfing me that he were going to of come back again. Larry were useless to fight so as I were trying to make plans what to do.

Inspector Nuts did of charf that he would sort Mr Dern out. I do of wished me and Sally were staying there by him rather an by Larry, but ma did of wanted us to stay with Larry so we was.

I reckon maybe ma wants Larry to be our new pa cause of our old pa are deaded. I aspose Larry are betterer as my old pa cause of he hasn't not donnered me or Sally or ma neither, but I don't not charf nobody nothink about what I do of thinked, not even Sally.

Larry did of maked us cheesy tomato zarms. I would of affered peanut butter, but I didn't not mind cheesy tomato that much. At least they weren't not egg. He did of also gived us coke to drink which were cool. All a time he were talking and charfing us that everythink were okay and that ma would of beed home soon and we must maybe make a big poster to charf 'Welcome Home Ma' and maybe we could get a cake and chips and have a party and we will all of us have to look after her cause of she will be still sore and he didn't not stop talking none.

What he were saying were nice and all, but anyone could of check that he were poeping his broeks big time. He didn't not once charf nothink about Mr Dern donnering ma. I knowed Inspector Nuts had of charfed us not to tell nobody, but I is not dof like Larry cause of I knowed that seen how me and Sally and Larry all did of knowed, Inspector Nuts didn't not mean we can't not charf each other nothink. But seen how Larry weren't charfing nothink, I didn't not neither.

It did of seem as Larry thinked that if he did of stopped talking about ma, then Mr Dern would rock up with his beanie and all and want to donner us.

We had of just started drawing a poster to charf ma welcome home and which Sally were doing really nice like cause of she can of draw lekker, when Inspector Nuts did of phoned.

Larry were all serious like on a phone and did of even call Inspector Nuts 'thir' which were lank funny cause of Inspector Nuts aren't not a teacher and Larry are one. Anyways, after he had of finished on a phone, he did of checked not so skrikked. He did of sit down on a floor where were were still drawing a poster and charfed us that a cops had of put Mr Dern into custard. At first I did of thinked that it weren't not fair cause of I didn't not donner Theresa and I did of get into kak. Mr Dern did of donner ma and he do got custard. But then as Larry did of talked more it do sounded like as Mr Dern were in chookie, not in custard.

That did of maked me feel less skrikked cause of if he were in chookie, he can't not come and donner me and Sally none. Larry do of also charf us that Inspector Nuts had of got edivince to of keep Mr Dern in chookie forever.

'I thtill can't believe it,' Larry do of charfed and it were like as he weren't not actually talking to Sally and me, 'Adrian Dern. I would never have though him capable of it. Murdering your ouma and father like that and beating your poor mother.'

There were somethink not right in what Larry did of said, but I didn't not charf him nothink, and Sally...I do of actually thinked that Sally did of got Selected Ammonia like what I did of had cause of she don't charf nothink neither. I aspose it could of beed maybe that she had of now learned when to stay schtum.

TWELVE

We had our man. Dern had no alibi and had made things worse by lying about being at home. The neat bruise across his shins matched the golf club from that belonging to Larry the Low Handicap, proving that Dern was guilty of the recent attempted attack on the lad. Then there were the gloves that the forensic guys unearthed at his house. They had gunshot residue on them and the lab crew matched the thread that we had found caught in the trigger of the murder weapon to them.

The *coup de gras* was the hair in the baklava, sorry balaclava. The DNA from that matched Dern.

When confronted with all this evidence, he broke down and confessed, almost arrogantly, as though he had done the world a favour getting rid of some 'white trash' as he referred to them.

But he didn't confess to everything. Yes, he had called the father. Yes, he had gone to the house to see the fall out. Yes, he was disappointed that the father didn't do more damage so had done that himself. The grandmother was an accident, he hadn't meant to kill her. She had surprised him and he only wanted to push her out the way. The wounded gangster was self defence. When Dern had gone into the room, he had been confronted with a gun. But Zakes' brother had been weak and dropped his guard. A struggle ensued and 'bang', one dead tsotsi. I didn't think that the prosecution would even raise a charge on that one.

He did, however, deny shooting the father. At first I thought it was a bit strange given that he seemed relieved to finally confess to all his crimes, then the obvious struck me. Murdering the father was the most serious of all the allegations against him. He would get done for assault on the mother and at best culpable homicide for the grandmother, but the father, that was murder.

The Public Prosecutor thought we had a strong case and could get a conviction without having to call the kids to the stand which I was rather relieved about. Despite his 'not guilty' plea and a vigorous fight against the murder charges, Dern was convicted and they put him away from a long, long time.

It was about a week after the arrest that I got the call from the lad.

'No, Inspector Nuts, Larry did of said I were allowed to use a phone to called yous.' He sounded insulted that I thought he would do anything he wasn't supposed to and I even felt a little guilty of accusing him.

'We is having a party cause of ma are coming home.'

'Yes?'

'And Larry did of said that I can invited my friends.'

'Yes?' I wasn't too sure where this was leading.

'And since you is a only friend what I do of got, I do of wanted to invite yous. Oh and Mrs Inspector Nuts too also.'

I realised then how much I missed the lad since we had resolved the case, but all I could do was swallow hard and say that I would be delighted to attend.

'Um, that are good, Inspector Nuts, but is you going to come?'

'Of course I'll be there,' I assured him and chuckled quietly to myself.

The next day, Larry visited me at the station and I realised then that the lad was in good hands. He may not be brilliant at fending off intruders, but Larry the Likeable endeared himself to me in that little conversation and I set about tying up the loose end he reminded me about.

THIRTEEN

I aspose Larry weren't not too bad as a pa. At first I didn't not like it so much there, aspecially when he did of maked me go to school again. But apart from that he were okay, and he did of never once donner me nor Sally neither. And he did of taked us to see ma every day and I could check that ma did of really liked him lots and if he were okay by ma, then he were mostly okay by me.

School were a bit weird. Some ous were like suddenly all friends with me and everythink. Miss Smit were even nearly crying like and all and Mr de Wit did of say a special welcome back for me in assembly which made everyone check me out and all which, even though it did of maked me shy, did of also maked me to feel special.

Cause of all a teachers were lank nice to me, I didn't not cause none trouble or nothink. If only growed ups were like this all of a time more, then I wouldn't not want to be naughty none. Some of a ous did of asked me to play cricket with them at playtime and everyone did of laughed when I hitted a ball and it did of donner Petrus Buthalezi on a head cause of he were too busy looking at Miriam instead of fielding proper like. Even Petrus did of laughed.

But a best think of all were that ma were coming home from a hopstibal and Larry the Lithp were making a big fuss about a party.

I were a bit worried that Inspector Nuts weren't not going to come cause of he did sounded like he weren't too sure when I did of phoned him and asked.

Our 'Welcome Home Ma' poster were actually looking quite lekker, and Sally's drawings were a bestest what she did of ever did done. I were so looking forward to having ma home, even if home were now Larry's place. But you know it were like Christmas or a birthday. You so much want it to of come that you do of scare it away and it do take lank ages to comed.

Adventually a day do come and Miss Smit are there by Larry's to help with a party and all. We had chips and cakes and coke and fanta and cream soda and peanuts and mini pizzas and mini hamburgers and mini boerewors rolls and all. I did of wanted to make peanut butter zarms too also, but a growed ups wouldn't not let me. Growed ups can of be a real pain in a arse sometimes, but please don't not charf them I did of said that cause of I would properly get a real pain there for saying a bad word.

So while me and Sally did of helped Miss Smit to put out all a food, Larry did goed and fetched ma. There were quite lank people there by a time they did of gotted home. Ma were in a wheelie chair and all, but when we did of all charf, 'Welcome Home,' when Larry did opened a door, she did cry, but that were okay cause of anyone could check that it were happy crying.

I were also so happy that I didn't not merember at first that Inspector Nuts weren't not there none, but a bit laterer after ma were sitting on a sofa drinking a coke and eating some chips, I did of merember.

I would have been lank cross with him, but I were just merembering he weren't not there when a door bell did of ringed.

'Hello, son,' he did charfed even though he weren't not my pa. 'Sorry we're late, but we've only just got back from Mpumalanga.'

'Mpumalanga? What was you doing there? Aren't not that where...' and now I do of stopped talking cause then I do check Zakes what were hiding ahind Mrs Inspector Nuts. He do of step out so as I can of seed him.

He do of check all shy and all and I don't not knowed if I should of still be cross with him or not, but afore I can do nothink, Inspector Nuts do charf, 'I think you two need to have a chat, we'll just go inside.'

So it were just me and Zakes standing there by a door not saying nothink.

Then old Zakes do of adventually charf, 'I'm sorry I left you like I did,' and he do of check out a flowers there by Larry's door.

'Howcomewhy did you of doed it?' I do asks.

'That man, the one with the dog. When you ran off, he told me that you had killed your father and grandmother and that you would kill me too if you got the chance. I didn't believe him at first, but he showed me the newspapers that said the cops thought that you did. Then you came back with that gun and shot at him. I got scared. That's why I wanted you to get rid of the gun and I thought that you had, but then I saw it in your bag and I decided to split before you killed me.'

'I never would of shooted you Zakes, you was my friend.' I can hardly not believe that Zakes did of thinked that I would of have shooted him.

'I know that now, but that man with the dog, he scared me something chronic. I should have known better than to listen to a grown up.'

'Ja, you can say that again. You can't not never trust a growed up none with nothink. I never would of have shooted you and I didn't not of deaded my pa and ouma.'

'I know,' Zakes charfs and we do of stand there not saying nothink.

Then I do of merember, 'Shaka are deaded.'

Zakes do of check up quick like.

'Dead? How?'

'I reckon he must of got hitted by a car.'

He do of check all sad like now so as I do of feel a bit sorry for him.

'Come, let's go get some chips afore a growed ups chow then all,' I charf.

FOURTEEN

It was a happy occasion that little welcome home party. The family, and they looked like a family with Larry as the new father, seemed comfortable together. The announcement of the engagement wasn't too much of a surprise, even when it was explained to the young lad what it meant. He just nodded sagely as if to say, 'well, duh!'

It had been a bit of a risk bringing Zakes along, but Larry felt in was necessary and, after tracking Zakes down and hearing his story, I realised that he was right, that this reconciliation needed to take place. And it was good to see that it happened so quickly and painlessly. I should have expected that though, kids don't hold grudges the way adults do.

We took our leave, promising to keep in touch and knowing that the pressures of my job would help me break that promise.

FIFTEEN

Zakes did of stayed for a few days afore Inspector Nuts tooked him back to his grandma and grandpa. Cause of his brother were deaded and he did got none ma and pa, it were a best place for him, a growed ups did of told me, but we do of knowed about growed ups, don't we.

Ma and Larry the Lithp did of gotted married and ma told me I did of have to call Larry 'pa' which were really weird, but I did of do it to keep ma happy, even though pa Larry did of put locks on a cupboard door in him and ma's bedroom. I don't not knowed howcomewhy.

There are only one more think what I must of charf yous afore I go. When I did of said that Mr Dern did of shooted pa, I were lying. After he had of shooted Zakes' brother dead proper like, he had of put a gun down and were checking all skrikked and all so as he didn't not check me none.

Even though I were poepping my broeks, I did of checked that he had of put pa's gun down on my table. I were really quiet and all and did of have a gun afore he checked me.

I have of never checked no one skrik so much never afore. I mean it were like Pooh Pants du Plessis had of poohed ten times in Mr Dern's broeks, that were how much he did of skrikked.

That were when I did of heared pa what comed into a front door cause of I did check round. It were then that Theresa's pa did pushed me and

202

runned out of a room. He must of have also pushed pa over too afore he runned out of a house cause of I couldn't not seed him and pa were getting up off of a floor.

I could check that pa had of beed drinking cause of his eyes weren't not so lekker. But he were lank cross, I could of checked *that*. He do of pushed past me and go into my room where he did of charf lank bad words afore he do of comed out and I can check that I were going to get donnered somethink chronic. Pa were like going on like as if it were me what did of killed Zakes' brother and that I were going to get it and all. He had of picked up my cricket bat and I knowed then that I were in a most biggerest kak as what I had of ever beed and pa were going to donner me for six. I were skrikking so much then that I couldn't not even have knowed how to poep my broeks if I had of wanted to. Pa were holding a bat above his head and were walking at me and shouting all a time.

Then there were a loud bang and he did of falled backwards and there were lank blood coming out of his tummy. He weren't not deaded proper cause of I could heard that he were breathink funny, like what Kevin Sykes did of breathed when he got hitted in a tummy by a soccer ball that one time. It were like as he couldn't not breathe proper like.

That were when I did of grabbed Sally and runned. I just do of hope that Sally don't not never stop having Selected Ammonia about what did of happened. I don't not want her to merember that she had of shooted her own pa.